MUTUAL LIFE & CASUALTY

Elizabeth Poliner

The Permanent Press
Sag Harbor, New York 11963

Library of Congress Cataloging-in-Publication Data

Poliner,Elizabeth.
 Mutual Life & Casualty / Elizabeth Poliner.
  p. cm.
 ISBN 1-57962-112-0 (alk. paper)
 1. Sisters - - Fiction. 2. Jewish girls - - Fiction 3. Jewish
families - - Fiction. 4. Insurance agents - - Fiction. 5. Marital
conflict - - Fiction. 6. Connecticut - - Fiction. I. Title: Mutual
Life and Casualty. II. Title

 PS3616.O5673M88 2005
 813'.6 - - dc22

                              2004065315

Printed in The United States of America

THE PERMANENT PRESS
4170 Noyac Road
Sag Harbor, NY 11963

Acknowledgments

Thanks to the editors of the following journals for first publishing these stories:

Connecticut Review, "A Meeting of the Minds;"
Crab Orchard Review, "Self-Choreography;"
The Crescent Review, "To Stand Before Children;"
Iowa Woman, "Swimming Like An Eel" (in slightly different form);
The Laurel Review, "Doubles;"
Other Voices, "Mutual Life & Casualty;"
Pleiades, "The Legend of Princess Topaqua."

Thanks also to The Corporation of Yaddo for time, space, and quiet in which to work on this book, and to the D.C. Commission on the Arts and Humanities for generous financial support.

Finally, for their help in bringing this work to light, thanks to Julie Langsdorf, Jennifer Unter, and Judith and Martin Shepard.

For Paul Hazelton, *in memoriam*

Part I

The Children

Renovation
(Hannah Kahn—1972)

We lived on Route 27, a two-lane country highway that blazed a trail through the heart of Wells, Connecticut. Our house stood just yards from the four corners, the crossing of Route 27 with Main Street, the major intersection in town. Wells spread out in all directions from this point, and drivers typically stopped at this crossroad, this core of activity that pulsated with the changing colors of the street light.

The town, near the center of Connecticut's northern line, lay twenty miles or so east of the Connecticut River. One of the state's minor players, Wells was too small to support even one clothing store, yet despite its size I was used to traffic sounds: cars honking and engines idling outside my window as I went to sleep each night. If I woke early sometimes I'd hear only the air's stillness and later the chatter of birds. Inevitably, though, the chirps would be interrupted by the moan of a car, the roar of a pickup truck, or the grind of a school bus chugging past our house toward Wells Elementary, down Route 27.

Though without question I loved Wells—it was all the world, after all, and I was determined to love it—I hated living on Route 27, plunked by circumstances beyond my control in the middle of everything, our yard, our house, our lives, exposed to every passerby from all sides except for the far back, protected by woods. It was bad enough that we, the Kahns, were the only Jewish family in town. It was bad enough that my father, Daniel Kahn, was a Hartford insurance executive—a professional—and not a machinist like so many other fathers at Pratt and Whitney where military planes were manufactured. It was bad enough that my father *hired* a man to mow our lawn, but did the whole town have to see?

7

Because my older sister Carolyn and I didn't believe in Jesus Christ, MaryEllen, who lived next door, told us we were doomed to eternity in hell. She was Irish and Catholic, a year older than me and a year younger than Carolyn, the sole girl in a family of five children. Her strawberry hair was a shade lighter than our rusty brown and auburn mix, and hers fell straight while ours was thick and wiry; still, on a few miraculous occasions someone would mistake us three for sisters. We'd eye each other then and giggle.

Eternity in hell. It was possible at least, and she thought we should know. In our best interest. I remember saying to MaryEllen quite sincerely, "Thanks."

Carolyn responded by doing what she did best: making a list. She titled it "God's Children," and began by writing down the kinds of Christians there were in Wells: Congregationalists, Catholics, and Lutherans. With some thought she added the other kinds of Christians we knew of: Presbyterians and Episcopalians. She finished with *Buddhists, Eskimos, Jews.*

Though only ten years old when I learned of my damned prospect, it didn't worry me. I had an idea about God. He was fair. For example, he didn't punish Jews who didn't believe in Jesus Christ. That would be as unfair as punishing us for being born to our particular parents, for being born at all. And that's how Judaism felt to me–less like a belief system than a physical state. I could ignore it but it was always there, like the loopy waves of my hair, marking me as different. *The Jewish race*, my fourth grade teacher Mrs. Fleming explained to my classmates, *celebrates the new year each fall at the start of school rather than after Christmas. Isn't that so, Hannah? And that's why you'll be absent these next two days. We'll miss you. We will.*

No, God didn't punish people for believing in different ways. What I sensed was this: he only punished people who didn't believe at all.

I had a problem, then, the next year when I began to question—against my will—if God really existed. It was 1972 and I'd just started fifth grade. I was on the verge of not believing but the leap was too radical; I couldn't make the jump. Imagine the rejection of God as a kind of pole vault. In my travels toward it I puttered down the runway, rather than sprinted, and the trip—a self-propelled one of flight and air and possibly freedom—was never mine to take. Instead I debated the issue over and over, with God, whose silent presence I sensed. As if he were a ghost, I dared to tell him I thought he probably didn't exist. Then again, if he did, something bad could happen if I didn't believe. I could miss out on eternal existence, a state I was banking on, something I equated, simply, with happiness. Each day I hoped for a sign like Abraham had received, or Moses, a bush or tablet to cling to that would put the questioning to an end. But it didn't end. God never signaled, never settled it. September came and went. By mid-October I figured there were just some things God didn't want me to know.

That fall my father was planning to vote for Richard Nixon. Like my budding atheism, this too was against my will. And my mother planned to duplicate his vote. Hers was a choice based on duty and loyalty to my father, not her own feelings, which in the fall of 1972 she had yet to discover.

I wasn't politically minded either. Most likely I'd never have noticed the election but my fifth grade teacher, Mrs. Tucker, whom I loved, hung her head whenever the name Richard Nixon arose. On the general subject of "the President of the United States" she maintained a proud demeanor. But Richard Nixon drove her to extremes. More than once she wagged an angry finger in the air as if telling him, as she told us sometimes, "Stop it. Just stop it." Several times she paced back and forth in front of the classroom's blackboard, E. B. White's *The Trumpet of the Swan* pressed to her breasts, the words she muttered barely audible, "Vietnam, children." After a minute she caught herself in what I knew she considered self-indulgence. "I'm sorry," she once said. "I have thoughts on these subjects. I don't mean to influence your political persuasions, children. But I'm human too."

She seemed beyond human to me. Superior. I worshiped her each night in the form of repeating the multiplication tables. Soon I knew them by heart. By day my response to seven times seven might have been a flatly spoken "forty-nine," so automatic as to be unconscious. But at night, alone in my dark room, whispering the times tables into my pillow, the phrase "seven times seven is forty-nine" had a hushed serenity, an oral beauty like prayer.

I knew that Mrs. Tucker would never learn about my parents' votes; they'd be cast behind closed curtains. This secrecy gave their voting an edge over their most flawed, most public, activity that fall: their decision to renovate our house.

Already it was monstrous, with twelve rooms and four bathrooms—more than any other house I knew. Once a farmhouse, by the time my parents moved in the farm was reduced to three quarters of an acre of mowed lawn, our house, two small barns that we used for storage, and an abandoned chicken coop built along one of the barn's back sides, leaning precariously, in its semi-dilapidated state, against it.

My parents were determined, and by renovation I mean they upgraded our house's every inch. Outside, they covered the old, modest, country red paint with an unusual terra cotta, a color I'd never heard of, one my mother insisted was "sophisticated," and the interior changes began with a flat wall-to-wall carpeting. By October stiff damask curtains clouded what used to be our clear open windows, new wallpaper dictated the atmosphere in six of our twelve rooms, tiles of simulated brick linoleum displaced our kitchen's old blue and pink speckled tiles, sparkling light fixtures glared above us and, when we were tired, we could always flop on our new blue velvet living room couch or its matching love seat.

Mitch Michetti, the handyman, grandfatherly and sweet, was the only benefit I found in this embarrassing display of our unique upward mobility. He liked me, Carolyn, and MaryEllen, and could whistle and whistled all the time. With this extensive a job, Mitch Michetti's lean frame became as much a fixture in our house as the stiff company of damask curtains.

"Your house looks so fine!" Mrs. Tucker said to me one day in late October. I'd just squirmed into my coat and was ready to walk the fifteen minutes home. My teacher wasn't exactly old, but she was graying and thick, a world apart from my young, wiry, energetic mother who, I knew, would spend the afternoon evaluating swatches of fabric and panels of paint colors. The renovation was stimulating my mother's curiosity as nothing ever had. Before this she'd been like a wanderer in the desert of her home, moving with little interest, though with great efficiency, from dusting to vacuuming, cooking to laundry. In redecorating she'd found a watering hole and her thirsty, undernourished self lapped it up. She was happy, absorbed.

I turned to Mrs. Tucker, grateful for the attention I needed but embarrassed too. As I whispered "thanks," my cheeks became flushed with a confusing collision of feelings. Didn't she really think it was too much? Should I be proud or ashamed?

"Are you okay, Hannah?" She pressed her hand to my forehead. "You feel hot."

"I'm fine," I said, quickly turning my face from hers, cutting short the meeting.

I limped home, my body weighted with conflict; a desire to have stayed longer with Mrs. Tucker clashed with an even more urgent pull toward solitude and flight.

My thoughts of Mrs. Tucker reminded me of Mrs. Howe, the elderly woman who used to rent a room on the first floor of our house. Mrs. Howe had moved to Restville the year before, the old people's home further up Route 27. By that day of the renovation what used to be Mrs. Howe's bare ivory walls were darkened with either oak paneling or the bookshelves and cabinets that Mitch Michetti had built. My mother had recently purchased a desk and two reading chairs, and, after a grave and exhausting grill session with a traveling salesman, my father had selected two sets of encyclopedias to fill the shelves, one set on science only and the other a social set, covering events and places the world over. None of my classmates had encyclo-pedias in their homes. "That's because your people—your par-ents, I mean—know the value of education," Mrs. Tucker once explained, beaming with an approval that I liked and spurned all at once.

My parents bought a stereo too, our first, and set it on one of Mitch Michetti's open cabinets. When Carolyn and I first lis-tened to a record on it, the sound-track from the musical *Oliver*, we sat as if frozen, mesmerized by the quality. The yearning of the orphan boy from London never sounded like this, as rich and intricate as the swirls of vines and flowers on the new Persian rug we sat on. My parents now called the room "the library" instead of "Mrs. Howe's room."

At home I found Mitch Michetti, whistling, bent over some small wooden boards he was hammering together.

"What are you whistling?" I stood by our new teak-wood kitchen table that Mitch had covered with a tarp. He wore white painter's pants with lots of pockets and a white shirt spotted with flecks of paint. His gray hair shined. Despite being more than sixty years old, his skin was smooth except for his huge hands, which were rough and calloused from his work. I'd never seen such tough hands. My father's were soft inside, like mine.

"The song is 'O Sole Mio.' Sometimes I whistle in Italian, my mother tongue." He stood straight, smiled my way, then tilted his head back as his jaw opened from the pressure of an enormous yawn. "Middle of the afternoon! My worst time of day!" I must have looked confused, because he said next, "Metabolism, sweet potato. That's what I'm trying to tell you."

"Mitch, how can you whistle in Italian when you don't make words when you whistle?"

Mitch pulled out a chair for me, then one for himself, and dropped his long body into it. He reached for his thermos, poured some coffee, and heaved a sigh.

"A song is words and music, yes? Just because I whistle the music without the words doesn't mean there are no words to the music." Mitch's answer came out flat as if it bored him to report the obvious. Yet I was amused; I'd thought my question would stump him.

"Hannah, I could use a thumb," he said.

I held my hands, midget-sized next to his, in front of his face. "Which thumb?"

Mitch picked my right and I held an old leather belt in place while he hammered it into one side of the open box he'd constructed from the boards. He whistled "O Sole Mio" the whole time and eventually I began whistling it too. When he finished he said, "Do you know what this is?"

"No."

"Your box."

"My box?"

"For Halloween. Just like you said you wanted. 'Tareyton Cigarettes! Get your Tareyton Cigarettes!'" I'd confided to him the day before that for Halloween I wanted to be a Tareyton Cigarette Lady, the kind of person I'd seen on TV commercials who'd "rather fight than switch." Patting the box, Mitch winked at me as if to say we now shared a secret. I grabbed the box in delight.

Later that afternoon when I went to the chicken coop roof, I wasn't completely alone. There was a dog there, a huge, fluffy St. Bernard. He was tied to a tree in our neighbor's backyard. The chicken coop, which that fall had become my own haven of privacy, extended out from the backside of our barn into a small patch of woods. The coop, which didn't concern my parents, remained exempt from the renovation, and I felt comfortable on its shabby wooden surface, dirty and worn, with a series of rotting holes running across its top edge. From my perch toward the lower edge, I sat staring through the trees at the dog who was on the other side of the little stream that divided my family's land from our neighbor's.

He could see me too. I knew this because when I'd first wandered up earlier that fall he'd barked and barked. But soon

13

he grew used to me and the roof sittings took on a routine that felt like ritual. Up I'd go, often followed by Teddy, our cat. I might lie down for a while and stare at the branches that hung over the roof and at the bits of sky broken up by the branches the way lines broke up a plain piece of paper in the scribble pictures Carolyn once taught me to make. That day, as usual, I sat cross-legged and had my round with God. When it was over I breathed deeply, then stared at the dog, who sat alert and still as if waiting for God's message too. Soon enough, as the minutes passed and the air entered my lungs, a song emerged, as inadvertent and effervescent as a hiccup.

I sang "Kumbaya" and "Five Hundred Miles," songs I'd learned the summer before at day camp that I was drawn to for their minor, melancholy keys. Then I sang what the camp counselors called "The Connecticut Song," beginning with the words, *I love the hills of my Connecticut. I love its valleys and its streams.* The singing, a kind of spontaneous meditation, told me what I felt in my heart right then, that it was possible to love Connecticut, that it was possible to love being home, and from the chicken coop roof hidden in our backyard I gazed longingly down the bank to the slow, trickling stream and across it to our neighbor's mowed valley. In these moments I forgot all about Route 27 and the renovation Route 27 exposed to Wells.

I sang in Hebrew next, the exotic language I didn't literally understand yet still felt close to. On Friday nights when we lit Sabbath candles I begged to be the one to strike the match and chant the blessing. And on the High Holidays I'd never minded missing school and leaving Wells for the synagogue in Worcester, Massachusetts, my father's hometown an hour's drive away, where his parents had sent him to religious services routinely. In fact we lived in Wells because it was between the two poles of my father's existence: his pious family in Worcester and his prosperous insurance work in Hartford.

At the synagogue I was struck by the prayer I heard there, the ancient language, like old Mrs. Howe and even Mrs. Tucker, moving in a way that was unhurried and relaxed, as if the

14

words, once uttered, were used to their existence, unsurprised by it in a way that contrasted with English words, which sounded as buoyant, energetic, and ambitious as my parents. And the older language was glued to melodies, wails and pitches, that sounded more ancient still. The songs were sad, serious, lonely. Everything I knew about God's personality—and my own, that I was just beginning to know—I could hear in those prayers.

When I came down from the roof I urged MaryEllen, who'd come over to watch TV with Carolyn, to come hear the stereo in "the library."

"Listen to this," I said. I put on *Damn Yankees* and Gwen Verdon's hearty voice burst forth. I sat on the new Persian rug and MaryEllen eased into one of the new reclining reading chairs. Her long legs stretched to the footrest, which I was leaning on. Of us three girls she had the distinction of being the fastest runner even though she was also the biggest. Her mother was from Boston and because of that sometimes MaryEllen pronounced words funny, like the word "Mom" which she called "Mum."

"Mum said I could only stay for one hour."

"Okay." I lifted the stereo's delicate diamond needle. I'd planned to play *Oliver* next, but instead moved the album case back into our narrow stack of records that Carolyn had recently alphabetized. I slipped *Oliver* in between *Fiddler on the Roof* and *South Pacific*, then put *Damn Yankees* in front of them all.

The contrast between Gwen Verdon's booming voice and the new silence was extreme: the silence felt as fragile as I felt the first time I'd climbed on the roof and the St. Bernard had barked and barked because I was there, a stranger, a threat.

I hadn't turned the light on in the library, and I glanced out the window through a crack in the damask only to see more dimness. It was almost time for supper. I heard the faint cry of cars on Route 27, slowing as they passed our house and neared the four corners' stoplight. The Persian rug's short wool pile scratched the palm of my hand. I stared at the rug, tracing its still unfamiliar border pattern around the library's periphery. I

15

felt sad, suddenly, for a reason I couldn't explain. Perhaps it was the dimness of the hour that brought it on, or the quietness of the moment when we two girls had run out of energy for play. Perhaps I would have liked MaryEllen to stay for supper. It was Friday, and I could smell the fish sticks my mother had already put in the oven. We now ate fish on Fridays—not meat—just like MaryEllen did at her house. This habit began last year and was practiced in case MaryEllen should decide to eat here. I knew I wanted Mitch Michetti to stay. And Mrs. Howe, who liked to sit still and to talk and whose presence was now barely visible—wouldn't it have been nice to have her here too?

It was an odd moment, but just then, just when MaryEllen stretched before getting up to go, something I could only identify as my rooftop mood—a kind of theology—overwhelmed me. "MaryEllen," I whispered. "We're average."

More silence. More thinking about average. The thought had suddenly arrived, that she and I and most people we knew—certainly our families, Mrs. Howe, Mitch Michetti, and possibly even Mrs. Tucker—were all average. And it hurt to say this because earlier on the roof I'd hoped, despite my doubts, to discover I was special, that God wanted to reach me in some objective, out-loud way. But here, back on firm ground, inside our newly decorated house and in the dimness of the library, this new thought emerged and it scared me. We were average. My parents were wrong. The decorating, the renovation, would make no difference. We weren't blessed. Not in the way I thought important, anyway, in a way that would lift us from the world of life and death and drop us in some other land, one guaranteeing a happy eternity.

I couldn't say all this to MaryEllen but simply repeated, "Average." And this time I felt a pinch of relief—to have said something true, finally, about *all* of us.

MaryEllen said, "Hannah, I have to tell you I never thought about it before," yet she agreed, finally, we did seem average.

My next thought—unwilled as ever—shattered the brief

satisfaction. *Like Mrs. Howe who lived here before us, we'll grow old and die. MaryEllen, that's how average we are.*

Four nights later, Halloween night, Carolyn and I modeled our costumes-in-progress for Mitch, who was in the upstairs hallway laying carpeting. As a gypsy Carolyn wore my mother's polka dot print cocktail dress, which fell below Carolyn's knees. She'd tied a floral kerchief around her head and covered one bare arm with a set of bangle bracelets. Gold loops burst from her ears.

I had on a plaid skirt, knee socks, and a plain blue turtleneck. I'd colored one eye black and painted my lips a brilliant red. My handmade sign, "I'd rather fight than switch," dropped over my chest.

Mitch let out a long, singing whistle. "Two lookers!" he said. "Two red tomatoes! How are you going to keep the boys away? Tell you what. I'll tell my grandson Tommy, when he wants to find a girl, come to Wells where the red tomatoes are!"

"Tommy?" Carolyn asked. I was surprised at her interest. But there she was, on tiptoes, her curiosity obviously peaked.

"He's fourteen." Mitch winked at Carolyn.

She sighed, then giggled and stared at the floor.

"*Tommy.*" I spit the word out in an instant, jealous fit.

"You too, Hannah. It'll happen to you too," Mitch teased. He picked me up and twirled me. But when I landed, I stood firm, shaking my head.

Carolyn and I were still in her room, fixing our costumes, when my father came home. I heard him greet my mother, who was preparing our meal. In the upstairs hallway my father then talked to Mitch, who announced his intention to stay until he'd finished tacking the carpet all the way down the stairs. He had momentum, he said.

"That's what I like about you, Mitch. You're determined."

"I get the job done." Mitch mumbled this as if his work habits didn't merit my father's compliment. I wished he wouldn't humble himself so before my father. After all, my father couldn't do the tasks Mitch could.

When my father reached Carolyn's room, excited and eager, he looked first at me, and laughed, then handed me a shallow cardboard box. It looked like the kind of box his white shirts came in, the kind he was wearing now, standing tall in the doorway in his business suit. He liked his suits, specially made for him by a Hartford tailor, which made him glow with importance. "Will this do?" he asked.

I looked at the box, then at my father, rocking happily in his polished wingtips. Mitch Michetti's box was on the floor in my bedroom down the hall. I hadn't shown it to anyone. It was still our secret.

I wanted to say that I already had a box, a handmade wooden box, a bigger, sturdier box, but I could see that my father was so proud of this box, his box, that was supposed to hang around my neck, not with Mitch's belt but only by string.

Mitch poked his head into the doorway then, lifting his finger over his mouth as he did, signaling "shush." Then he gave me another wink. "Hannah, sometimes it's better to switch than fight, yes?"

I took the box from my father's hands and muttered my proverbial, "Thanks." As I dropped onto Carolyn's bed, the weightless box floated down beside me, then bounced with each movement of the mattress.

When my father turned to Carolyn, he didn't laugh at her costume but seemed taken aback. "You look—" he paused, coughed, and blurted, "sixteen!"

Carolyn spun around, delighted. She was only twelve-and-a-half but I could see where my father got that idea. The gold loops. The bracelets. My mother's polka dot print.

"Carolyn's going to marry Mitch's grandson, Tommy!" I said—another unwilled thought that bubbled up, surprised me. But I'd begun to envision it and it didn't seem so bad. Carolyn in white. Me, behind her, in yellow. Tommy, somewhere in the distance, approaching. . . .

"Is Tommy Jewish?" my father asked, his mouth suddenly

straight, his voice quiet but firm.

His words were calm, but still I jumped, perhaps at the sound of that firmness, its implicit message slapping me awake. There was something unnerving to the words, a demand we'd heard so many times before, and something unnerving to the long, threatening pause that followed. I looked to Carolyn, who stared at my father in the doorway. Carolyn's red face registered the same confusion I felt. Mitch Michetti, standing in the hallway, couldn't help but hear, and he looked dismayed as well, his mouth twisted and puckered.

Though my father hadn't addressed Mitch, Mitch nevertheless responded—by stepping back, away from my father, away from us. He looked down at the carpeting he'd just laid, his shoulders drooping as much as his head, and began to whistle, softly, in what I knew was Italian. Sitting on Carolyn's bed I felt adrift, as if cast off on an island. Carolyn, who, like Mitch, now hung her head as if she'd been punished, seemed equally adrift. "It's only a costume," she mumbled. The hair brush in her hand trailed by her side. She collapsed on her bed next to me and rubbed the handle of the plastic hair brush as she would a set of worry beads. I knew what she worried about. The demand. The seriousness. The sudden end of fun. And was it our fault, how we didn't know even one Jewish boy?

As my father approached us, arms outstretched, an offering of comfort and peace, the sound of his words, "Is Tommy Jewish?" echoed in my mind.

I stared into my empty cardboard Tareyton Cigarette box. *Tommy*, I said to myself, sadly. I said this as I heard Mitch walk away. *Tommy*.

That Halloween, like every Halloween, a parade of school children marched in costume from Wells Elementary, up Main Street, swerving onto Route 27 until the parade reached our house. A fire engine led the marchers, and it angled our way as it neared the oak tree at our west end, managing an easy turn-around in our especially wide driveway, which served as the parade's midpoint.

19

Everyone knew to march to the driveway's far side and wait for the truck to back out, then the parade would resume in reverse order as before back down to the school.

Carolyn, MaryEllen, and I waited on our front porch for the first sign of the fire truck. We rushed to the oak as the hum of engine and children's shouts approached. Despite the anticipation, we managed to pull our gazes from the road for a final once-over. Our costumes were now covered by coats; still, we had to agree: we looked good!

As always Halloween began with the wait before the parade. The air was crisp and cool, hinting of winter's chill. The sky had been dark since supper. We knew what boys did, how they'd stockpiled a night's supply of eggs, slipping boxes by the dozen into thick paper bags.

I hated our house, our location on Route 27, every day, every year, except on Halloween. Come Halloween night I lost my envy of my classmates, living on quiet streets in standard homes with normal yards hidden from view in the back. Come Halloween night my classmates put on their masks and trod to our oak. A fire engine, a red palace of a vehicle, turned into our driveway, leading the pygmy parade. Come Halloween night, despite our awkward place in the community, in the center of town, sticking out in our odd house like a palm tree in New England, I knew we were marked. Not average. But not different either. Very much part of things, yet still, somehow, special.

By the time we joined the parade I'd forgotten about the better box I'd left home and my father's divisive—or was it loyal?—comment. I was lost, deliciously so, to the swirl of masks and chatter around me. Later at the party at Wells Elementary, even though I didn't win a prize for my costume, Mrs. Tucker, clapping as she saw me, kissed my cheek. For the rest of the evening, while Carolyn, MaryEllen, and I went on to trick-or-treat, I could feel Mrs. Tucker's sweet touch.

We trekked up Main Street, all the way on North Main and back, up Route 27 past Restville, to which we shouted, "Hello Mrs. Howe! We love you!" And home again. Carolyn had mapped our route and she'd figured how to stop at enough homes so our candy would last through December. "The trick," she explained, trailing behind me and MaryEllen, "is to eat only one candy bar a day. The treat is that the days go on forever."

Though MaryEllen, the fastest, complained a lot, "Come on, you two, come on," as we parted she agreed our long haul was worth it. We'd made it home without one egg breezing past us and our loads were now heavy with sweet jewels.

Inside, Carolyn and I dumped our stock on the living room floor. Milky Ways, Tootsie Rolls, apples, and a multitude of Baggies filled with bite-sized treats obliterated the geometric design of yet another new Persian rug. Carolyn had another plan. We should separate our candies into piles, the ones we liked best, second best, and so forth, down to the ones we could envision sharing with our mother, whose sweet tooth we knew would be activated by our lot. I began by putting everything with mint, my least favorite, to my right.

My mother was racing from the kitchen to the front hall, an empty bag of Hershey bars in tow. "Over two hundred visitors!" she announced, pausing to stare at our neat stacks of candy, her gray eyes dangerously wide.

"Two hundred plus! A record year!" my father said. He dropped onto the blue velvet love seat, exhausted.

I could hear Mitch Michetti whistling something American this time, "When the Saints Come Marching In." He was now in the front hall, just finishing his work on the stairs.

The doorbell rang again.

"Avon calling!" Mitch followed this with a hearty laugh.

"I'm out of treats!" My mother jumped from the couch, leaped across the Persian rug like it was a huge, colorful puddle—one she mustn't step in—and surged toward the kitchen. After noisily opening and closing cabinets, she yelled to my father, "Only raisins! Little boxes of raisins!"

From the front hall where my father was answering the door, I heard a loud, "Ho, ho, ho. Come on in! Ho, ho, ho."

Oh, no! I thought. He has it all wrong. He's doing

Christmas!

My mother now stood by me, kneeling by my bundles of candy, reaching toward my favorite pile of chocolate and caramel.

"No!" I placed my body between my candy and my mother. Carolyn's bangle bracelets rattled when she reached to clutch her several bags of M&Ms.

"Please?" My mother was asking for the world, but she was doing it rather nicely. Her voice was soft, beseeching, and she gently rubbed my head and patted Carolyn's arms. "It's for them. Your friends." Her gaze drifted to the doorway where my father stood, beaming at what looked liked three blind mice. They were mice, all right, and they were wearing sunglasses too.

"I don't know them," I said.

She gave it her best shot. "You'll feel better about yourself later if you just do this one thing for me now." She said this with her gray eyes, which were sadly blinking, as much as with her voice.

I went for the pile of mint. "Here."

She whisked the load toward the empty wooden bowl in my father's hands. Carolyn, always more generous than me, walked out of the room with several full-sized Baby Ruths. She turned to my mother and spoke firmly. "In return, I expect you not to sneak candy this year." Her footsteps up the stairs were as heavy as Mitch Michetti's hammering thumps. Her bangle bracelets sounded like dim bells of mourning.

I stayed on the rug, rearranged the remains of my candies, then moved them from the carpet to the cardboard Tareyton Cigarette box. The door bell rang again. I raced to reach it first but my father beat me. His "Ho, ho, ho!" drowned out my simple, appropriate, "Hi there."

I knew them. It was Bobby Crane, a pirate, and his sister Cindy, some kind of witch. Bobby was in my class at school. Both of them smiled and I admired how they'd each blackened out one front tooth.

I turned to the wooden bowl but my father's soft hands filled it first. He dropped a candy bar into each of their bags, telling them while he did this what terrific costumes they wore. "Terrific!" he said. "Ingenious!"

I watched Cindy, who was looking past the front hall into our living room. Her eyes traveled methodically from the new damask curtains to the Persian rug to the blue velvet couch and love seat and finally to Mitch Michetti, the hired man in white painter's clothes, whistling as he tacked red carpeting onto the last, bottom stair.

Cindy looked to her brother next. My father was staring beyond them at several ghosts who appeared to be drifting toward our front porch. He called to my mother, "More! We need more!"

I'd turned to go back to my Tareyton Cigarette box, to donate my next-to-least favorites, when I saw Cindy mouth the word, *Jew*.

I tipped back, dizzy, almost falling, until Mitch caught me. Bobby nodded. With a raised hand he rubbed his thumb against his forefinger. He mouthed back, *Money*.

"This your Dad?" Bobby asked me. He pointed to the man on the porch, standing tall in his suit, his arms outstretched as if he planned to hug the first ghost to arrive. My father had heard Bobby's question and his head turned slightly toward us, enough so I could see his cheerful face glowing with pride.

No! I thought. *Not my Dad! Not my house! Not my fault!*

But I didn't say anything out loud. Before I knew it I'd grabbed the closest thing next to me: Mitch Michetti's rough, workman's hand.

The next afternoon when I climbed on the roof, the dog hardly flinched. He lifted his head, his big St. Bernard ears drooping, his jowl hanging. He gave me a great, blasé stare.

I'd had a rough day at school. Though Mrs. Tucker had whispered in my ear, "You were so cute in that costume," I didn't feel cute or special or even average. "Hannah," Mrs. Tucker had said, crouching by my desk, "when you walk pick your head up. I noticed when you were at the party last night. You look down and don't let people see you!"

That afternoon, because my head felt too heavy to hold high, I lay back on the roof's mildly sloping surface. My eyes clung to the branches above me that I knew so well from a season's worth of longing. Looking at them was like clutching a security blanket.

The day before I'd betrayed my father for Mitch Michetti. I hadn't fought; I'd switched. He'd seen me grab Mitch, and I'd seen him, his drooping mouth, his sagging head and neck, his shocking instantaneous deflation.

When it was time to sing—after having no talk with God who was maddeningly beyond reach—only one song emerged, the Connecticut Song. The St. Bernard, whom I decided to call "Oliver" after the orphan boy from London, seemed indifferent to it. At least he never lifted his head to acknowledge the tune. Still, I was determined. I sang what I had to sing: *I love the hills of my Connecticut. I love its valleys and its streams. I've got my heart set in Connecticut, and it's always in my dreams.*

To Stand Before Children
(Mrs. Tucker—1972)

Mrs. Tucker had no children of her own, but each morning at five past nine when she took roll of her class of twenty-three fifth-graders, she felt a distinct pang of satisfaction that she believed compared in spirit to a mother's. At that time of day, especially on rainy mornings, the children moved slowly, sluggishly, allowing her a good look at each of them.

There was Peggy Hardley, her wispy hair newly permed, yet accenting rather than hiding the pale mouseyness of her face. Peggy wore, as usual, a lace-collared dress, flowered in print, short in sleeves, and covered by a large, unshapely cardigan sweater, each garment a hand-me-down from her older sister, Louise. Louise was in the sixth grade now, having passed through Mrs. Tucker's class the year before. How different the two were, she often thought. Though smarter and prettier than Peggy, Louise was self-satisfied to a fault, and last year she'd had to prod the girl into paying more attention to her classmates. She hoped, for Louise's sake, that even though the girl was out of her reach—in another classroom on another corridor—she still remembered to keep her eyes at least sometimes off herself. Perhaps she'd go find her and tell her so?

For the younger sister's sake, because Peggy was a liar, Mrs. Tucker sat her in the front row where the girl could receive what she hoped would feel like personal touches: special glances, comments under her breath, and the like. Peggy couldn't seem to help but tell lies. When they began their geographic study of North America, for example, Peggy raised her hand and insisted that she'd traveled alone, by train, across the whole of Canada. When Hannah Kahn sat at the piano one day early in the fall and played for them the first lines of Mozart she'd ever learned, Peggy stood up, almost shouting, almost in tears, to tell Mrs. Tucker and the class that she could play the accordion. She could! Her father had taught her, she explained. But Mrs. Tucker, who'd taught Peggy's father so many years ago, knew that no child of Frank Hardley, that withdrawn farm boy with no artistic inclinations whatsoever, had ever learned the accordion from him. "Peggy," she said. "You sit now and think hard about all the chores you do for your Daddy's farm. Think hard, because I'll call on you later and ask you to tell us all about them. Why, it's 1972." Frowning, she paused. "What I mean is, there's barely a person around here anymore who knows a *true* thing about a farm!"

So Peggy sat, and later that day, after she explained that a sticky coating surrounds each newborn calf, she gave a virtuoso's description of shoveling cow dung and carrying chicken feed. To Peggy's delight, the class laughed and laughed, and when the principal, Miss Hullman, passed by on her way down the hall, she stopped to tell Mrs. Tucker what a pleasant sound her cheerful class made. "You make my ears ring, students," Miss Hullman said. With that Mrs. Tucker could see from the children's posture—taut necks, raised heads, stiff spines—how they realized they'd done something magnificent, for Miss Hullman had a bad temper and had, just that morning at assembly, slammed a folded metal chair onto the floor to scare all of grades four through six into keeping a quiet that would hold.

After Miss Hullman left, Mrs. Tucker thanked Peggy and thanked them all. She said, "Class, I owe you thanks because you've just earned your first compliment. And when you're complimented"—she gave them a tantalizing, teasing grin—"I'm complimented." She stepped up to the large blackboard and erased the morning's math equations. The children, sitting quietly and watching—wondering, she sensed, what it was she planned to do next, proud, it seemed, to have given her a compliment, thrilled, moreover, to have been part of a compliment themselves—followed her as she put down the eraser and lifted a piece of yellow chalk. She reached high, her blue-checked blouse coming slightly untucked from her corduroy skirt, and at the top right-hand corner of the board she made a short, vertical line. "One," she said. Beside it she made another. "Two," she added. Turning, she smoothed her blouse and faced her class. "One for the compliment Miss Hullman gave you, and one for the compliment I'm giving you now, for being so quiet as I do this, so alert, so good. Two compliments. By the end of the year maybe you'll have earned *fifty* compliments."

Fifty compliments. She knew it seemed impossible to them, as impossible as memorizing the fifty states. Yet geographic region by geographic region the states were indeed conquered, and, that accomplishment intact, she ordered that they revisit each region for the purpose of learning state capitals. In all, she awarded the class five compliments during the time they studied across the street, in Wells's cramped public library, poring over encyclopedias to learn states' birds, crops, industries, populations, and nicknames. Someone had named their state, Connecticut, the "Nutmeg State," and she watched with relief as the children devoured the "Indian" pudding, heavily flavored with nutmeg, that Diana Nicholson brought in the day she reported on Connecticut's basic facts.

Diana Nicholson was three years older than the others, having stayed back twice already and having started school a year late to begin with. With her blossoming bosom and widening hips, she was a lone weed in a flower bed of ten-year-olds. Several times when on recess duty Mrs. Tucker hadn't been quick enough to stop a group of boys from circling Diana— "dumb," as they called her, "dumpy" Diana—and taking turns snapping her bra strap. Apparently, because the taunts didn't let up, Diana had given in; by late fall rumors were out that she was in the business of selling feels of herself to boys.

"Diana," Mrs. Tucker began one day after school. "You mustn't let them touch you like that." To her dismay, Diana claimed that she didn't mind, that they weren't so bad when you got to know them, that it was a lot better this way, giving them feels and having them be nice to her.

"No!" Mrs. Tucker said. She rubbed a hand over the grooves of her forehead. She was fifty-two years old, and in thirty years of teaching she'd never known a student to sell feels like this. "Dear God, Diana," she mumbled. And then it hit her. The knowledge—pellucid, sure—that Diana wouldn't graduate from high school before having a child of her own. God only knew if she'd make it through junior high. She spent several more afternoons in the empty classroom teaching Diana the facts of life, facts that she—modest, infertile, not to mention worn with fatigue at the day's end—couldn't pass on as easily as she did the workings of the multiplication tables each morning.

Sitting one afternoon beside Diana, both of them squeezed into chairs meant for littler people, the light having dimmed, it seemed, with the absence of the other children, she said, "Diana, you must listen to me." Yet Diana's gaze incessantly drifted away from her, pulled, she noticed, by the strange ocean-like patterns on each floor tile.

"You don't want to bear a child when you're but a child yourself, dear." A pause followed, during which the last afternoon bell rang, a bell that signaled nothing, really, yet echoed with inflated importance as it traveled through the near-empty school yard.

Diana turned her face then, freckled, and for the moment wide-eyed, toward her. "Oh, yes," the girl said. "I do want a child, Mrs. Tucker. I want a baby! All my own!"

And Mrs. Tucker, sensing she really meant it, sensing the loneliness that caused the longing, wrapped an arm over Diana's shoulder and said, "When you're married, Diana. That's when you'll have your baby." A twinge of that same longing startled her. For a moment the pain drew her into herself. Her arm slipped from Diana's shoulders. She paused, sighed, pushed on. "Promise me you'll wait until you're married."

So Diana promised, and Mrs. Tucker, standing guard at the window, clutching her sagging, now-menopausal belly, watched as the girl ran eagerly for home, her breasts bouncing, her legs strong, her skirt flapping and lifting in the wind.

Overall they were a good class and often they gave her moments of intense pride. Like the day they wrote letters in their best cursive script to Roy Peterson, twenty years old and far away, in Vietnam. "Children," she began. "You all know a little, I suppose, about the war." And they nodded. One boy, at least, squirmed in excitement. From the back of the room came the jutting sound of a machine gun and she snapped quickly, instinctively, at Marty Littleton. "I'll have none of that," she said, and there followed from the group a deep, regretful silence, for it was mid-year by then and the children, even pugnacious Marty Littleton, obviously felt something toward her, loyalty perhaps, attachment, surely some trust.

She feared for this Roy Peterson, she told them, who was a

fifth-grader once himself. Her student. A good student. A lot like Marty Littleton, she explained, attempting a quick revival of Marty's spirit. She knew she snapped at him too often. Marty, who'd been staring into a book, looked up, quizzically, into her face. "Good at math!" she exclaimed, and the class nodded, offering Marty a collective salute because, indeed, Marty—who mumbled when he spoke, seemingly embarrassed by his knack for thick books with small type the rest of them wouldn't tackle, and who started fights now and again to make sure everyone knew he was adequately tough, and whose thick glasses were constantly shattered in those fights—was never-theless comfortable in his emerging role as their most brilliant mathematician.

It had taken all year, but each morning after she'd written five equations on the blackboard—having directed the children to do them at their discretion before the earliest bell—there would be Marty, squinting behind his glasses as he figured how to multiply the complex fraction before him or how to manage, step by step, the process of long division. He finished all five each morning, getting a few wrong answers at first, then, with time, becoming quicker and more accurate. "Five out of five," she'd heard him say each morning that month. He'd say this while poking Hannah Kahn, his most serious competition when it came to the equations. Hannah, kind and naturally encourag-ing, always smiled a broad, toothy smile at Marty. This made him blush and he'd then sock her, awkwardly, a little too hard, in the arm.

Hannah Kahn. This was the student whom she'd targeted from the start for becoming a teacher. She had it in her, the easy concern for others, the ability to encourage where it was most needed. Just that morning she'd written to Roy Peterson: *I don't know much about Vietnam. But I was once at camp, away from home. I hope you are not lonely. I sing songs when I am lonely. Richard Nixon has won the election. Mrs. Tucker worries about us all.*

Mrs. Tucker read that letter out loud and because each letter was like this—so beautiful, so full of good will—she awarded them a total of six compliments. Roy Peterson will be pleased, she said. Roy Peterson will visit us when he comes back, she added with as much confidence as she could muster. She gave an extra compliment, a personal one, to Jackie Thunder because he'd drawn Roy Peterson a picture of a horse, and Jackie Thunder, the class artist, drew wonderful horses.

Hannah Kahn and Jackie Thunder were nearly inseparable that year. All Hannah had to do was look at him and Jackie Thunder—short, round, a mixture of Pequod Indian and Italian Catholic, usually good and quiet and shy—couldn't help but giggle. At any given moment of the day she could catch them rocking red-faced in their chairs, gasping for breath. Still, Mrs. Tucker didn't scold. They were friends, becoming truer each day, she believed, and she couldn't help but indulge herself in watching the development of something that reminded her of her own friendship with Kenneth Tucker, her husband, now four years dead, who had once made her, when she was a little girl and he a little boy, laugh and laugh.

Each March she offered them poetry. Over time she came to think of it as her special gift, her best treat, something they most likely wouldn't get at home, an offering over and above that of the average Wells mother. Experience had taught her that some classes would take to it better than others, and she sensed that this one might be of the more skittish variety. Nevertheless, she was determined. "Poetry is more sacred than compliments," she began, by way of introduction.

The difficulty emerged at the start. She instructed them to memorize a poem. The next day each would recite it, aloud, before the class. Marty Littleton groaned first, and he made a sour face. Ignoring him, she told them that another New Englander, Robert Frost, had written the poem she'd selected, and that he'd strung together in his lines of verse certain familiar and valued events: snowfall, horseback riding, traveling home, sleeping.

"Oh, I love poetry, Mrs. Tucker," Peggy Hardley insisted, but the next day when she volunteered first to recite, she started off at a trot, her voice rising and falling with the bumpy motion of the poem's rhythm, her cardigan sweater nearly falling from her slight shoulders, and soon she strayed from coherence altogether, reciting at a gallop's pace.

Mrs. Tucker clapped her hands, cutting short Peggy's performance. "Beware of the sing-song sound," she warned. She raised her eyeglasses, which had been hanging on a chain around her neck, and put them on as if to punctuate her point. "Yet don't be too stiff. Say it with *feeling*, children." Removing the glasses, she recited the poem herself, something she'd done each year for the last thirty years, and the class settled down and in their stillness seemed to hear it. She then asked, "Who's next?"

Diana Nicholson's raised arm flapped like a wing preparing her for flight. "Me, me," she pleaded. Surprised, Mrs. Tucker told her to begin. Diana stood, her faded plaid dress draping over her wide hips, her freckled face glowing with a red flush, her greasy hair hanging in her eyes. "*Whose woods these are,*" she began, slowly, as if in genuine wonder. "*I think I know,*" she said modestly, not thrusting the assertion at them. She went on, each line following the next in a careful, considered, conversational tone. She spoke the last line in a whisper, as if sleep crawled nearby, a real predator about to take her. At the end she paused, a silence she'd created hanging in the air. She dropped her head in final, dramatic closure.

Snickers . . . titters . . . and within seconds the laughing spread, a spontaneous combustion of raw emotion. Jackie Thunder, beet-red and beet-round, nearly rolled off his chair. Marty Littleton pounded his desk and hissed at Diana, "You dumb cow." Hannah Kahn looked around in bewilderment, unsure, Mrs. Tucker could see, whether to laugh or hold still. Looking for guidance, the girl turned her way.

But she could only fume. Poetry was *her* offering—*her* unique gift—and they were close to rejecting it. She pushed on her glasses, gave the class a quick once-over, then pulled the glasses off, the view more than she could bear. Desperate, she pointed an index finger first at Marty Littleton, then at Jackie Thunder, and said, "You. Out." The boys stood. Marty tucked his head as he carried his bony frame toward the doorway. Jackie sheepishly followed.

In the now-silent room Diana Nicholson continued to stand by her desk, her head hanging and her greasy hair falling further into her face. The children, not daring to look at each other, not daring to look at *her*, raised their heads to follow Matt's and Jackie's slow saunter.

Once they'd gone she said, "That was lovely, Diana. Sit now." Holding her head high, she turned from the class, walked to the blackboard, and reached for the eraser. In one sweep she expunged precisely seven compliments.

The compliments were not to be regained until the next month when Joshua Cooper, a visiting artist from Hartford, came to teach all the fifth-grade classes about the joy of murals. The joy of murals had to do with thinking big. Small sketches on small pads were quickly transformed into big pictures on huge sheets of newsprint. The joy of murals had to do with getting along with your neighbors. The children formed teams of artists: Jackie Thunder led a pack of three other boys, while Hannah Kahn grabbed Peggy Hardley, a defense from being excluded from Jackie's group. Hannah explained to Mrs. Tucker that because she knew that Jackie would paint horses, she would paint the most opposite animal she could imagine: fish. Mrs. Tucker watched as Jackie and his boys splattered as background the predicted red and green, the colors of barns and pastures. Then she heard Hannah order Peggy to slop blue everywhere, for her picture, unlike Jackie's, would be "the under-the-sea view of things."

For the better part of two weeks painting murals occupied a portion of each afternoon. At first Mrs. Tucker walked from group to group, checking how the children were getting along.

Satisfied that each had found a niche, she began taking long breaks in the hall, pulling a chair out with her and sitting there alone, in the quiet of the afternoon, thinking, daydreaming, and re-reading her beloved Robert Frost.

Within days Joyce McAlley, who taught across the hall, joined her. They'd been neighbors for ten years and she noticed how Joyce, always vivacious, especially vibrant with a softball in her hand, was showing in her newly frosted hair and thickening frame the first signs of age. "This painting's a wonderful treat for us all!" Joyce said, huffing a little as she slid her chair toward hers. The two women sat side by side, nodding. Later, when Joyce said she wanted to go to the lounge for a cigarette, Mrs. Tucker held her plump arm. "Stay," she said to the younger woman. "Stay and talk to me."

As always their talk turned to one topic: the children. Though in general the thought of being maternal merely in attitude and not in fact made her squirm and blush—made parent-teacher conferences often unendurable—while in the confines of the school yard, particularly in the hall where her classroom was, she felt this tension ease, felt a little in command. Without hesitation she talked about children all she wanted. She ruminated about how poor Hannah Kahn was paying the price for having that needy Peggy Hardley on her painting team. Then she told Joyce about discovering in Diana Nicholson something she never imagined possible: "A natural ear," she said, "for poetry!"

And Joyce, herself a mother of two, responded to her as she always did, as if Mrs. Tucker were an old pro, considering her without question to be *something*—rather than the less than something that at that moment, beside this mother, beside *any* mother, she suddenly sensed she really was.

Did other women feel this way?

She dared to ask Joyce what she thought she would be like if she hadn't had her children.

The younger woman laughed, a quick, nervous sound. "Without the kids? It'd be like—" she paused, thought, then

chuckled again. "Quiet. I can say that. It'd be awfully quiet."
Sitting still, Joyce crossed her legs and folded her hands over
her lap.

Mrs. Tucker wanted to say, *not it, you, what would you be
like*, but she stopped when she felt Joyce's hand as it clasped hers.

"What you are, Bev, is the best teacher this town ever had.
Everyone knows that," Joyce said.

"Yes, yes," she answered, quickly, dismissing the compliment. "Problem is, Joyce, that's all."

Within a few weeks the two returned to their respective class-
rooms for the entire day. They often met later, though, after the
last school bus rolled on, to stand before the mural that Jackie
Thunder mastered. "That Joshua Cooper reached our Jackie,"
Mrs. Tucker commented one afternoon as she shook her head at
the wonder before her. For the first time since she'd known him
Jackie hadn't painted horses. Instead he'd painted a covered
bridge, *their* covered bridge, the one that lay just inside Wells's
town line. He'd painted the covered bridge that connected
opposite banks of the Branch River. The sky hung in a clear
blue, the Connecticut River valley, hilly and green, was splayed
in the background, and in the foreground the river, dotted with
boulders, twisted, then slid beneath the shade of the wooden
bridge. Mrs. Tucker heaved a deep sigh when she first set eyes
on the finished mural, and she hung the large painting—carried
it out and tacked it herself—not in the classroom, but on a wall
in the hallway so all the fifth grade would see it, would file past
it, on their trips to the lavatory, lunch-room, and playground.

There in the hall, by the stairwell that led to the cafeteria,
she and Joyce stood, drawn there by this picture of a bridge
they'd both known their whole lives. They leaned their faces
toward each other, their shoulders brushing, their voices low,
and sighed, deeply, with pleasure. "He did it, Joyce," she whispered. "Our Jackie painted New England!"

Hannah Kahn's mural didn't turn out so well, yet to Mrs.
Tucker's relief Hannah chose to hang it, a blue-green mess, in

the corner of the classroom—the one the door opened onto and hid most of the day by its being open. No matter, by the end of the two weeks Hannah had all she could take of Peggy Hardley's tiresome lies ("I can play piano, too!" "I've gone snorkeling, too!"), and she appeared elated just to have Jackie back. Mrs. Tucker rearranged the children's seating, as she did every so often, and this time she sat Jackie Thunder right next to Hannah Kahn. After all, it was spring, the best time for a friendship to blossom. And possibly, she thought—or was she merely indulging herself again?—theirs was a friendship that would last.

So much didn't last, after all. Their annual spring trip to Old Sturbridge Village in Massachusetts came and went. Then Field Day—a day spent outside while the children ran all kinds of races—came, despite cloudy weather, and went. So too the annual teachers-versus-students fifth-grade softball game, organized and pitched by Joyce McAlley–who that year almost didn't have the energy to play it. Even the science fair, with its overflow of display booths, the hamsters dragged in for experimentation, and the overuse mainly by the sixth-graders of the word "simulation," came, she noted, quickly, and went.

By June she had the satisfaction of knowing the class knew it was special. They'd earned their fifty compliments. Like a pot of tapioca pudding, becoming with time thicker and richer and more congealed, they'd finally become, with just a little stirring from her, one thing.

She so liked the class. They *were* special, she often told herself. Then she'd shake her head. No, she'd admit, they were no different from other classes. That last day she wanted to say so much to them before they left, for their sake—to hold onto them, protect them a little longer—and for her sake—to make an impression, indelible, lasting . . . but what could she say? Don't change? Things will happen to you, children, but don't let that interfere with who you are, right now, this last day of your fifth-grade year?

How absurd.

No words, she knew, could alter the fact: teachers were teachers of one class per year.

They left. Peggy Hardley and Hannah Kahn had lingered some, waiting for the others to go before they raced back to kiss her cheek. She sat in her chair which put her at their height. Feeling the silk of their faces, she jerked her head back.

"Go on," she said. "Don't be late for summer."

When she lifted herself from her chair a half hour later, she walked into the hall and ran a sponge under the flow of a water faucet. Inside her classroom she washed the blackboard once more. Walking up and down each row of tiny desks and chairs, she scanned the floor.

A pencil here, a crayon there. Hardly anything at all.

Seated at her desk, she leaned her head into her raised palm. How sleepy she felt. How tired all this teaching made her. It wasn't supposed to be like this. She wanted to say that to Kenneth, her husband, to remind him of the pact they'd made some thirty-two years ago, how she'd only teach until the first little one arrived, or maybe the second one—after all, she'd come to like teaching . . . but Kenneth wasn't here and longing for him reminded her that no life was supposed to be the life it ultimately was. We dive in, head first, optimistic! We never know how long, how hard, the swim will be . . .

Yes, yes, she told herself next. Aren't I the sage? What's that, Kenneth? Kenneth?

"Mrs. Tucker?"

It was Diana Nicholson, standing beside her, peering at her with a questioning gaze. Had she been talking out loud?

"I wanted to say bye bye."

"Bye bye?"

"Mrs. Tucker, you're a nice teacher."

"Diana, you're a nice girl."

"Thank you."

"Thank *you*. Will you have a good summer?"

"I don't know."

"What will you do?"

"I don't know."

"You can read, Diana. Go to the library. Tell Mrs. Ellridge I sent you and want you to read Robert Frost." She ripped a piece of paper from a pad and wrote the poet's name.

"Bye bye." And with that Diana dashed off, clutching the paper to her chest.

"Bye bye," she answered, anyway.

That evening, when in the middle of a solitary dinner she put down her fork and said out loud, "There are no children. There never were," she felt surprised at the satisfaction that suddenly surfaced and ran parallel with the despair. She knew she couldn't compare this satisfaction with a mother's. It had only to do with being herself, Beverly Tucker, fifty-two years old, barren, menopausal, a relatively new widow and by now, she figured, an old, but damn good teacher.

After dinner she wrote the first of the many entries she'd write all summer in a journal dedicated to "Kenneth, of course, and to Robert Frost."

On teaching: I had a class once. We took Styrofoam cups and planted, each one of us, our favorite spring flower. We put those twenty-three cups on the window ledge. Each day I told the children the same thing. Children, I'd say. Children. Now you breathe on them. So they breathed on them. And soon enough the little things they'd begun, rose.

She learned that Hannah Kahn and Jackie Thunder were assigned to different sixth grade classes. She knew they'd meet again, near strangers by then though, on the ninth grade pre-college track. Marty Littleton wasn't in Hannah's sixth grade class either, but he sat across the hall from her. From the glimpses Mrs. Tucker caught, she saw that he was punching again, needing to act tough, and standing, often, in the hall. Once she spotted him there and she frowned when Hannah walked by him and refused to even say hello. Should she give the girl a talk?

No. If she learned one thing it was to be firm about letting them go. To refrain from scrambling after them in those new corridors. They were never hers to begin with. She could accept that now as she never had before.

One day, soon after, Hannah Kahn knocked on her classroom's door to tell her that she couldn't bear the sight of Marty Littleton anymore—bored and in trouble, standing always in the hall. "Can you help?" Hannah asked.

Mrs. Tucker walked to the doorway and looked down at the girl. She knew her so well, the earnestness in her eyes, that appealing, toothy smile.

Her eyes drifted then toward her new class, her present class, twenty-six in all, who were just beginning to find common denominators in fractions.

She glanced from Hannah toward Belinda Early, a small girl in the third row. Belinda's blonde head was bowed and she leaned her body over the paperback workbook on her desk. She scratched with her pencil, erased, scratched some more. Beside her, John Beard, cute, carrot-topped, and fidgety, popped his hand up, waiving it to flag her attention. He knew the answer. He always knew the answer. She motioned John's hand down while reminding Belinda to go on, but slowly, to take her time.

Hannah tugged at her arm. She looked at her, then at the class. Once again at the old student, then toward the new ones.

"Don't be late for summer," she heard herself saying to Hannah Kahn, or was it Diana Nicholson? "Good, good, good," she heard herself whispering to Marty Littleton. "Not now, a little later," she was saying, right then, to John Beard, while in her mind she was saying, "Yours is a friendship that will last," to Jackie Thunder, then to Kenneth and to Roy Peterson, even though they were both dead. "Tell me about a farm!" she urged Peggy Hardley and Peggy's father, Frank Hardley.

Hannah Kahn was tugging at her arm. John Beard was trying so hard, she knew, to keep his hand down. Frank Hardley was Peggy Hardley's father. Diana Nicholson had an ear for poetry. Belinda Early was taking her time. Time was swirling all around her. It wasn't supposed to be like this.

A moment later Hannah was leaning over Belinda Early's workbook, helping her. John Beard was listening to Hannah, spellbound. Mrs. Tucker was still seeing a blur of faces, hearing a blur of voices.

She would ask Hannah to leave. She would get back to her class, her present class, just as she'd planned.

She was about to whisper to Hannah, "It's not a good time, maybe later," when the blur ceased, the air cleared, she saw something new. How right she'd been about that girl, how she *would* become a teacher.

She cleared her throat to make an announcement. Work by yourselves, she'd tell them, then she'd quickly nod Hannah's way, letting the girl continue to teach Belinda math, to teach John Beard about patience, about teaching.

Rows of bright faces peered at her, and she looked back into the rows of faces. There they were again. The old ones and the new ones. How strange, she thought, to be given such a gift. The chance to stand before children. To tell them something of yourself. To see them unfold.

She opened her mouth to speak. She had one hand on her stomach, the place where other women ballooned with life. She was ballooning too, buoyant and a little off balance, filled with a startling sense that she had it wrong again. It wasn't the children she had to let go of but herself, her incessant resolve, her constant planning, the tug of war she'd created years ago between having and not having, the arrangements she made to gain a sense of her worth, to cover that other sense of not mattering at all. It didn't have to be like this: an existence in extremes.

Her feet shifted beneath her, her arms, now loose, moved like snakes with lives of their own. Her voice propelled itself up and she took a deep breath. What would she say next? What would she say?

Mutual Life & Casualty
(Carolyn Kahn—1973)

Our shopping sprees began with a blank check. Mom would send one of us, me or my younger sister Hannah, to Dad's checkbook, a large, heavy ledger laid open on his desk in the upstairs den. Three business-size checks comprised each page with a column on the side for writing the amount and purpose of each withdrawal. If I got the check I'd invariably write "Loehmann's" as if that explained everything. If Hannah went she'd sometimes note the same, though at times she insisted we shopped "to buy beauteous garb for the gallant girls," or "for styles to make you smile." Dad liked those lines. All it took was a check stub entry with some pizazz to make him feel part of things—keep him from mumbling that evening that all he did was provide, provide. With the right entry he'd smile brightly and kiss Mom's cheek, then each of ours. These were the times when we—Mom, Hannah, and I—were nothing but Dad's beautiful girls. And then the money came freely.

I had two fathers, really. My father in the morning, in his plaid PJs and robe, his rusty beard yet to be shaved, reading the paper at the dining table while Hannah and I had breakfast. This was the father who made our lunches for school, who took delight in knowing the particularities of our tastes: no mayonnaise for Hannah, not even to moisten tuna fish; for me, always a dab of mustard, but only a dab.

"This angel wants a little spice of life. Say, Carolyn, hand me the lettuce?"

And if he had to leave for work early, there'd be the lunch bags in the fridge and the note on the counter. "Carolyn—extra zip." "Hannah—plain and basic."

But my father in the evening didn't know us so well.

40

Arriving home, he'd throw his suit jacket over the stair's banister. He'd shuffle through the mail. Tense and demanding, he'd sit at the head of the table expecting Mom to serve dinner pronto. His long face, often serious, now looked grim. He'd eat fast, hardly noticing what he ate, it seemed. At least he never commented on the meal, Mom's work. Then, pushing his chair back from the table, finally relaxing some, he'd talk. Not about us. Not even to us. He'd begin by uttering his daily report about the latest at Mutual Life & Casualty, the insurance company in Hartford where he worked, thirty miles south of Wells.

His day involved matters of money mostly. He was a vice president, in charge of a certain company portfolio. And so it was stocks and bonds, then company policies and county politics. The county couldn't contain him, however, and he'd invariably move on with increased vehemence, and volume, to state and national politics. Then world economy.

Mom got up and down from the table as Dad talked on. He'd mark her entrances and exits by calling, "Naomi, you listening?" She'd nod each time, even when she was in the kitchen where, from his seat at the table's far end, he couldn't see her. I'd sit in my chair and soon enough all the songs I'd ever learned roamed through my mind. When Dad stopped, signaling dinner's end, the family of songs simply vanished.

We'd wake in the morning to our other father. The one who paid attention. The one whose perspective wasn't on the whole world.

"How about a little jelly with that peanut butter, Hannah?" he'd say, teasing her as he winked in my direction. And we'd laugh, Dad and I, as Hannah came charging in, demanding, "Plain!" Dad would whisk her up and set her on the counter beside him.

"Say, Care," he'd sing. "Maybe we'll go with rye bread today. Yes?"

If as provider he did a lot for us, that was the extent of what he did with us. Mom, then still a homemaker, was our companion parent. Insofar as her looks were concerned, those years, during the early 1970s, were her best. She was of medium height, with broad shoulders and a slim waist that gave her a curved, nearly perfect, figure. High cheekbones marked her face and when she smiled her cheeks rose from her olive skin like twin moons. Her dark brown hair, fine and parted on one side, hung to her shoulders in a blunt cut. She feared losing her hair, going bald like her mother, and to preserve it she had her doctor prescribe a zinc formula—a remedy Mom had discovered in a magazine. As a teenager she'd plucked her fragile eyebrows to the point where they never grew back. That's why each day, in a ritual I remember seeing over and over, after Mom had dripped liquid zinc with an eyedropper and brushed it through her hair, she bent forward, focused on her image in the mirror, to pencil her brows back into existence.

Hannah and I escaped the fate of Mom's thinning hair. In fact we looked almost nothing like her with our matching manes of auburn—mine long and Hannah's short—and our lighter freckled skin. We were both unmistakably Dad's girls, fair and tall, with long torsos balanced on pairs of skinny legs.

Mom amazed us. Beautiful and friendly, she reigned queen of the dressing room at Loehmann's. After ambling through racks of clothes, Mom, wandering through size six, and Hannah and I, separated from Mom and each other by sizes ten and twelve, would pile clothes on our arms and carry them off to Dressing Room One or Two, or, on a busy day, which meant an extra room was available, Room Three.

The rooms were public: big square halls lined with mirrors, hooks for clothes, and low benches. Typically we'd scout for three hooks in a row to hang our clothes on and by doing this we'd stake out our dressing room territory. Mom, always hauling in the most, would confidently strip to her underwear without regard to what piece she'd try on first. But I lacked Mom's ease and would organize my selections so that I never had to present myself to the dressing room crowd in only underwear. I'd try on a blouse, say, then, leaving it on and shimmying out of my blue jeans, I'd sample a skirt. Just once, in eleventh grade, when I'd slimmed down on a kelp, lecithin, and complex vitamin B diet, did I dare try on bathing suits at Loehmann's.

Mom's good looks and shape, complimented by an instinct for style, drew admiring stares from the semi-naked ladies crowding the room. The dressing room at Loehmann's was overwhelmed by underwear and skin, by half-dressed women posed before mirrors, reflected in them—the reflections, in turn, bouncing between mirrors on opposite walls. The effect multiplied, seemingly exponentially, all the different kinds of underwear: padded bras, strapless bras, high- or low-cut panties, girdles, and hose, and all the different kinds of skin: smooth, taut, tanned, dimpled, flabby.

Mom conducted experiments. The styles then flipped so frequently—from mini to maxi to midi—and Mom's hems, like manic moods, were driven up and down. Usually she'd try on clothes just to see herself in them, a way of testing the limits of who she thought she was. Now she was a business woman. Now she was set for a safari. In blue jeans and a sweater, Mom approximated Gloria Steinem. When she looked confused enough over an outfit—asking Hannah and I repeatedly, "Is it me?"—one of the ladies, an unknown from the mass of shoppers, would finally offer help. "It's fabulous on you," the stranger would tell her. "You can get away with it. Not me. But you. You!"

In this way Mom came to rely on the help of strangers—fellow Loehmannites, you might say. These women were more often than not Jewish, and, aside from the synagogue we attended a few times yearly, Loehmann's was our other major tie with Jewish life. For Mom it was a party in the dressing room at Loehmann's. She'd make new friends, receive compliments, dish out fashion tips like party favors, and even hear a bit of gossip about a rabbi as she befriended his estranged, shopping daughter.

It was August 1973 and I hadn't yet entered ninth grade when

Mom bought her first bikini. That morning I sat at the dining table doing crosswords as I had each day that summer after breakfast with Dad. Hannah, then eleven, was there too, munching a second bowl of cereal.

We always ate breakfast with only Dad. Mom didn't like to rise early. She never felt energetic until well after Dad left. "Just can't," she explained. "Too . . . I don't know. Just can't."

This day even Dad hadn't eaten breakfast with us. It was fishing day—an annual event, a day he took off from work to go out with his buddies. The men had met at four o'clock in the morning in our backyard. From my bedroom window I'd seen them pile into Stan Hanson's station wagon for the drive to New Haven where I knew their captain, a rented soul, waited to take them out to sea. I knew little else about Dad's trips; girls weren't allowed on them and I wasn't all that interested.

I'd recently begun drinking tea at breakfast, and all summer I'd been lingering at the table long after Dad had left for work, reading the comics and Ann Landers, sipping the hot drink, waiting for Mom to come downstairs to join me.

When I heard her walk into the dining room I assumed she was dressed as always, in her blue terry cloth robe. I only caught sight of her—a compact, slender woman revealing more flesh than usual—from the corner of my eye. Hannah, facing her directly, squealed.

"Mamma mia! Where'd you get that?" she said.

Mom, headed for the kitchen, slowed to a stop. "Talbots." Facing us, she broke into a laugh. "Sorry. Couldn't help myself girls. Loehmann's! Where else?"

She held her arms at her sides, keeping them uncrossed so as not to hide her middle. "I bought it on the sly. Now what do you think? Can I get away with it?"

I didn't know. She was our mother and had an ever-so-slight potbelly. It showed in the bikini as it never had in her waist-high underwear. Her tan lines were shaped by the one-piece she'd been wearing and, though parts of her back were tanned, her belly was a soft, doughy white. We were her daugh-

44

ters and even we didn't wear bikinis. We had slight potbellies too, and skinny legs and no hips. The question was complicated. Could she wear a bikini? Could we? I sipped my sugary tea and stared.

"In all fairness imagine it with the right tan," Mom said. She paused and raised her drawn eyebrows, winking at Hannah, then turning to me, her eldest, with a serious look. "Carolyn, what do you think?"

"I don't know," I said. The tea made me hot. My sweating legs stuck to the chair. "I mean, yes, I guess with the right tan."

Mom's eyes and shoulders drooped and she folded her arms to hide the whitest part of her belly. The bikini, a swirling pink and orange print, shimmered as it stretched around her.

"I'm foolish," she said. Still facing us, she didn't move.

"Not foolish." Still stuck, I didn't move either.

"I'm too old, is that it?"

"Not too old," I said, though it was the first thought that crossed my mind. Other mothers were still in one-pieces, and I wondered why mine, at thirty-six, wanted to split her bathing suit in two. I took another hot gulp.

Mom turned to go back upstairs to her room.

"Give it a try!" I yelled. I didn't want her to feel bad, to leave us. "I think we need time to get used to it! You already look pretty good!"

She returned to the table.

"It's the tan, that's all. You can sure wear a bikini, Mom. Not me."

Her frown became a smile and she settled into a chair.

"Me either," Hannah said. "But *Mama mia*, it's you!"

At that Mom hugged each of us, briefly. Then, forgetting Hannah didn't drink it yet, she politely offered, as if we were guests: "A fresh cup of tea?"

Later that day when Dad and the other men returned, Hannah and I stood on the back steps watching them. They gathered around our picnic table and Dad began flipping fish from side to side, slicing meat from bones. Soon, the smell of fish, almost rancid in the hot sun, spread, and the neighborhood cats began to mill around the group of smelly, sweat-stained men, who in turn surrounded the bass. Then bees were drawn to the scene, and Mr. Hanson was the one who finally yelled, "These God-damn bees!" Then all the men, including Dad, began a chorus of happy, unguarded swearing.

Soon the picnic table, where Hannah, Mom, and I had eaten our cottage cheese and melon an hour before, was covered by the wet insides of fish, by bones and dismembered heads with eyes that stayed open and stared.

I stared back, and what fun I'd initially found in the scene vanished. I felt wary of these men suddenly—Dad included. Their swearing was frightening, their fillet knives were fright-ening, their dead fish were frightening. When Dad yelled, "Carolyn, would you bring us a drink?" I dashed inside to the kitchen where Mom was talking on the phone. She sat, her head lowered into a hand, staring at her bare feet. Occasionally one foot would swing as if in rhythm to the words at the other end. Her words came in her typically quick rush, yet had a consol-ing ring to them. "I know," she said gently. Then, "I can just imagine. You poor thing." I felt a need just then for these famil-iar, soothing words. As I opened the refrigerator I heard her exclaim, with enthusiasm, "Yes, I've felt that way too!"

Every day Mom talked on the phone to one of a slew of women friends, housewives all of them. Whenever Dad asked her what she had so much to talk about, Mom retorted, "Everything." From the conversations I'd overheard all my life I knew that "everything" was limited to the goings-on in our home, what Hannah and I were up to, what social events were upcoming, and the like. Yet "everything" involved something else, less definable, like a mood. It had to do with how these women were doing. "How are you doing?" they'd ask each other daily. "I'm doing okay," I'd hear Mom sometimes say, or, "I don't know. Too much to do, I guess. I feel . . ." There was something compelling and ever-changing about the "everything" they were always after. And so they called each other every day about everything. On a good day Mom had four or five of these sympathetic conversations.

I was staring into the refrigerator's cold insides, listening to Mom's voice, figuring out what drink to bring Dad and the men, when Dad came in. I must have been taking too long. I was the slow one. The slow eater, dresser, runner. Slow, compared to Hannah who was a tomboy and quick.

He stood behind me. I smelled him first—a fish smell—then felt his stomach and chest press lightly against my back. Reaching over my shoulder, he pulled out a cardboard carton of orange juice. I lifted my head backward, gazing at the ceiling, and he leaned over and gazed down at me. His thickening beard, which he hadn't bothered to shave at four o'clock in the morning, made his long, thin face look not older but younger, like a boy who'd gotten dirty playing in mud. He smiled. It was the middle of the day but I recognized this person: my friendly morning father. I smiled back. How could I have been afraid?

"Here's the ticket," he said. He turned to Mom then and waved the orange juice as if to tell her he'd be taking it outside.

She was still in the chair by the phone, her head cocked to her left, her eyes cast down. When Dad motioned with the orange juice she looked up, her drooping mouth registering instant dismay. She tucked the phone between her shoulder and ear and motioned with her arms that he leave the kitchen.

"What?" he said, confused.

"I'm busy," she whispered. "It's a weekday, Daniel," she hastily added. Her arms still gestured him out. "For God's sake, it's the middle of the afternoon."

That night when she showed him, Dad didn't like Mom's bikini. Nor did he like the pantsuit that preceded it the week before or the dress, black and strapless, soon to follow. "Who do you think you are?" he asked Mom the night she modeled the dress. He read the paper as he sat on the living room sofa. When he glanced up to look at Mom, he spoke in a voice that challenged.

"I think it looks good. I like it," she said quietly.

"Where do you think you're going?"

I was sitting across from him, on the love seat, asking him from time to time if he knew the answer to the crossword I was doing. He was busy being the evening father now—engrossed in public affairs—but to my delight he didn't mind the interruption of a question requiring a certain amount of authority. But now I grew quiet; I never dared answer that intimidating tone.

"What do you mean where?" Mom's voice, usually gentle, rose to a new pitch. "Why are you ruining this for me? I'm going nowhere. This is me, and these are my clothes." She stopped for a moment, then continued in what was now a raised, quavering voice. "Why are you ruining this for me? I'm going nowhere. But this is what I wear, what I *choose* to wear, while I'm going there!"

After some silence he said, indifferently, "Do what you like."

Though his words were not encouraging I was still relieved, because when Mom challenged Dad—even with her odd explanations—he could grow frustrated and yell. She'd recently begun to confront him more often but she could never score. He could be louder. He *was* bigger. He read two different newspapers daily and knew more, and recently I'd heard him hurl that fact at her too.

As I sat, listening, I watched how he stared at her in her outfit. Despite their quarrel, Dad was as proud of her looks as ever and his eyes gleamed with pleasure. Yet I knew he didn't admire some of her other qualities. Like how she'd "shooshed" him that night at dinner when his voice rose excitedly—he'd tapped his fork angrily in response. And at breakfast that morning he'd complained to me that she spent too much money.

"He doesn't let me know how much money we really have," she said the next morning, once she'd gotten up, defending herself over a cup of tea. "*He* totals the figures and keeps it from me. He brags we have plenty, then criticizes. Not rich, mind you, but comfortable. Plenty, but don't spend it. Plenty! Plenty!"

Dad's complaint against Mom registered in my mind, yet, as I knew firsthand—and as Dad couldn't—in her own way Mom shopped wisely. Recently she'd become relentless about her trips to and from Loehmann's, in good and bad weather, thirty-two miles one way. "You never know what'll be there," she explained. "It pays to go often. Besides," she added, sighing sadly. "It's fun."

Once there she'd frequently notice items hanging from and traveling on the automated discard rack, a track that led from Dressing Room Three, past Dressing Rooms Two and One, to the sorting room where the clothes would be arranged to go back onto the sales floor. She'd nudge one of the salesladies and request that she find the pink blouse or the scoop-necked dress that had just passed by. "I think it was a dress," she might say. "You never know. Belted, it might be a long top. Perhaps it could be worn as either. So interesting!"

If the saleslady knew Mom she'd trot off happily because it was exciting to help Mom, with her near-perfect shape, her dressing room popularity, and her genius—or so I came to think of it—for shopping at Loehmann's.

Watergate. It dominated national politics and that meant it dominated the verbal course of our evening meal. Dad, as dedicated to President Nixon as he was to Mutual Life & Casualty, as to his job as our provider, defended Nixon against the increased evidence of scandal.

"He's too smart. Has to be. You don't get where he is and make that kind of mistake. God dammit, you don't!"

But by late August Mom had become angry, impatient, accusatory, and when Dad lectured at dinner Mom finally attempted to interrupt him with her different point of view. That day she and I had talked it over. She'd turned from the TV news and said, "It makes me sick. I feel—"

"Betrayed? Cheated? Royally P.O.ed?"

"Yes. All of it. Carolyn, I feel just like you!"

And I had to smile because I loved being in harmony with

this fun, special person, with Mom.

At dinner that night she'd started with, "How I feel is—"

Dad looked at her and impatiently sighed. "Naomi, give me some facts, please. Can you support what you feel with facts?"

Her eyebrows wrinkled, her voice faded.

Dad began to knock his knife tip against the table top.

I dropped my eyes and focused on my plate of food. It seemed that whenever Mom tried to say something serious that Dad didn't agree with, Dad did this: forced her to talk on his terms, answer his questions, which worked to shut her up.

Didn't he want her to speak? Wasn't he *for* her? For *us*?

I looked to Hannah, wanting to signal something—anything. Confusion buzzed in my head and I felt a pressing need to connect. But Hannah was beyond reach, in dreamland, ignoring our parents' verbal battle, staring blankly out the window at the oaks in our backyard.

Ninth grade wasn't going well. My marks, usually solid, plunged, especially in Ancient Civ where we were forced to memorize key dates and names. Without the nerve to make a crib sheet and cheat, like so many classmates did, I brought home C's and once a D+. I also brought home a hatred for the history teacher, the pontificating, all-knowing, red-faced Mr. Blay, for his laziness and his willingness to settle for a grading method that meant, as far as I could tell, nothing.

On a near-weekly basis I began to leave school. I'd drop into the main office and speak to Mrs. Tull, the principal's secretary, a thin, elderly woman, who, with her small bones and shrinking frame, had an affinity for fragility. "I'm not feeling well," I'd explain. "Carolyn, you do look peaked," she'd agree, handing me the phone to dial Mom. Each week I looked peaked to Mrs. Tull. I'm not sure how I managed except that I probably did look peaked, always tired, always grumpy, always mumbling under my breath about lazy, red-faced Mr. Blay.

Once home I'd drink a cup of tea with Mom. She didn't mind the regularity of these sick days nor did she notice that I looked especially peaked. At least she didn't mention it. After tea, from a pile stashed on a bath towel under the dining table, Mom would pull out a block of wood and a piece of sandpaper.

"You sand, I'll varnish," she'd say, thus divvying up the tasks of *découpage*. Mom had discovered *découpage* that fall in a magazine. Taken with it, she shopped card stores for pictures that would look good when their edges had been ripped and burned—the antiquing effect. Soon she developed an eagle's eye for such prints and at the height of her *découpage* enterprise she plucked from our incoming mail New Years cards and the occasional, well-drafted birthday card, no matter whose birthday was being celebrated.

With the coming of *découpage* our dining room was transformed into a craftsman's workshop, our table cluttered with hammers and glue, with varnish and wood stains. And on days that I skipped school, dinner, if it was cooked at all, was served in the living room on trays.

Dad didn't go for this. He preferred the classic meal of meat, vegetables, two starches, dessert. But Mom, not a bad cook in the least, was quickly losing an appetite for her own food. "Good," she'd now typically quip, finished with dinner. "Only *6,432* meals to go!" As if on cue, Hannah and I would laugh and Mom would join in. Dad might have offered a thin smile, but this was our joke, girls only, and it was clear that his smile was forced, that he didn't really get it.

Hannah once explained: "Counting meals, Dad. It cracks us up!"

It was early in January when Dad came home with news of Mutual Life & Casualty's growth. By then Mom had taken on another new endeavor, volunteering to write news blurbs announcing functions of the PTA, the nearest Hadassah, and, less frequently, the county's Y.M.C.A. She didn't care about the functions themselves, but she liked discovering a way to make each event sound special and important. "A must," she liked to say. She was becoming proud of herself as she discovered more and more that her sharp observations—the very kind that brought her such success at Loehmann's–served her well when she tried to pitch events. And I was excited for her. She was starting to get up earlier too—to look forward to the day.

That day she'd begun to write about the upcoming Y.M.C.A.'s 10-K run, the first long-distance run ever held in our area. "Listen to this, girls," she said. Hannah and I sat still as Mom began to detail the "impossible dream" of running all that way, the "satisfaction you hadn't felt in years," once you finished, not to mention the money you'd help raise "just by putting one foot in front of the other." The dining table was covered with scraps of Mom's notes and photos clipped from magazines of sweaty, jubilant runners, and Hannah and I each had a pad too. "Just in case," Mom said. "You two might get an idea. We'll band together, girls. We'll brainstorm!" The dinner hour had long passed and none of us was even hungry.

"Well," Dad said, speaking unusually brightly. He stood just beyond the doorway and rubbed his hands together. "Today Mutual Life & Casualty joined the prestigious tribunal of Lloyd's of London."

"Oh," Mom said defensively. "Today we started a new blurb."

"Oh." Dad's tone was the same.

On my pad I doodled a stick figure running off, escaping through an open doorway. I scrawled "impossible dream" beside it.

Hannah broke a length of silence. "Lloyd's of London . . . must be something!" After he left the room, Hannah asked, "What's a tribunal?"

"A big old business word." Mom glanced over her shoulder toward Dad in the kitchen. There she'd left him a pastrami sandwich. That's as far as her cooking went anymore. "It means a club, but it's for businessmen, and they say 'tribunal' to justify the extra money they'll make from being together."

Hannah slammed her pencil down. "That's horrible!" She paused, looking confused. "Isn't it, Mom?"

I said, "Who knows if it's good or bad, Hannah? The point is, who cares?"

"I don't know either," Mom said. "But I'd like to." With that she ripped her blurb into tiny pieces, and, like confetti, let them fall haphazardly, everywhere.

After that, new activities developed in the house. Hannah, though only in sixth grade, took to arguing with Dad about current events. I'd hear them going back and forth, Dad's voice rising, seemingly in enjoyment, while Hannah's voice rose too, not with the same satisfaction as Dad's, but with increasing, even tearful, frustration. He'd keep the talks going by withholding what she most wanted him to say: that she could be right too, that she had a valid perspective. Though Mom never joined in, she was pleased with Hannah, cheering her on when she began to falter. I couldn't see how Hannah bore such battles— they were too heated to be solely for sport. We were growing apart, Hannah and I.

"I can't help myself, Carolyn," she explained. "I need to make a point."

I felt I needed something too: physical space. If Dad walked into a room, for example, I'd find a reason, soon enough, to walk out.

My behavior may have differed from Hannah's, but, like her, I felt it couldn't be helped.

Simultaneously I found a new way to spend more time with Mom. We went shopping, just us two, the last Tuesday in January. Not feeling well, I hadn't bothered to attempt school that day. I knew I'd be missing my best friend Anita's birthday and I was sorry for that. I'd been up late the night before planning my annual "Birthday Salute." That morning, though, the prospect of leaving home seemed too much. I felt as stuck as ever as I sat alone, lingering over my tea, Dad and Hannah having left already. Finally pulling myself up, I climbed upstairs to watch reruns of "I Love Lucy" and "Leave it to Beaver."

In time, Mom brought me more tea and toast, the standard sick food fare. It was snowing outside, and the cloudiness cast a dim glow on the day. In the nearly dark den I munched and watched and heard Mom in the distance doing chores. Finally she sat with me. We watched "Andy Griffith" together and the sight of little Opie was almost too much for us to bear.

"Adorable!" Mom exclaimed.

"You said it," I agreed. Despite the weather's gloom, I felt better. Three reruns, two pieces of toast with butter and jelly, and Mom, sitting on the floor beside me and laughing.

Later we drove to Loehmann's. Because of the snowfall the drive was especially long and I sat on the seat's edge the whole time helping Mom steer. That day our arrival was a triumph of sorts. I no longer felt sick. In fact, marching beside Mom into Dressing Room One, I felt lucky, had a strange sense that this could be *my* day.

I brought in several sweaters. More often than not Loehmann's styles were too adult for me, but that day in the sweater aisle I'd noticed something new: Pierre Cardin.

Mom had with her the usual assembly of skirts, slacks, and her latest favorite: the one-piece pantsuit. Upon stripping off her clothes, she slid her legs into a pair of plaid slacks. She'd brought more items in than I had, so I didn't rush. I wanted our timing to stay in sync.

Mom struck up a conversation with a lady—overweight and over fifty—on her left.

"Looks great." The lady, wearing an awkward combination of undergarments and high heels, trotted around Mom. "A knockout. My God," she said to Mom, "don't you have a dynamite behind!" Mom smiled, and her high cheekbones rose in their round fullness. I knew that's what she came here for, the easy compliments, the nurturing attention. When she turned my way, I readily agreed; she looked great.

I pulled off my sweatshirt, then tugged a Pierre Cardin over my bare, freckled shoulders. It was brown and one hundred percent wool. Mom had taught us never to buy cheap blends and I was proud of the fact that even without checking labels I'd somehow developed an eye for textured purity.

I looked at myself in the mirror. My frizzy auburn hair complemented the stark brown wool. So did my red face, flushed from tension at the unavoidable display of myself in the dressing room. Yet this time the added color helped. Upon first sight I knew I loved this Pierre Cardin.

I tapped Mom and asked, tentatively, "Is it me?"

Both women faced me and stared. The lady, nodding vehemently, said, "And your daughter. I never would have guessed she's yours. But what a bloomer!"

"Thank you." Mom looked surprised. In her shock, her cheek bones vanished. "How much is it?"

The price tag dangling at my wrist read, "Thirty-nine ninety-five." I mumbled the words, knowing this price wouldn't match Mom's strict conception of "a buy."

Mom, staring now at my mirrored image, said, "You're only fourteen."

I nodded. There was no reason to say more.

In the end I purchased with Mom's approval a simple navy button-down blouse for twelve dollars. Mom bought a sweater and a shawl and a peasant dress she was sure Dad would find "too hip." She turned to me and winked. Pulling out Dad's check, she called the day a success.

I called it a success too. I didn't own a Pierre Cardin but that didn't matter. Even without it my sense of luck had been fulfilled. For while I'd modeled the sweater Mom had said something I'd never heard. Her eyes were wide and her face was strangely serious. "Carolyn, I have something to confess," she began. "You do look good in brown!"

Other confessions soon followed. Mom didn't feel good in the mornings. Mom didn't sleep well at night. Mom didn't like Dad. She began to tell me this in short sentences sheepishly uttered during my days home. She talked to me now like I was one of the women on the phone, or one in the dressing room, and the intimate connection felt good. I loved Mom's confessions.

"I can just imagine," I said after a time. And I could, had for a while now, though I hadn't realized it before. Why, I knew her life from the inside, how she experienced it. "You poor thing," I said. "Mom, if I were you I'd feel that way too!"

She smiled at me, then frowned. "If I left, Care—divorced—what would I do?"

"Work!"

"At what?" And she quickly laughed, a defeated, feeble sound. "I can't do anything. Not really. I'm so afraid. Incredibly afraid."

By then I'd become a kind of personal fashion consultant for her. To do this I'd stopped visiting Anita and my other friends so much. I didn't mind. I loved being Mom's confidante.

On slow weekend afternoons we'd often wander into her bedroom to try on clothes. I'd lie on her bed and watch her change. As always, she was tenacious about her changing, swapping identities as she moved in and out of several outfits in an hour. She'd put on one combination and I'd nod. She'd try on another and I'd offer advice. No criticisms or challenges; just an idea to make the look even better.

Best of all, every so often she'd throw me something. Then I'd get off the bed, put the piece on, and gaze at myself—ungainly and freckled and pale—dressed in Mom's clothes, posed in Mom's mirror. I never asked, but always wondered, would I ever look like her?

Only once did Dad ever wander in and we'd yelled, in unison, "We're changing!" At that he'd backed out—a swift, sure retreat.

The very next morning Dad seemed especially eager to help me prepare my lunch.

"Cheddar, Care, or Swiss?"

"I make my own lunch now." I gathered the makings close to my body.

"Can't a father help his angel?"

"Hand me the mustard and the lettuce, then." He wouldn't back off.

"Not too much!"

"I know. It's me. It's *for* me." I wouldn't look at him but I felt his intrusive stare.

"Can't a father help his angel?"

"What do you think, then? Rye or wheat?"

Suddenly he pulled me into a fierce, unwanted hug. While I stood there, stiff, holding my breath, Dad said, "Carolyn, angel, how you always loved rye."

That's when I stopped having breakfast with Dad. Instead, I stayed in bed—like Mom, only I wasn't sleeping—until Dad left for work. I'd know because I'd hear the sounds that marked the progression of his morning routine: the running water in the bathroom, the creaking of our heavy front door while he retrieved the newspaper, the chatter of the radio that now often accompanied him while he read and ate breakfast, the slam of the back door, and, finally, the choked cough of the car engine. Then I'd get up and race to school.

Once he left me a note: "Angel, feeling all right?"

I never answered. As far as I was concerned I had no father in the morning. There never was a father in the morning. There was only my father in the evening. Demanding. Critical. Bossy. And by now it was clear. I wanted a divorce from Dad.

One day in the gloom of late February, a mood augmented by one of Mr. Blay's endless monologues, my friend Anita passed me a note. "Unbelievable," she wrote. "Over the weekend my father moved out."

Her father. I saw him whenever I visited Anita's house though I couldn't say I knew him well. Like Dad, hers worked in insurance. And, like Dad, her father kept to himself while we were together in her house, essentially leaving us alone.

In contrast to her father, Anita's mother oozed affection. "Dearie," she'd call me. And, "Sweetie." Immediately upon meeting her I liked the easy warmth. Like Mom, she was adept at making things, yet she was even professionally accomplished. She didn't work per se, but she was a wonderful artist, sketching in her notebook at every spare moment. Often while I visited she'd bake for us, then stay near us, sketching us while we read or drew our own pictures. I imagined her and Anita having even more time together now that it was only the two of them. And I imagined them using that time well: their mutual talents—their *selves*—developing and blossoming without the stagnation, or intimidation, of a man.

"How?" I asked Anita once we were in the hall going to our next class.

"How what?" She hung her head as she walked, which caused her to nearly bump into several people.

"How'd you and your Mom get rid of him?"

She stopped then and looked up, surprised. "Get rid of him? Carolyn, where'd you get that idea?" As we continued down the hall she said, sadly, "Didn't I tell you? He left *us*."

That next Saturday I spent the afternoon in the upstairs den, watching, for at least the third time on TV, *The King and I*. I'd been with Mom all morning and was wearing a luxurious mohair sweater of hers, her latest from Loehmann's. In it I felt sophisticated, irresistible, chic. I felt like a vision of Mom.

I lay on the carpeted floor with stacked pillows under my head. I was by myself and happy. Mom and Hannah had gone off to a lumber yard to buy some wooden boards for *découpage*. No thoughts of the red-faced Mr. Blay or Dad plagued my mind. Anna was falling in love. The King was as adorable as his flock of children, and, like Anna, I was falling in love with him too.

Just then I heard Dad climbing upstairs, his stomp as distinctive as his voice. As his footsteps drew near, my body tensed. I didn't want to be interrupted, certainly not by Dad, and certainly not when romance was about to swell, like a cumulus cloud, and ride on the air.

He came into the room. By then my body was rigid, as frozen as a mannequin's. We didn't speak. I folded my arms across Mom's mohair, waiting for him to leave. This meeting, even with him holding back in the doorway, felt like a colossal collision.

He asked, "Where's your mother?"

I rubbed the arms of Mom's mohair. "Out."

After a long pause, he said, "What's this?"

"*The King and I*," I finally mumbled.

From the doorway he continued to peek at the television. With him nearby, I'd lost the ability to watch with abandon and all I wanted then was to salvage what abandon I could.

"I want to be alone."

"What?" He sounded confused.

"Please leave. I want to be alone." I paused, then added, "Why are you ruining this for me?"

For a moment we were silent. I coiled my legs and tightened my crossed arms.

"I'm ruining?" His voice sank to a rumble.

Sitting upright, I yelled. "Yes! Ruining!"

A long hallway ran between the den and my parents' bedroom. Though I managed to squeeze past him at the door, I knew I was a hunted criminal, and I fled as if racing toward a border into freedom down the hall.

I slammed the door to my parents' bathroom, within their bedroom, but before I could lock myself in Dad was there, pulling the door open.

At first, when he grabbed my arm, twisting it behind my back, it hurt, but then I didn't feel it. All I heard was Dad's low growl—an animal sound—and deep within my heart I felt I was getting what I deserved.

In compliance, I fell to the floor.

Nothing happened for a moment except a lot of breathing. I was gasping and I could hear that Dad was too. Next he started growling, "How dare you? How dare you?" Then he kicked me, with his knee, with his foot. A pause. More breathing. Then again—the knee, the foot.

Slowly, grabbing the edge of my parents' bed, I pulled myself up. Dad helped. The smell of his breath, sour and over-heated, hit my nose. I felt drowsy with fatigue as if all the tired-ness of the year had just jelled in my bones. Mom's mirror, over her dresser, held me captive. Oddly, her sweater now looked absurd, clingy on my frame, clearly no fit.

From the den, down the hall, music streamed. The King would soon put his arm around Anna's waist. She would hold his hand and teach him the dance steps—one, two, three.

Dad had both his arms around me, gently now, and though I didn't will them into motion, my arms reached for him.

He said, quietly, "Oh, my God. Carolyn, oh, my God." The voice, I couldn't deny it—it was my father in the morning.

In the other room I heard the King ask Anna: "Shall we dance?" At that I knew their careful twirling had begun. They'd step together, slowly at first, Anna's head nodding as she offered the King her boundless encouragement. His skill and confidence would soon grow, and they'd twirl faster and faster until they'd spun nearly out of control. Breathless, they'd stop and gaze into each other's eyes. Shall we dance? Is this love? "Oh, my God." One, two, three.

I felt Dad patting my head. He was holding me up and I was leaning into his chest. "I didn't mean it," I heard him say.

I let Dad lead me to my bedroom, tuck me under a blanket, and pat and pat my head. He mumbled all the while, "I didn't mean it. I don't know how this happened." But before I could answer, "me either," I dropped into something Mom knew well: a deep, long sleep. A-way-to- avoid-things sleep.

My dream is a memory made bright. I'm ten and Hannah's seven. It's Saturday and a blizzard whips outside. Wind is visi-ble in the air, sweeping through it like a huge, gray flag that's been so precariously raised it dips from the sky and into our world. At the dining table Hannah and I cut out paper dolls from Mom's stockpile of *McCall's* magazines. It's late morning and Mom's just up and dressed. Now she's with us, flipping through a cookbook. She snaps it shut and Hannah and I look up at the sound. Is Mom angry?

She rises, leaves us.

When she returns she wears her coat, gloves, boots. "Come on, girls," she says. "Let's go shopping."

Outside, Mom scuttles through the snow, her head bent in determination as she makes her way to the icy car. Hannah and I take more time, prancing about the slippery sidewalk, laughing and taking delight in the cold, wet snowflakes that blow into our faces. At Mom's urging, we've left the brightness of our dining table and have moved into a wondrous yet tumultuous gray land. For a brief instant I marvel at Mom's choice of activity that day, her recklessness—desperate though it is—not with herself, but with *us*.

I turn and see Dad peeking out a window in the upstairs den where he's spent the day reading the paper and watching football on TV. I kneel, make a snowball, then throw it toward him, knowing as I do the distance between us is too great for me to reach my intended goal. As if on cue, Hannah does the same, and we continue in this way, dressed in clownish hats with huge pompons, putting on a show for Dad.

The car engine sputters, then works its way from a low growl into a steady roar. Exhaust clouds the air and Mom yells, "Come on. I'm leaving!"

I glance one more time through the grayness toward Dad. His eyes look worried. Be careful, his expression seems to say. You never know what could happen. I flop on my back in the snow, spread my arms and legs, and jump up. I point at the white angel I've left behind. I see Dad nod. He steps back from the window.

I can hardly see him at all. Then just his hand. Goodbye, a shadow waves. Goodbye.

Part II

Like Happiness, Like Love

The Legend of Princess Topaqua
(Hannah Kahn—1993–Thirty-one years old)

Our lake was called Topaqua after the Indian princess who drowned in it, self-sacrificially, to bring needed rain to her tribe. Who told me that story? I came by it in the way that most town history in Wells is passed: by no one in particular. Most likely I came by it in the same way I came upon the lake itself, having been brought to its edges as an infant, then returning day after day, year after year, swimming in summer, skating in winter, boating in spring, until finally the lake was part of me, with no first time and no last time, just the sense—the same one that I have of my mother—that I knew it completely, that I always had.

Because I assumed the legend of Princess Topaqua was unique, I was shocked when in my last year of college I heard an anthropologist—a squat, sharp-tongued professor visiting our Worcester campus from Boston—tell the tale of a beautiful Indian princess, the most beautiful, most compassionate, in her tribe. This tribe lived in a small New Hampshire town, with a lake. The tribe lived by the lake, the professor recalled, and one year the lake's water sank dangerously low. Drought threatened. The tribe, dependent on the lake for its survival—not so much for water as for fish—spent a season frozen in anxiety until the princess volunteered to appease the gods with her life. She threw herself from a large rock into the lake and drowned.

The anthropologist's lesson was simple: all the New England states were strewn with these lovely princesses, now all dead. My story was everybody's story; my home town, any old town.

The class was called "New England Folklore" and I got an A, having written my term paper on French-Canadian Folk

Cookery. To do this I'd collected recipes from four dislocated French-Canadian sisters, octogenarians all, sharing a house and a four-car garage on a quiet, dead-end in Worcester. I was thrilled when Worcester's Historical Society accepted the recipes as relics of historical dimension. But what I really couldn't get over after having taken that class was the news that no matter where one looked in New England, so long as there was a lake, nearby there would likely be a large rock too. Bet a town local someday and you're sure to win. Ask, isn't that the rock an Indian princess once threw herself from?

And here I sit, on Lake Topaqua's infamous rock, one among an outcropping of boulders. Surely this is the rock. Bigger than the others. Growing up I remember the teenagers, older, tougher, terribly remote, sitting here smoking cigarettes and talking, occasionally growing rambunctious and diving off it, despite the shallow water and rocks below. They wouldn't dive so much as push themselves, headfirst, from the rock out into the lake. They'd surface in an instant, screaming or smiling, and inevitably a whistle would blow. *No diving off the rocks*, the lifeguard would call. We had a small public beach— still do—and this is where that legendary rock stands: at the end of a pebbly jetty, by our pebbly public beach, by our lake, named for the sacrifice of Princess Topaqua.

My husband's words: *There comes a point when you just have to take the plunge. Don't you see that, Hannah? We're ready.*

This pregnancy was Jack's idea. A step forward, he said. So here I've come, to wait for her arrival. I know she's a she.

And I wait for Jack.

For a time, before she moved away from Wells two years ago, my mother had been giving me gifts of lace: a pair of hand-crocheted gloves, a small, delicate evening bag with a drawstring handle, a collar that slips like a poncho over my head and across my shoulders. I don't know why the lace. Perhaps she saw me as a relic of the past, a twentieth-century woman with a nineteenth-century soul that only hand-made lace could fully reveal.

The other night I stood naked in front of the mirror, swollen belly and all. I put on the lace gloves. The lights in the bedroom were off; only a glow from the hallway brushed my skin. I thought of lighting candles, but that would have meant leaving the room to get them, and Jack was in the living room watching TV and I didn't want him to know what I was doing.

Holding the gloved hands in front of my face, I spread my fingers wide, peered through the slits between the fingers like a child cheating at peek-a-boo. I pulled the elastic band from my hair and shook it loose. Then I reached for the collar.

Time must have passed as I stood there, staring into the mirror at my form. I was an exaggeration: my stomach full of infancy, my neck and head and hands full of time past. Yet what I felt most was that something of myself was coming alive. I stood, staring, and tried to reach back, to place this vague burden I've always felt—my sadness—at its source.

How do we pass on what's inside of us? How does the pain and confusion that belong to someone else's life infuse another's? I wondered then, as I do now, will I pass this sadness on to my daughter? What will I do when she wakes up that first morning, as bewildered as her mother, as helpless, and cries?

My mother once told a story of me and her and Lake Topaqua. I'm two. She's twenty-six, five years younger than I am now. It's summer and we're here at this scraggly public beach. So are the other mothers, twenty-six, twenty-seven years old; two, three, four kids apiece. My sister Carolyn plays happily among her friends, swimming and building sand castles. The lake is breezy as usual. Every so often the whine of a motorboat engine interrupts the quiet on the shore. There must have been someone on water skis, my mother concluded, and I've imagined this person sliding over the wake of a motorboat's wake, creating in the process a second, similar wake.

We were there for several hours already. That would mean my mother and the other mothers would have been sitting on a large, pilly blanket playing endless rounds of bridge. One of them would be wearing an unbuttoned cardigan sweater over her bathing suit, another, a broad straw hat. My mother would be wearing as little as possible, tanning, tanning.

Her skin would have been so warm. I came to her, she said, at exactly eleven o'clock in the morning. On time, always. I crawled into her cross-legged lap. I curled there like a kitten. I made her feel so loved, so needed.

"I needed you too," I explained, leaning toward her.

"Of course you did. Hannah, I was your *mother*," she responded, stepping back ever so slightly.

The breeze. The sunshine. The mothers' voices telling soft tales, bidding small bids, gossiping between plays. My mother's warm skin. Sweet dreams and sleep.

That's the story. The Regularity With Which I Napped, I've called it. When I told her that title, two years ago when we were still such good friends, it did what I'd hoped—made her laugh.

I wonder, did I breathe in something else while resting on her legs? Something not so sweet? She hadn't yet begun to fall asleep midday herself. That tendency developed years later.

"I always loved my babies!" she's said whenever we've recounted other things—PTA meetings, car-pooling, my father's tone of voice—that she didn't like so well.

The Regularity with Which I Napped is a happy story and as I sit here contaminating it with gloomy speculation I feel guilty. And drowsy. Like most women I've become in certain key ways like my mother: I'm so full of something, some heavy something, I crave sleep.

My mother's idea that I'm someone attached to another time would stem from her private, romantic side. She grew up, an only child, in a working-class neighborhood in Bridgeport. The city became her springboard for dreaming. Ugly and industrial, Bridgeport was a haven for the kind of labor that could make its Greek, Italian, and Polish immigrants achieve their better American lives. Her parents were not Greek, Italian or Polish, but Lithuanian-Jewish, and together they ran a small dry-cleaning and tailoring operation.

My mother liked to read. She had trouble reading at first. Coming from a non-reading family, she entered school and found the piecing together of the alphabet's sounds cumbersome, more a block than a route to the escape she longed for, even so early in her life. But with time her reading pace quickened; and, in time, with her rise through Bridgeport's schools to her entrance at Connecticut College on full scholarship, her escape from Bridgeport's smokey drudgery became complete.

She sang in a chorus at college and met my father, a Clark University student, born and raised in Worcester, who sang in his. The schools joined ranks for some regional concerts and my parents found each other that way, their mouths wide open, their voices in tune. When they married, my mother dropping out of college early to do so, my father brought her to Wells, hilly and green and near enough to his insurance work in Hartford. My father is a cautious person and his steady career in insurance—guarding, for a price, against even remote dangers—has suited a certain rigidity in his character. He doesn't like change. Given a new situation, he'll alight on possible dangers before he ever sees possibilities.

If my mother felt alienated in Bridgeport, a dreamer unable to find a niche in a noisy industrial city, she felt just as alienated in Wells living amidst its amalgam of working-class Christianity. Perhaps to compensate for my parents' oddness—their Jewishness, their uniquely collegiate backgrounds, my father's professional standing—my parents began to socialize rigorously. Back then, in the 1960s and early 70s, cocktail parties and bridge groups were the rage.

Their rage, and by that I mean their very best performance, came in the form of an annual formal evening party, drinks and hors d'oeuvres, for the few other professionals in Wells and a good many of the doctors, lawyers, and insurance executives in and around the northern Connecticut River valley. As hostess, my mother would dress in one of her many full-length gowns, tease her hair, bare her dark shapely shoulders, and don glittering clip-on earrings. She was sexy, and once a year she let it unabashedly show.

My father played bartender. He prepared during the afternoon. First he turned our rectangular dining table sideways so that it reached nearly wall to wall across our dining room, with only a sliver of open space on the left side that he'd squeeze his gangly frame through. He'd cover our table's gleaming surface with bottles of gin, vodka, whiskey, a black ice chest, and small glass bowls of orange and lime slices, olives, and maraschino cherries. These, Carolyn and I would sneak all night.

Carolyn and I handled the arrivals. We'd answer the front door, and then I'd follow Carolyn upstairs where we'd heave our guests' coats onto our parents' bed. For the women, the range was from real to fake mink; "fashion," for lack of a better word, dictated such a sad, limited sphere. Yet "fashion" equally constrained the men. They'd wear ties and jackets, distinguishing themselves only by the singularity of the tie's print or the texture of what was most likely a navy blazer's weave.

On a good year the turnout was such that women's fur obliterated my parents' cotton-chenille bedspread. Midway through the party, when the din downstairs peaked, Carolyn and I took turns modeling stoles and jackets. One year, 1971—before my parents' estrangement moved in—Mrs. Klass, Dr. Klass's well-spoken yet matronly housewife, arrived in a knock-out, full-length fur coat that dazzled even my mother. In the contrived romantic lighting of my parents' bedroom, Carolyn tried it on first. "It sends you," I told my sister, lost inside the coat's bulk. I was imitating my mother who, when shopping, especially liked when clothes "sent her."

The morning after their party my parents woke in an excited state, something combining mild happiness—relief—with a slightly more acute, more negative, anxiety. They'd have stayed up late the night before to start cleaning, but the downstairs would still be a wreck, paper napkins littered about, half-filled glasses lying on table tops, some drinks with cigarette ash floating in them. My parents would assess the night's events. The count was always crucial. How many showed? How much booze was used up? How high were the coats piled on the bed? They'd run through these questions between themselves, then turn to us as if we could offer a fresh perspective. Weren't there a lot of people? Wasn't it noisy? Weren't the gowns lavish (at least for Wells, my mother would add)? Did we—Naomi and Daniel—look okay? Weren't we having a good time?

They continued hosting until I turned twelve in 1974. That year my mother stopped socializing so much. No more "obligations," she said, "just friends." She packed up her fake mink, stashing it on a remote shelf in our linen closet, away from her everyday wear. She dressed more simply: jeans, t-shirts, a tweed blazer with big wooden buttons, occasionally a silk or cotton scarf. She and her best friend, Candice Eastman, "puffed" a little marijuana. The year before she'd stopped preparing full dinners. She didn't want the fuss— "the waste of time." She was thirty-seven years old and in a hurry. With a vengeance she took a slew of continuing education classes: basic accounting, assertiveness training, transcendental meditation, rug-making. I've always found knitting relaxing, but when my mother learned how she worked her needles into a frenzy, producing in just one season piece after piece after piece.

"Let's go!" she says. She seems tall today, especially tall in her ice skates. I'm twelve and have entered that age of adolescent dismay. Like her, I'll be of medium height and well-proportioned, but for now I'm all out of balance, all over the place— long legs, short waist, round face, wide eyes. A strong wind gusts about the lake. Because of the wind, the ice has frozen in lumpy ripples, but the sun shines relentlessly, creating an illusion of perfection. See? We have a perfect lake. This is perfect skating weather. And my mother, swirling backwards and gesturing for me to come along, is elegant and graceful and, this afternoon, here with me, only me.

This was her idea. We hold hands. Push and glide, push and

glide. She lets go to practice cross-overs and I do the same, with less success. She stops, breathes deeply. We're surrounded by puffy clouds of our breath. The brightness of our red cheeks matches our hats, multi-colored striped things bought just that morning at The Dollar Store, a new store at our town's first mall. My mother is wearing a black woolen jacket and red, stretchy slacks. Her fingers, covered by black leather gloves, look like crows, distant and V-shaped, as she lifts her arms, fluttering her hands about her.

She points toward the middle of the lake.

Lake Topaqua is six miles around and one across. As we head out, the breeze, steady and refreshing, invigorates. I push to keep up with my mother who glides two paces or so ahead.

"Fun?" she calls. Her voice is charged with excitement, with motion.

"Fun!" Pushing on, I feel the first tingle of perspiration under my hat.

She points again, and we head toward a split between two of the islands in the lake's middle. There, it's like skating on an ice road, for the split is just wide enough for a boat, maybe two, to get through. And it's quiet. Ahead of me my mother swings around, digs with the points on her skate blades, stops. Her breathing continues, though, in quick spurts.

"Whew!" She pulls off her hat. Most of her hair lies flat against her head, giving her a new, relaxed look.

We continue to catch our breath. She holds her head high, glancing about her. I do the same. The trees on the island, though leafless, still form a kind of shade. It's almost dark in this split in the middle, at least as compared to the glaring shine on the open lake. With one of my mittens I wipe the sweat on my forehead. My mother doesn't seem to be sweating at all.

She folds her arms across her chest and shudders. Her frame collapses as she tightens it into a ball, pulling into herself for warmth. "Got to keep moving," she says, straightening. I nod. We push on.

Once through the split we're back out on open, frozen

water. We skate clear across the lake. Topaqua Park, the public beach where we began, isn't visible anymore. The islands block it. An ice fisherman is sitting on a crate near the edge of this foreign shore and we skate to him.

"Cigarette?" he offers my mother. He leans over the hole he's chipped. No catch.

"Oh, no," she says. Then, "How do you stay warm?"

He laughs, pulls out a small bottle of brandy from inside his thick parka.

"This, mostly," he says.

My mother and I eye each other. Then she does something daring, new. She grabs the bottle, takes a swig, laughs. She hands it back, then pushes off.

"Got to keep moving!" she calls.

My father doesn't want to hear any more.

"What?" he exclaims. "You took her across the lake?" He's already slammed his fist on the kitchen counter. His ruddy complexion has turned into the red of alarm. Loosened, his tie swings with the heaves of his chest. My sister and I, cleaning up after dinner, tiptoe around him.

"Yes, it took no time. It was clear and cold. We went right across, through the middle." My mother answers as she carries dinner plates to the sink.

He repeats these words—*through the middle*—in a low, grumbling voice, taking his time with each one as if chanting them. He's tall, and as he stands in the doorway, moving from the dining room to the kitchen, he pauses to touch the beam of the door frame above him. This gesture is his habit, one of his many strange stretches, a vestige of his year of college track, a move I've never understood. Does he think he might hit his head? How disillusioned; he's not that tall. Or is it for security's sake, touching the beam to reap the comfort of repetitive motion? Once through the doorway, his hand back by his side, the bellowing begins. "Naomi, do you know what might have happened?"

73

"But it didn't," she insists, quietly. She closes the refrigerator, then walks, her back to him, to the sink.

"But it could have! You know that. Don't you?"

"It was frozen solid. It *was*." She's rinsing now. She's refusing to say more. I can tell. I go to the dining table in the next room to clear off any dinner remnants. Carolyn's there—waiting, it seems. We've come to know what to expect.

When he finally lets loose, my sense is that my sister and mother share my relief. At least it will be over soon, I tell myself. *Soon.*

"*Dangerous!*" he thunders. "*Careless!*" Then, overcoming a verbal inertia, the words spill out. "*You could have killed her—you could have been killed yourself—go ahead and do it— you fool, you stupid, stupid, Goddamn fool—do what you like— whatever you like!*"

Later that night, I brought my mother some orange juice and aspirin. She was in Carolyn's bed—temporarily, she promised. It was okay with Carolyn. She liked sleeping on the couch in front of the TV. She liked old movies and she liked watching them by herself in the deep of night. TV felt good, Carolyn told me once when I asked her how it was she never grew tired.

"Don't tell Dad," were my mother's orders, and, dutifully, I snuck into the kitchen for her medicine. Turning the light out behind me, I silently crept back upstairs.

I sat with her for a while as she lay on the bed. In the dim room we made soothing small talk.

"You and Carolyn got your clothes figured out for tomorrow?"

Yes, we had.

"You and Carolyn planning any weekend events?"

I wasn't sure. Carolyn was older and didn't like to hang out with me anymore. I might plan something by myself, I said.

"You have a nice day at school today, Hannah?"

I turned to her, to correct her—my day was better than nice, it was wonderful, but I didn't have it at school, I had it with *her*.

74

By then, though, my mother was asleep.

Jack and I complement each other. People have always said that about us. Me, the piano teacher, easygoing, nurturing. Jack, the successful home builder. My mother's bragged from the start that we're a perfect couple.

We've known each other always, tolerating kindergarten through high school in Wells's impoverished public system. When we were small I used to tease him. He was shy and stocky, an odd mix of Pequod Indian and Italian Catholic that gave him a lovely dark complexion, though not much height. All through grade school I'd make him laugh, easily. A mere glance Jackie Thunder's way undid him.

By high school, though, I'd lost the touch. We'd pass each other in the hall and Jack would look right past me. One day I was playing piano for the spring drama production—*You're a Good Man, Charlie Brown.* I was working through the finale, a song called "Happiness." It was after school and he was on his way past the auditorium to baseball practice outside. He lingered in the auditorium's doorway, and I became self-conscious, making so many mistakes I had to start over again and again.

The fiasco drew his sympathies. That was late in our sophomore year. We began to sit next to each other in classes then, still not talking, not acknowledging anything between us. He was always serious—a cover for his shyness—and I was always giggling—high on dope—and he didn't like this. Unlike grade school, he'd only bear my giggles now, not join them. Once, in eleventh grade pre-calculus class, he turned to me. The minute before, our teacher had solved an equation on the blackboard, which made me laugh—an out-of-control, dope-induced tantrum. It was first period and a morning buzz controlled my mood.

"Do you get it?" he asked.

"No. Actually, no." I laughed more, but the question forced me to pause.

He paused too, tightening his brow and catching my eye in the brown sea of his. "Hannah," he began. "Do your fucking homework."

Do your fucking homework. To me, these were magic words of love. No one had cared, in so long, whether I did my homework—or anything.

After that, no more morning buzz. Dope, only on weekends for me. No more inane giggling fits in school. At home I didn't feel like I had a family anymore; since my mother began changing her habits, changing the rules, and my father began resisting that, everyone had gone off in a different direction, spiraling into intense, unbearable autonomy. My mother had her classes. My father had his work. Carolyn had TV. And now I had a boyfriend, I had Jackie, and whenever I was confused—which I suddenly wasn't anymore—I knew I could ask Jackie Thunder just what to do.

There comes a point when you just have to take the plunge. Jack said this one evening, nearly a year ago, after we'd returned from grocery shopping. The trip was routine, the drive home as silent as the trek through the store. After he'd popped the trunk, we opened our car doors, slammed them shut, walked around the car, our feet breaking the thin coat of ice that covered the year's first snow. Our steps made an intrusive crunching sound. We met, in perfect, rote sync, at the car's open end.

"Shake it up, Hannah," Jack began. His voice was quiet as usual, though adamant, imploring. He didn't look at me but at our groceries inside the trunk. He heaved as he lifted two bulging bags. He was angry. I knew what he was referring to: our circumscribed life.

"But I feel safe."

"You *are* safe. *Too* safe." His words formed clouds of condensation.

"We're not making mistakes." I whispered, but he heard me well enough. His mouth tightened and he drew in a deep breath of air. He was willing himself into patience.

76

He stepped closer. His footsteps sent echoes spiraling into the night. When he let out his breath he began to speak at a pace set deliberately slow, as if I were a child. "You won't make a mistake. I trust you."

"I trust *you*." I didn't move. I knew how the ground would give beneath me.

"Then go for it!" Underneath it all he was exasperated. Another cloud of words hit my face.

He put the bags back in the trunk, stepped toward me again, and held the ends of my scarf in each hand. He'd calmed down some, and, gently, he tugged one end, then the other.

He spoke quietly. "It's what we've wanted for years now. It'll be good for us."

After a moment he grinned broadly, picked up an icy chunk, and threw it. When we heard it land, he turned to me, his dark eyes sparkling with excitement. I hadn't seen that glimmer in the longest time. "I hope it's a boy!" he said.

After twenty-three years, my parents finally split. The act was their only mutual one in a decade. My parents had endured by living in a haze of stormy silence. We'd known that my mother wanted to leave, but she never could. For one thing she didn't know what she would do: she didn't work, didn't have any particular skill. Once, coming inside after rewiring the car radio, she suggested she couldn't do anything. It seemed so obvious, but my mother wouldn't agree: how she could do, if she wanted, nearly everything.

My father didn't force her out or leave himself. During the years that my mother took classes, my father thought she was going through a phase, like the terrible twos, from which she'd emerge not older, but younger, the wife she'd once—in my infancy—been. And, hiding behind the newspaper each night, my father could pretend he didn't see the changes, could keep at least the idea of her old self alive.

During the first six months after the separation, he visited Jack and me each month from his new home in East Hartford.

These were forlorn, timid visits, filled with stilted small talk, trips to movie theaters, forced dinner parties. I noticed how my aging father walked through doorways now with his head bent down, his arms no longer reaching.

His new habit was to get up early and walk. His first morning with us he came into the kitchen after the walk, his cheeks flushed. I sat him in the breakfast nook, poured him tea, and slapped two eggs, sunny-side up, on his plate. Jack, who slept in on weekends, eventually joined us and the two men passed the newspaper between them. It was silent but not too sad.

When my father handed me his empty plate, he thanked me, told me what a wonderful breakfast it was, what a wonderful morning it was. He'd launched into a discussion of what wonderful weather we were having when Jack cut him off.

"Why?" my husband, always direct, asked. "Why'd you divorce after all those years? Why not work it out?"

My father looked up, seemingly unsurprised by Jack's question. "I did things to her, she did things to me. We were drowning in anger," he said. "Maybe we drowned. Who knows?"

Jack nodded, satisfied. Then he looked at me. His face was grim and he began to tap his fingers impatiently on the table. I didn't like that look, those fingers drumming out our frustration.

Not sure what to say, I leaned over the table, poured my father more tea.

More than Jack, my mother had been nagging me to get pregnant—for years already. But I wouldn't. My life felt full already.

When Jack and I moved back to Wells to be closer to my mother after the divorce, the pressure was severe. It let up, though, the day she met Louis.

That day was almost routine. In the morning I'd practiced piano, as usual. Scales, then technical exercises, then a piece or two. Then a phone call to my mother. We had nothing urgent to say, just chitchat. Soothing talk, easy connections. I invited her over for lunch. Again, nothing unusual. We ate lunch together almost every day.

After she left I did a few household chores, laundry and dusting, all to Beethoven's Fourth blasting in the background. At four o'clock my first student arrived. At five o'clock, my second. The lessons were fine. Still nothing unusual.

At six, Jack came home. We had dinner near seven or so. Afterwards he went into the living room to read. Again I dialed my mother. We would talk for another half hour.

This was all part of a habit, each aspect of the daily routine falling into place much like the notes in the pieces I played, without thinking, day after day. Because I always played the same repertoire of pieces, I knew them by heart.

I called my mother, but there was no answer. I tried fifteen minutes later, then fifteen minutes after that. I tried each of the next three ten-minute spells.

"What are you doing?" Jack asked, coming in for a drink.

"Mom's not home. We've got to find her."

"Don't be crazy," he said. He opened the refrigerator. "It's probably nothing." He scooped me into a quick, reassuring hug.

I tried to leave the kitchen where our phone was, but I couldn't. I paced, lifted the receiver, put it back down. I raised the receiver again, dialed, then hung up before it even rang. The next time Jack walked in I rushed to the sink, pretending to be busy. I was embarrassed because I couldn't control myself.

But this missing of the nightly phone call was like missing a note in one of the pieces I'd memorized so long ago. Compulsively, I returned to the phone, to dial again, to make it right.

The next morning my mother's voice was excited. She'd met a man, she explained. The day before. A very nice man. She'd gotten a flat tire— "not to worry, in a parking lot"—and he was kind enough to help. They'd had dinner together. No, she didn't think to call. What was I so upset about? Wasn't I happy for her?

"I'm pregnant," I said, though I knew it wasn't even possible. What I meant was: *Don't leave. Don't change. Mom, don't move.*

Jack tells me I look terrific pregnant. Like a big, round jolly thing. My face, painted with blotches, is ruddy, he says. Never looked healthier. I tell him, please, no need to patronize. But he says, "Really, Hannah. Really."

This was last night. So I put on the lace again. The gloves, the collar. I left the handbag on the dresser. "Jack!" I called. "Come look!"

I stood, trying this time to be proud of all that I carried: this baby, this legacy of delicate, outdated, fragile lace. I was naked in the middle of the room.

Laughing, he said, "Hannah, just look at you!" He lifted my left hand first, peeling off the glove as he held it. He took each finger to his lips. Then the right glove. He played with the collar for a while, covering my face with it, kissing me through it. He hummed a little Mozart, something he'd learned from me, and as he did he lifted the collar over my head and let it fall.

Last night we slept peacefully, like babies.

This morning I felt different, hopeful. I picked up the collar from the floor, folded it, tucked it away in a drawer. I decided that my experiments with another, earlier time were over. When I saw Jack having his usual toast and coffee for breakfast, I turned to him. "Shake it up," I said.

Then I announced: "There will be rules."

Jack said, "Loosen up, Hannah. No rules. We'll be fine."

But I said, "*Rules.*"

I began to lay them down after breakfast. My hopefulness had transformed, quickly and inexplicably, into my old routine: anxiety, caution.

Rule number one: respond to the baby's cries promptly.

Jack said, "Hannah, are you kidding? Why wouldn't we? We don't need that rule. It's insulting." He put his coffee down.

He pushed his chair out from under the table.

Rule number two: There will be storytelling and they'll be happy stories. Each night we'll read to her, but we'll choose the stories carefully. *Carefully.*

Jack said, "We can't protect her forever. Not every story is a happy story." He gets up, paces, then stops and scratches his head. "All right, when she's a child, of course, only happy stories. All right, calm down." He lowers his voice. "Happy stories." He walks to me, head down. "Come on, Hannah. We don't really need this."

"Because I tell you, Jack, we protect her from certain things. We're her parents and we protect her, and if I *ever* hear you mention a word—about sadness, about losing things—not just people, even toys—"

Jack crosses his arms, turns his back to me. I yell louder, hear myself yelling the way my father used to. And the words, for the sake of what I think are love, are familiar words of hate.

"—*you tell her those things, you teach her those things, you get her thinking along that track, and I swear, I'll do it, Jack, I'll do it—*

"Do what?" he asks.

I swallow the words in my mouth: *kill you, leave you.* Absurd words.

"Stop you," I whisper. "I was going to make you stop."

I felt drowsy all morning. I didn't practice piano and I hadn't yet come here to the lake.

Mid-morning I decided to drive the two hours to my mother's. She was sewing—she's as good a tailor as her parents were. She was making a jumpsuit, in gender-neutral green, for the baby. She brought the garment into the kitchen where we sat with our herb tea. The day was brilliant, the October chill having scattered any clouds. Sunlight streamed in, streaking the wooden table top, yellowing the dark brown. The green of the baby's outfit looked almost translucent. My mother loves this new home in Litchfield, which she describes as a life-time away from Wells. She lives here with Louis, that nice man.

"It's about time I had a grandchild. Don't you think?"

"Jack says so too," I told her. We weren't in the habit of phoning daily anymore. By now we're almost out of touch.

She was redecorating the kitchen. She'd stripped the floor of its worn linoleum and underneath had found, to her delight, well-preserved floor boards. "Pine!" she exclaimed. "Hannah, the real thing!" By her delight I could see that she'd transferred to the house the authenticity she always dreamed of for herself.

She pulled out wallpaper samples and began to leaf through several heavy books. She works now part-time in an upholstery shop and her work gives her access to materials that she loves: textured and printed fabrics, curtains, table cloths, woven rugs. For this room she wanted something with red and green. "Warmth and growth," she said.

She fed me lunch, a cold turkey sandwich and a pickle. I drank more herbal tea and she had coffee, a drink she and I had taken up together years ago after she'd begun to drop off to sleep. Turning our attention back to the wallpaper samples, we settled on a light, floral pattern. She was glad I'd visited.

When I had my coat on, ready to leave, I pointed to my bulging stomach and asked, "Do you think I'll be good at it?" I looked into her face. Her cheeks were flushed with a rosy glow as if she were the pregnant one. Her gray hair fell in waves almost to her shoulders. She looked good—even better than that. My mother looked happy and beautiful.

She smiled. "You won't even have to think."

She pulled my collar up over my ears, then hugged me, leaning for a moment into the folds of my coat. I liked the feel of her holding onto me like that. In an instant I knew it was what I came for. I could have stood there a long time, my bones warming, my heart lifting, as I lent my mother my body for her support.

"I've never had to worry about you," she said, stepping back. "I've always trusted you." She patted my cheek and opened the door. "Trust me, kitten. I know you."

* * *

Jack still wasn't home when I returned, and I left him a note, telling him I'd be here at the lake.

There's a story I want to tell Jack. Not the one about Princess Topaqua. He's bound to know that one. It's the other one I want to tell him. About napping in my mother's lap on the shore of the lake. It's been a long nap, I'll tell him. But I'm rested now. I promise, Jack, I promise to wake up!

And I'll tell him this.

It was after my father had exploded about our having crossed the lake on skates. My mother hadn't yet crawled into Carolyn's bed. I was unfolding an extra blanket, smoothing it out, readying the bed for her.

"Not stupid," she remarked defensively. She wasn't talking to me, so I didn't answer. Then she turned, stood straight, and smiled a magnificent, rare smile. There was abandon in it, genuine abandon.

"Hannah, if you're not afraid, we could do it again, tomorrow!"

And I said, *Yes! Yes!* That, despite the precariousness of the lake, despite my father's warning, despite that now I was desperately afraid. My mother looked so happy just then, smiling, going "Whoosh," pretending to shove off and glide forward, away.

In ten minutes, of course, she would have forgotten that I was even with her that day, asking me instead about school. Then she'd fall asleep.

But this was an earlier moment. And when she was happy like that she looked so beautiful. So beautiful, there was no choice to be made. That's what I'll tell Jack. How I would have crossed that lake again, following her. To see her happy, I'll explain—I'll have to explain—I'd have followed her onto the lake, through the middle, or right into it. I'd have gone to the ends of the earth if that's where she needed to go.

Self-Choreography
(Carolyn Kahn—May 1975)

The 1970s were particularly stressful for our family. In addition to my parents' relationship, deteriorating throughout the decade with the steadiness of a John Phillips Sousa march, the health craze was beginning to take shape and it threatened us. Come Saturday afternoons, when families could be seen across the American landscape collectively elevating their heart rates, we were still sitting at our kitchen table, occasionally the four of us together, reading the paper and licking the remainder of blintzes and sour cream—whole cream—off our plates. Actually, from our dining room in Wells we couldn't see the expanse of American landscape, but we'd watched enough TV to overcome the geographic limitations of our front yard. Later, on a typical afternoon, my grandmother, Mom's mother, would arrive with homemade chopped liver in tow. I'll spare you the ingredients. You get the idea.

Sometime in that decade I began water ballet lessons at the county Y.M.C.A.—an attempt at athletics—and my mother formed the annoying habit of raising that fact as compensation for who we were.

"Carolyn's in shape," she'd plead. This would be to a friend, a house guest, who happened to jog. If my father were in the same room he'd add, authoritatively, "Has to be. Water ballet requires real muscular coordination and two hell-of-a-good-shape lungs."

Mom also developed the habit of volunteering my services, as a family representative of sorts, to run with the children of other jogging families. If Hannah were available she'd get chosen first–as a tomboy she really did have two hell-of-a-good-shape lungs. But sometimes I had to do. Had to—or risk shattering the

84

mask that we wore, so determinedly, to hide our collective anxieties.

Thus it was that in early May of 1975, on the eve of my sixteenth birthday, I found myself chugging beside Clarissa Eastman, daughter of Brett and Candice Eastman, the latter being my mother's best WASP friend.

Clarissa and I had little in common beyond our mothers' friendship. She was my age, and I'd known her for years, but we didn't hang out together in school. My group was the smart, unathletic-to-mildly-athletic type, all girls, not one boyfriend among us. Hers was the perpetually hitched set, a clique of savvy-looking teenagers, boys and girls. They'd stand together in the hall between classes in a big clump, and, upon approaching them, my friends and I would split like a fork in a stream and trickle in single file around.

Mind you, Clarissa was no more enthused than I about our anointed rendezvous. But she happened to be with her mother when she stopped by our house, and our mothers were so keen on our duet, a little show of modernity, that we both caved to their embarrassing prompts. "You two could jog together!" It was better than, "You two could be friends!"

We began our jog at a slow pace, down the street, around the corner. As I worked to maintain my breathing I focused on how Clarissa's blond ponytail swung rhythmically behind her. I tugged at my two, thick auburn braids. No, they were not swinging; whether I jogged or stood still, they hung with the solidity and shape of down-turned icicles. When traffic picked up at the downtown intersection and we were forced to stop, Clarissa bent over, fidgeted with her right sock, and pulled from it a hand-rolled cigarette. She smiled broadly.

"Come on," she said. "Let's get high."

Clarissa was a confident girl and when she said, "Let's get high," I wanted to tell her right off that I'd love to but, really, I'd never done it before and wouldn't she prefer to smoke with an experienced person? Instead, I took a step back—into the road—and a car honked at me as it passed and I leapt back on the sidewalk landing slightly off-balance.

"Let's," I said as calmly as I could.

We walked a short distance on Main to the elementary school playground. It was mid-afternoon on a cloudy, brisk Saturday and only a handful of small children played on swings. We aimed toward the baseball diamond, then dropped into the home team's dugout.

Clarissa's sportswear served multiple ends: she carried matches in her left sock and a lighter in the pocket of her sweatshirt. She smiled at me, lit the tightly wrapped stick of white paper, inhaled several times, then held the joint in front of her while she held her breath. I studied her moves. Still holding her breath, she handed me the joint.

I took it between my thumb and forefinger, mimicking her as best I could, but she could see I had the tentative technique of a neophyte.

"Suck it," she said once she'd exhaled. The acrid smell of pot swirled around us, prickling my nose. "Then hold it in as long as you can."

We passed it back and forth for ten minutes. On each try I pulled on the joint a little harder until finally I felt that soreness in my throat I'd heard about. I waited to feel a visceral understanding of the word "high."

I waited, but twenty minutes later I still felt like me, a bit heavy, terribly self-conscious, more than a little worried. We were jogging again, this time past the new condominiums–Well's first–being built on Main, then up the street, toward my house, toward our mothers. Our pace had slowed, and even Clarissa's ponytail didn't bounce anymore.

"She's making me model," Clarissa complained. Since we'd emerged from the clubby baseball dugout Clarissa had opened up, had been talking no end. "You know, the fashion show next month at the high school? In front of everyone I know! It's embarrassing. I'm going to have to wear *mainstream* clothes. The Talbot's catalogue! What's that got to do with *me*?

I'm not telling anyone. I mean I'm telling you—" We rounded the last corner and entered the driveway to my house. There, we stopped the pretense of jogging. "But I'm not telling anyone. You know what I mean?"

Our mothers were in the kitchen, not eating. That's what they told us as soon as we came in. They'd been there the whole time, in the kitchen, but had not had one bite of anything to eat.

"What about that?" Mom asked, obviously pleased. "And how about you two? You two young health nuts. Can I get you some juice? A little yogurt? How about tap water!"

I looked at Clarissa, who was not happy. Her mouth drooped in a frown and her arms were crossed over her thin chest. "I wouldn't mind some of *that*." She pointed at a freshly baked banana bread. Holidays aside, Mom didn't bake much anymore. These days her time went into the continuing education classes she and Candice Eastman continually enrolled in. But banana bread—ever-practical as a way to use rotting bananas—had survived these early years of Mom's delayed individuation, her "second adolescence" as my father called it, not without condescension. "Go ahead, girls, we'll watch. We'll watch how you two young things wolf down food and don't put on a pound." Mom patted her nearly flat stomach as she said this and looked at Clarissa's mom, as if seeking her approval.

Mrs. Eastman sighed. "Ah, yes, to be young. Young and hungry." Clarissa's mom had short, teased, frosted hair, a thin face noticeably made-up—blue eye shadow, pink lips, smudges of rouge on her sunken cheeks. She had long nails too, with pink polish chipping at the edges.

Clarissa and I took to the banana bread like prisoners would to a home-cooked meal. We sliced, then ate. Sliced, then ate. By the time we finished, two-thirds of it was gone.

"Wow!" said Mom, finally pulling the bread away from me as I attempted one more slice.

Mrs. Eastman reacted with a crisp, cutting, "Enough!" Instantly I recoiled from the sweet bread.

87

As Mrs. Eastman and my mother said their goodbyes, I stood with Clarissa for a moment in the driveway.

"I don't think I actually got high," I confessed.

"You mean you ate all that straight?" She laughed. For a few minutes she couldn't stop.

Before she got into her car she turned to me. "Good for you. This is the only way I let myself eat. I have to turn it all off." She raised her arms and gestured vaguely, at me, our house, our neighborhood, our town. At nothing and everything.

"You probably caught more of a buzz than you know," she told me. Then she added, "Let's do it again."

Her friendliness startled me. "Catch you later, Clariss," I said.

The next Monday at school Clarissa acted like she didn't know me and I acted like I didn't care. I'd expected as much. In English class I told my best friend Anita that I'd gotten high. I'd finally done it. Soon enough, I said, wouldn't I be having sex?

"It was weird," I told her. "I felt older and younger at the same time. I felt like I knew what was going on in everybody's head: my mother's, Mrs. Eastman's, Clarissa's."

Anita said, "You always know what's going on in others' heads. Carolyn, it sounds like you were you."

"I was," I said. "Only more so." I felt compelled to lie like this to Anita, to blow the weekend's prime event out of proportion. I paused, then added, smiling, "Clarissa hates herself. At least, she's not so happy as you'd think."

My mother was asked to be in the fashion show too, a fundraiser for the county hospital. The request to model pleased her to no end. If Mom lacked a certain verbal confidence, she made up for it by her elegant appearance, her deep, hopeful eyes, her thin, well-proportioned frame. In fact, dressing and not talking was her forte, though I knew that with her continuing education classes and her growing independence she wasn't content anymore with this limited a stance in the world.

Still, she wasn't about to give up looking good. The clothes for the fashion show were being imported from the best stores in the area, and Mom, avaricious as ever in her shopping, valued the opportunity to be dressed by someone else, to expand the range of her look in exciting ways. That year a new women's clothing store, A.K. LaBett's, had opened only sixteen miles from Wells, and Mom had become a steady customer, turning away from Loehmann's suddenly, finding A. K. LaBett's flashy New York styles irresistible. At the fashion show Mom was to be the A.K. LaBett's representative.

"Maybe he'll do me in leather!" she exclaimed. She was talking on the phone to Candice Eastman. Mrs. Eastman had a loud voice and I could hear her response.

"Maybe he'll just do you!"

Mom burst out laughing.

Nobody was doing me, but I felt ready. Anita and I confessed that we wanted to marry young, just after college, and have kids, say, at twenty-three. Though we were enlightened enough girls to assume we'd get a college education, we didn't expect to actually *use* the education. Life beyond college meant marriage, and what we planned was to be next door neighbors, always. We'd take turns baby-sitting for each other. We'd carpool, too. Our lives would be rich with the mutual goings on in both our busy houses.

At the county Y.M.C.A., two towns outside of Wells, I'd begun to grow curious about the boy who handled towels at the front desk. He looked like he was eighteen or so, but it was hard to tell exactly. He defied categorization and for that he charmed me all the more. He had a rather vacant stare, a stringy body, and disheveled light brown hair. I didn't know his name but by his shy smile and reticence I figured he was my type. Quiet, serious, hard-working. A little out of it, in a way that made me feel I had a chance. After water-ballet I'd shower, brush my frizzy hair, pinch my cheeks—a manipulation I'd learned from old movies—and head out to the lobby where I'd hand him my damp towel. Week after week I'd tried to think of something to say. But for three months I'd just smiled, a mysterious Mona

Lisa smile that I'd hoped would look so alluring as to override any need for words. I didn't believe in words. That would be tantamount to believing I could affect, even control, a situation. Like Mom, I didn't yet trust that my voice mattered.

Despite my smile, each week he'd only taken the towel, thrown it in a bin filled with other damp towels, and said a quick, indifferent, "Thanks."

Clarissa Eastman and her current boyfriend, Mark Hansly, made out in the halls at school between classes. From the corner of my slightly-averted gaze, I'd see how he'd pull her in close, their bodies pressed against each other from toes to lips, her arms raised over his shoulders and dangling limply over his back, his thicker arms around her slim torso, stroking her back and her blond pony tail, and plucking, occasionally, at her bra strap. Once I saw him do that and Clarissa whispered, "Not *here*. How many times do I have to tell you?"

Despite Clarissa's ambivalence about the bra, about the display of it all, I envied her. And whenever I'd see Mark pluck like that my back would begin to itch. At night I'd imagine myself in the same situation. I'd be with What's His Name, the stranger at the Y. We'd be by my locker at school, relocated in my dream on a main corridor, where the public location added both excitement and validity to our affair. He'd sneak up behind me, tap my left shoulder, then quickly leap to my right. I'd turn, wonder, who did that? Then he'd jump in front of me and grab me, pulling me toward him, kissing me until the next bell rang.

In every dream we always felt perfectly at ease with each other as if we'd been best friends for life. Our comfort was so real, our intimacy so complete, we never had to talk.

That year Anita became metaphysical. She'd been given the book *Jonathan Livingston Seagull* for her fifteenth birthday and she wanted to live like that, a life of purity, of seeking, of experience on higher ground. I brought her down to earth.

"We could get high," I said, imposing the literal. This was

a week after my experience with Clarissa.

Anita clasped *Jonathan Livingston Seagull* to her chest. She wore jeans and a flannel shirt. She would have been pretty if she'd cut her hair, but vanity bored Anita, especially that year. She read *Jonathan Livingston Seagull* the way some people read their Bibles, carrying it around with her, pulling it out in moments of unstructured time. "I'll do it if you get it," she said.

I wasn't sure who to ask. I could ask Clarissa, but I'd have to stop in the hall, interrupt her love-making. I could ask a host of others whom I knew smoked regularly—by then practically all of Wells High—but I wasn't a likely candidate and the situation proved too demanding. Then, the following Thursday night, while discarding my wet towel at the Y, I noticed What's His Name's red eyes and the faint rusty odor of marijuana that seemed to be issuing from behind his ears.

Dope, I realized, would make the perfect icebreaker. I took a deep breath. "Do you sell?"

He looked at me with the same vacant gaze he used when handing out towels. "Sell?"

"Yes, you know." I lowered my already low voice. With my hand I made a quick rolling motion, then pretended to pick up a joint and to suck. He nodded.

"Can I get some?"

"It'll cost you ten." He looked only slightly more engaged than before.

"Next week, then." I worked my mouth into my best mysterious smile. He didn't flinch.

On the same Saturday that I was to meet Anita for the purpose of what we called "transcendence," Gram visited. As usual she arrived with home cooking. She'd baked strudel filled with jelly and raisins that she'd arranged on three plates. She also brought over a package of pink marshmallow rabbits, Easter candy that she'd picked up at Woolworths, post-holiday, on *sale*. She emphasized this fact above all else. Besides, she added, she didn't want Hannah or me to feel left out of what she called "the goyish hoopla."

"Mother, you're just satisfying your own sweet tooth," Mom said, whisking the bunnies from my grandmother's over-sized pocketbook and tucking them in the back of a cabinet behind cans of soup and tuna. The cellophane that covered the bunnies crackled, as if in protest.

"What's the matter?" Gram said. "You used to like to eat." She frowned. Like Mom, Gram was not a tall woman, but she radiated a warmth that made her plump presence feel enormous. She liked cooking on a gas stove, and when she came to our house she'd stand by Mom's electric, her hands on her ample hips, her face drawn, her double chin drooping.

"What is this?" she'd say. "I don't understand. Cookie, what is this?" Mom was "Cookie" to her. But only her. She made sure of that.

"And, Cookie, you look thin," Gram would typically add. This would make Mom calm down.

"I'm healthy," she'd say, patting Gram's large upper arms. They were wonderful, flabby, grandmother arms, and when she'd raise them her underarms would swing the way Ethel Merman's did as she belted one out.

When Candice Eastman came by to see Mom's latest from A.K. LaBett's, Mom and Gram were sitting at the kitchen table with Anita and me, drinking tea. The fashion show was in three weeks and A.K.—whoever he was—had given Mom four out-fits. Clarissa was with her mother.

As they walked into the kitchen I noticed Clarissa's feet. She wore sneakers. So did Anita and I. If our mothers got wind of it, I realized, they could very well conspire, jointly volunteer us for a jog. To avoid yet another imposed display of modernity—or even a fuss about it—I began to yawn madly, then got up to make more tea.

Soon, Mom, Gram, and Mrs. Eastman disappeared into Mom's closet, leaving Clarissa downstairs with me and Anita.

With what I hoped was an air of authority, I pulled from my pocket a joint. Instead of buying a Baggie's worth, What's His

Name had handed me a bag of four slimly rolled joints. "It's the same deal," he explained.

"Sure, I know," I said, and quickly passed him ten dollars. He actually smiled at me as I stuffed the bag of joints into my duffel. He laughed some too. Stunned, I simply walked away.

At the sight of my joint, Clarissa's eyes grew wide. She nodded, and we jammed ourselves into the downstairs bathroom, opening its sole window.

We took turns sucking, holding our breaths, and exhaling out the window. We didn't talk. I could see that Anita was excited, but shy. Looking at Anita in her untucked flannel shirt, then at Clarissa in her neat blue cotton sweater, I wanted to reach over and fix Anita's appearance, at least to slap a soft smile onto her otherwise rosy face. As for myself, I was almost relaxed; at least I knew how to smoke the joint this time. Clarissa broke the ice.

"I've got my outfits too." She sounded angry. "Girly," she complained. "A prom gown. 'The Big Night,' it's called." She explained how each of her outfits had a name, like they were paintings. "An Average Day at School" was another. She'd model that before she did "Weekend Fun!" and "Young Wedding Guest."

At the sound of "Young Wedding Guest" Anita started to giggle. Then I did too. Clarissa still pouted, but soon even she broke into a choppy laugh. We were cramped by the window in the downstairs bathroom and once we were laughing—not just giggling but all out laughing—we began to fall onto each other.

"A Better-than-Average Visit with the In-Laws!" Anita yelled.

"Happy Grocery Shopping Attire!" I added.

Clarissa thought for a while, then suggested, "Saturday Afternoon Fuck!"

The words stopped Anita and me cold. We might have thought such words, but we'd never have uttered them. Clarissa looked up, her forehead working its way into a knot. "Saturday Afternoon Fuck," she repeated, quietly. "It's a joke. Get it? One of those things we'd never do?"

"Right!" I said. Anita let out a breath of air.

I heard Mom calling my name.

We scrambled out of the bathroom, leaving the window open and the bathroom door shut. We'd already sprayed ourselves with Lysol.

"You kids want strudel?" Mom yelled the question as she wandered from room to room looking for us.

In the kitchen, we each went for one of Gram's three plates. Gram watched as I downed mine, her eyes wide and twinkling. Mrs. Eastman, who faced Clarissa, wore an expression as frosty as her hair. Mom stood stock still, aghast at how often Anita's mouth opened wide. "Girls!" she cried, as if that could stop the spontaneous gluttony.

Mrs. Eastman was more direct. She reached for Clarissa's hand, slapping it as she whisked away the next piece of strudel.

Gram didn't move, though. She stood before me, her thick arms stretched forward. She said, smiling, "Carolyn, that's my girl."

The next week a scale appeared in the bathroom that Hannah and I shared. Mom had bought it for herself, to weigh in before the fashion show, but since her bathroom was carpeted she needed to put it in ours where it could lay flat on our tiled floor, registering what she called "truer value." It was blue with a white rim, and the numbers flashed in red. An all-American scale, I thought. We'd never had one in our bathroom and I wasn't in the habit of weighing in.

That first morning I cautiously stepped on it, causing the numbers in the small plastic window to whir around as if for a lottery. Would it be my lucky day?

The numbers settled at one hundred thirty-three.

Okay, I thought. Okay. Not so bad.

I decided that I wouldn't obsess and step on the scale every day. Only once a week, on Saturday mornings, before breakfast, after I'd peed. But each morning in the bathroom the scale called out to me. "Carolyn," I was sure I heard it say. "Come see."

It was awful. Within three days I could not *not* step on the scale. On the fourth day, while I brushed my teeth in the bathroom, I covered the scale with a towel, but the mere presence of the flat, square podium was enough. "Carolyn," it called. It even had a distinct voice, a nasal one, that sounded only slightly muffled when covered by a towel.

Anita weighed one hundred twenty-one, which made me jealous, but I acted like I didn't care. Hannah weighed one hundred nineteen, but she was younger. Mom, I figured, weighed less than me too—she never disclosed her weight, though I spotted her checking in at the scale every day. This difference made sense too. I was taller than Mom, and more busty. My shape now approached Gram's build.

Gram's build!

I looked in the mirror, dread welling up inside me. Though my underarm flab was not nearly at the Ethel Merman stage, already I could see the signs. Cringing, I reached my arms out in front and swung them back and forth. I pinched the looseness. What I felt about myself was this: disgust.

Protein, the diet guide said. I bought it the next day at the Food King. It was a *New York Times* best-seller—over two million copies in print. Still, I was embarrassed—all three checkout clerks were my classmates. So I got milk and eggs and bread and, at the checkout stand, snuck the book in between the items, not looking at either it or Barry Crane the whole time Barry rang up my total, even when he said, "Hey, Carolyn. How's it going?"

At home I read the advice: go all out on protein. Cottage cheese, meats, eggs. Cut back on fruit and carbohydrates. No need to count calories.

I boiled the eggs I'd just bought. Each morning that week I ate an egg with cottage cheese. Luckily, Dad liked deli meats and kept us well-stocked. For lunch I filled Baggies with slices of meat. I ate what the others did for dinner. I didn't want anyone to know I was on a diet. It was my secret.

One hundred thirty-one . . . one hundred twenty-nine . . . one hundred twenty-seven-and-a-half. Within days my protein diet was working. I began to look forward to hopping on the scale. "Good morning, Carolyn," it began to say, taking on a tone of respect. A week before the fashion show I hit one hundred twenty-five and I felt like a person raised from the dead. Leaving the bathroom I was certain I heard, in a most wistful tone, "Catch you later, Carolyn."

In water ballet my favorite move was called "the clamshell." It was the only move I could do with any semblance of grace. I'd lie on my back, fluttering my hands lightly by my hips to keep my body afloat, trying to be still. Then, in a swoop, I'd raise my arms over my head, lifting water as I did. At the same time, I'd bend at the middle, thrust my feet into the air, and point my toes.

In this clamshell state—bent in half—I'd sink, sink. After I lost momentum I'd unfold, and, doing as smooth an underwater breaststroke as possible, I'd swim away, resurfacing somewhere else. The clamshell was the move of the elliptical.

One night during my second week of crash-dieting I had a fantasy. I was floating, but not in the Y's swimming pool. I was on a bed, a water bed. What's His Name was there, leaning over the bed, ready to hand me a towel. I smiled my mysterious way, luring him closer. Eventually he smiled in his familiar distant way. He leaned toward my face and I could tell he was ready to move onto the bed. Just as we were to join, our bodies collapsing into each other like Clarissa Eastman's and Mark Hansly's, I collapsed into myself, bending in half into the clamshell, suddenly able to penetrate through the water bed's surface.

As I sank I heard What's His Name say, "Carolyn, catch you later." But his voice was different than the one I'd heard, briefly, at the Y. It was the whiny nasal of our bathroom scale.

I woke in a near panic. That What's His Name had spoken

had ruined the fantasy. And that he had the same voice as my scale, who knew my weight, my most private—my worst—secret, made the disappointment more severe.

Love could never happen this way, with this kind of knowledge, this intimacy. After my dream I was sure of it. Love would only happen if he didn't know anything about me.

In the next week I perfected my mysterious fake smile. And I lost another pound. Mom noticed the change in my body and gave me a nod of approval.

"What have you been up to?" she asked, smiling.

"Nothing," I said. "The change is all natural. I'm just being me. Only more so. And it's working."

That seemed to make sense to her. She nodded and went away.

The night of the fashion show I sat with Anita and Hannah. It was a Friday, early in June. We arrived early to help Mom lug her A.K. LaBett's outfits into the high school, along with makeup and changes of shoes—A.K. didn't provide those. Candice and Clarissa Eastman arrived at about the same time. Mrs. Eastman was excited, walking in with a lift, but Clarissa looked dwarfed under her load. Parts of "The Big Night" were entangled with elements of "Young Wedding Guest," and it looked as if she were purposefully dragging "Weekend Fun!" on the ground.

Watching Clarissa's discomfort, I was glad I wasn't in the show. Still, I wished I'd been asked to be in it and had the privilege of declining. "The Big Night" and "Weekend Fun!" had been easy to mock, but in truth they suggested a world I felt I lacked access to, a beauty club that Mom and Clarissa were part of and I wasn't, though I thought my diet would help. I longed to know the password to gain entrance to this exclusive club of thin, pretty women who had a better chance than me of getting certain things from life—like happiness, like love.

The high school's stage had a make-shift runway covered by green indoor-outdoor carpeting. When Mom stepped onto it, in a black blazer, plaid slacks, a kerchief on her head, and her own flats, Hannah and I didn't recognize her. Her hair was the same, a shoulder-length blunt cut, but she looked taller than normal, and thinner. She smiled at Mrs. Rudman, our principal's wife and the fashion show's moderator, who announced that this outfit had the casual-yet-classic, timely-yet-timeless, look of Grace Kelly. The nearly all-female audience sighed. Mom peered out, radiating a kind of superiority. A.K. LaBett's had brought her to new heights.

As Clarissa predicted, she and Mrs. Eastman were essentially mainstream. Less Hollywood, more suburb. Mrs. Eastman came out first in a corduroy work dress. Like Mom, she looked exceptionally confident as she strode down the runway.

Clarissa was next, wearing "An Average Day at School"— pastel plaid slacks and a matching sweater vest. She carried a red notebook in her left arm. As she walked stiffly toward us, I could see the blush in her cheeks, as bright as the notebook. It wasn't make-up, I knew, but sheer embarrassment.

Mom's next outfit was a bathing suit coverup, short and pale yellow, and she wore huarache sandals with it that she'd bought just that week. Because they weren't broken in yet they squeaked, and Hannah and I squirmed for her sake. Yet she didn't seem to notice. She gave that same superior, elated look.

Mrs. Eastman's outfits continued to be sensible. And Mom was timely-yet-timeless to the end. But Clarissa kept changing. As she walked down the aisle in "Weekend Fun!" I noticed that her face had relaxed. In her jeans skirt and jacket she looked tough. She strutted forth.

She modeled "The Big Night" next, a slinky navy prom gown with a big bow that curved over her buttocks. Her blond hair hung loose, and she wore dangling earrings that her mother had borrowed from mine. Looking up at her, I knew her outfit was exactly the kind I could never pull off. But Clarissa wore it with ease; in fact, she was so comfortable as to appear giddy. Standing at the runway's end, her mouth hung open, awkwardly, and it looked as if she might be laughing. But no sound came out. I looked at her eyes.

"She's high!" I told Anita.

Walking back, Clarissa slowed down. Then, before dipping offstage, she lingered. Mrs. Rudman finally urged her off with a curt, "Thank you, Clarissa. That will be all." It was the same line her husband, our principal, used after disciplining students.

The fashion show was a success and Mom was the star. "A natural," Mrs. Rudman said, holding Mom's hand while she thanked her for participating. Mom still looked classy in just blue jeans and a turtleneck sweater. "You remind me of Liv Ullmann," Mrs. Rudman told her. Liv Ullmann was Swedish, fair-skinned, and blond, and Mom was Lithuanian, olive skinned, and brunette. Still, Mom loved the identity. She beamed a smile, and I beamed one back, imitating Mom's imitation of Liv Ullmann.

Mrs. Eastman had held her own all night, just like her teased and frosted hairdo. After the show, she and Clarissa came to our house for a post-fashion-show debriefing session. The mothers drank white wine. My father and Mr. Eastman had come to the show but they hadn't lingered, and Dad was upstairs. He knew enough not to share white wine with the women. White wine had become a ritual object in Mom's and Mrs. Eastman's private, single-sex, mid-life education. Clarissa and I drank tea. Hannah had gone to bed, and Anita had gone home after the show.

When Clarissa motioned I knew what to expect. Grabbing our sweaters, we crept to the side of the house. In silence we passed a joint.

"I did it," Clarissa said, handing me the joint. "Humiliating! But I did it."

"You were great," I said. "You looked comfortable, especially once you got going. I could never have carried off those outfits."

She smiled, but only a little. She was furious. She angrily tugged at her sweater, snapping the ribbing, pushing the sleeves up then yanking them down. As we re-entered the house I heard her mumble, "I can't stand it. A stage. Always a stage!"

I didn't move closer toward her. By the way she stamped her feet and swung her arms she gave me the sense that her rage had so encased her as to leave her impenetrably alone.

In our kitchen she opened the refrigerator as if it was hers. She pulled out several packets of deli meats, a loaf of bread, and my bowl of pre-peeled hard boiled eggs. From the freezer she grabbed the fudge swirl ice cream—Hannah's and Dad's favorite. At the counter she began lifting slices of meat, not making a sandwich—just stuffing her face. She opened a cabinet, looking for a bowl, I guessed, but instead she confiscated the box of pink marshmallow bunnies. She found a spoon by the sink and dug into the ice cream, balancing a whole bunny on each full bite. In the next instant she spread mayo on a piece of bread, slapped slices of turkey on it, and ate that. Then, spotting the ripening bananas by our toaster, she took not one, but two.

I shook my head, thinking she meant to give me one, but I was determined not to be hungry no matter how I actually felt. I'd lost too much weight to let a thing like hunger ruin me.

But Clarissa kept eating. And eating. And eating! As if I were invisible, she hadn't noticed me at all. She was halfway through the carton of fudge swirl when her mother walked in. Clarissa froze. Though Mrs. Eastman disapprovingly eyed the meats and bread, the ice cream and banana peels, she couldn't tell how much Clarissa had downed in the last five minutes. Only I knew that. And I knew that Clarissa needed this to be a secret.

"I'm hungry!" I said, stepping between Clarissa and her mother. "I didn't eat before the show," I explained.

Mrs. Eastman was silent, but her pink lips were puckered into a tight ball and her grim look said, *I feel sorry for you, Carolyn.*

From behind her mother, Clarissa gave me another kind of look. Through a film of sadness, I read, *Thanks.*

As Clarissa followed her mother out, I surreptitiously handed her one last marshmallow bunny—a treat for the road, a habit I'd learned from Gram.

The next day Gram brought us more homemade strudel and chopped liver. I didn't touch the strudel and she seemed disappointed. She walked over to me several times to feel my forehead. But when she saw how I heaped chopped liver onto a plate, eating it without crackers, her worry lifted. She didn't know I was protein-loading—avoiding carbohydrates. She thought I just couldn't wait to take the time to spread it properly on a cracker.

"Carolyn," she said. "My girl."

That night I had another clamshell fantasy. I'd been having them, perfecting them, for weeks. By now I weighed one hundred twenty-three-and-a-half, and I was becoming confident that by summer's end I would break the one hundred ten pound barrier. In my fantasy I was in the pool at the Y swimming naked. I was on my back, floating, readying for the thrust that would begin the clamshell. My stomach, flat and hard, broke the water's surface. My breasts rose up, majestic, firm.

What's His Name was in the bleachers this time watching me. I knew, but pretended not to. I was on display, fully, frontally. Every so often I'd bend my knees, pull my legs up, then spread them apart before pulling them together. I knew I provoked him with the last part, where I lingered.

Whenever I had the urge I'd lift my arms, fold my body in two, begin my clamshell descent, swimming underwater, elliptically, as graceful as a mermaid.

When I'd surface the routine would begin again. It was my own, self-choreographed water ballet.

Preparing to go under one last time, I heard What's His Name's nasal voice. "Wait for me," he called. "Wait for me." He was speaking to me but he wasn't calling me by my name anymore, and that made all the difference.

In my dream we were What's His Name and No Name. And

I was sure by his intimate nasal tone and the longing in his voice that our union was complete, that our love would last forever.

I descended that last time with such happiness and confidence I actually believed I was a mermaid and swam on and on. Yet a moment later, my chest and head pounding, I clambered to the surface.

In my post-fantasy confusion I had to work hard to remember. Who was I? And why was I gasping so for air?

A Meeting of the Minds
(Helen Grobar—Fall 1975)

Helen Grobar sat on the wooden deck of her home, a compact cabin that overlooked Lake Topaqua. The lake was calm today, the last tumult of motorboats and water skiers having ravaged its surface Labor Day Weekend, several weeks ago. Because of the lake, Wells had attracted a small population of "summer people," and this cabin, which Helen lived in year-round, was originally built for such seasonal use. Though she'd moved there in 1971—it was 1975 now—Helen had never bothered to change the drab indoor-outdoor carpeting that covered the cabin's downstairs, but over the years she'd embellished its plain walls with her own sketches of the lake, the local ducks and birds, and her family, Anita and James.

Helen's legs were crossed, and her kneecaps protruded, like arrows, pointing toward the lake where Anita and her friend Carolyn were swimming. Her kneecaps were connected to calves not much bigger than lemons, to thighs noticeably too thin. In the last year and a half, since James's leaving, she'd lost twenty pounds—as inadvertently as she'd lost him. Helen wore her old black bathing suit, a simple one-piece that now bagged around her frame, and she enjoyed the warmth of the sun on her skin. Though late September, the weather had turned unusually mild. Despite the heat, Helen had shrugged when Anita yelled up to her, a few minutes before, "Water's great! Come on, Mom. Come swimming!"

"Not now, sweeties," she called down. "I'm swimming in the sun. Delicious!"

"You're not swimming. You're going blind," Anita said. Then she added, "I give up!" and abruptly dipped underwater.

Helen turned a page. She reached for the glass of water beside her and sipped. On her lap lay a legal text, a book filled with judges' decisions about disputes over contracts. The book, over thirteen hundred pages long, felt like a large paperweight that served to bolt her to the deck's wooden surface. Without it, she knew, she'd be susceptible to the wind's every whim; these days her daily posture was as tenuous as a grass blade in a rainstorm.

She'd been in law school for just over a month. Each day since she'd begun, she'd come home from her classes, shed her denim skirt and blouse, and slide into either blue jeans or her bathing suit, depending on the weather. She'd fill her cup with water, grab a sweater—just in case—and head out to the deck. There, she'd sit cross-legged, underneath the stabilizing weight of whatever case book she needed to attend to: property, criminal law, contracts, torts. These books were good, she told herself, turning one thin page after another. The book's print was invariably small; its decisions, slow to read and precise. Though she hadn't been hungry for food in a year and a half, she was hungry for these brooding, flimsy pages. They filled her up; they used up time. She liked how judges tended to go on and on.

When the girls squealed, Helen looked up. They were pulling themselves from the water, onto the dock. It was a comfortable dock, about twenty square feet, and it jutted from the bank into the lake, rocking gently whenever the lake did. Anita and Carolyn stood on it, tipping themselves sideways as they squeezed water from their hair. Then they collapsed onto the dock's sunny surface. Helen smiled. Anita was holding up okay. Recently she'd grown excited about the prospect of choosing a college over the next year. After a long hiatus, she was entertaining friends again.

The girls' chatter became a soft background sound and Helen resumed her slow reading. Rolling her eyes over a column of nearly solid black print, she learned that to be valid, contracts required a meeting of the minds. That meant that all parties to a contract had to be agreeing to the same thing. The case before her was about the sale of a cow. A barren cow named Bertha. Both the buyer and seller knew Bertha's barren status and a price was set accordingly. Cash was tendered, accepted, and the execution of the contract was complete. There had been a perfect meeting of the minds.

Helen turned the page. Bertha wasn't barren after all! Though unknown at the time of the sale, the buyer found out as much several months later. And he celebrated; he'd gotten Bertha for a steal. The furious seller sued, arguing that the contract for Bertha be canceled. There was no meeting of the minds. There couldn't be a meeting of the minds when you didn't know the real nature of the thing you bargained for. It wasn't fair.

Or was it? Helen asked the girls. They were passing her by on their way inside.

"The way I see it," Anita said, thrusting her chin forward and wrinkling her forehead in thought, "is that this is just hard luck. There *was* a meeting of the minds. They just met over the wrong thing. That's life, isn't it? It happens all the time, Mom." Anita crouched down to talk to Helen face to face. Her skin was tanned to a radiant nutmeg tone and her wet brown hair hung over her shoulders and dripped onto Helen's legs.

Anita's assurance stunned Helen. "But if you think you're agreeing on one thing, and in fact you're agreeing on something else altogether . . . I don't know. I just don't know." She looked blankly at Anita.

"Mom, you're too nice. How are you ever going to be a lawyer if you think so much?" Anita stood up, and she and Carolyn smiled down at Helen. The two girls shook their heads. How would she ever cope? they seemed to ask.

She didn't mind their pity. Law school wasn't for the future as much as for now. Oh, she had told everyone it was for the future, it was her *plan*, and to her relief people nodded encouragingly. She had been encouraged by it herself, the idea of a profession, of something worthwhile that she could have, she figured, for a long, long time to come. But now that she was in it she had to admit she didn't know what kind of lawyer she would make, nor could she actually see herself performing lawyerly tasks, assuming a lawyerly air of authority. But that didn't matter. The point of it all had shifted as swiftly as the winds did on the lake. That she'd made a fool of herself earlier that day when she didn't know the answer to the question her contracts professor asked—was it of any real consequence?

"Would an economist, Miss Grobar—" A long pause while the professor cleared his throat, a gesture she knew he made deliberately, for her sake, granting her a moment to adjust to the surprise of having been called on. She'd noticed how he did this with the several women students, though he didn't hesitate when calling on men. Helen was less surprised than disoriented, a little lost; no one had called her *Miss* since . . . when? When she was a girl?

The professor continued. "Would an economist agree with the court's decision?"

Yes or no. Yes or no? And silence. A room of one hundred students, utter silence, and the answer, a flip of the coin. She stared into the fluorescence streaming from the lights above. Her heart beat madly.

Beside her, a student whose name-card read "Landers," a woman who looked barely twenty and who invariably chewed bubble gum while in class, slipped her a piece of paper. *Yes*, Miss Landers wrote. *Absolutely*.

"No," Helen said, a knee-jerk reaction to being fed the

answer undeservedly. "An economist would not agree with this decision."

"No?"

"I don't think so."

"Would you like to think some more?" When the professor smiled gently, determined to be both Socratic and kind, a patter of laughter issued from several rows behind her. Miss Landers sighed loudly and popped her gum.

"A little more thought," the professor said, "and Miss Grobar, I'm sure you'll conclude that an economist would agree with this decision. Now, let's talk about it."

She didn't have to say anything at all. He'd move on to the next person. She knew that and spoke up anyway. "Yes," she said. "Let's."

"Soufflé for dinner, girls?" She still held her finger at the point where she'd stopped reading. She turned her attention, which had drifted, back to the girls.

"See?" Anita said. "Too nice."

Helen dismissed them with a flick of her hand.

She didn't go back to her reading. Instead she closed the book, lifted it off her frame, and lay down on the deck, staring at the leaves of the tree above her. They'd begun to turn already, with red and orange tints bleeding from the outside edges in toward the leaves' green core. She gazed at them, dangling like ornaments against the sky's clear blue backdrop. The word *elegance* came to mind. The elegance of the curve of the branch above her, the elegance of the cumulus cloud, dropping in from the west, lightly, adding just a touch of moodiness to that all-too-perfect, one-dimensional sky. She raised her left arm and squinted as her wedding ring, which she still resolutely wore, glinted in the sun. Then she waved her arm back and forth as if sketching the scene above her. On her mind's canvas she painted the branch, the leaves, the cloud. Then below them she painted herself balancing on the dock as she tipped to one side, ringing out her graying hair. She painted the water and gave it a few glistening waves. She painted the sun, its rays falling just to the right of the dock, just outside her reach.

Sighing, she dropped her arm over her concave stomach. From inside she could hear Anita and Carolyn at the piano, playing tunes from *A Chorus Line*, their latest favorite. She rolled over, curled into a ball, shut her eyes tightly.

When had James stopped loving her? The question was always there, like a recurring dream, whenever she closed her eyes, whenever she paused. When she thought of Pauline, the woman he left her for, the woman to whom he was now engaged, the woman he "loved dearly"—telling her in one swoop not only that he loved someone else but also that he'd stopped loving her—Helen thought how conventional Pauline was. She had met her at functions over the years—Pauline and James worked for the same insurance company—and she would never have guessed that this woman would attract James, a woman her age exactly, an insurance underwriter who wore silk dresses, pearls, and blazers, and had obviously dyed her graying hair, a woman who talked in a voice that rose and rose until she'd gasp and acknowledge, "Well, I'm getting carried away again!"

When did James start wanting something else, something she couldn't help but characterize as *more*? They'd moved to their cabin in Wells to avoid the trappings of always wanting more, of the severe materialism they saw around them. They would live a simple, spare life. *She* was a simple, spare life. She thought he was too.

He'd always worked long hours and she assumed he had to. At home, he'd spend much of the weekends out on long, solitary sails and she didn't think of this as anything other than a fragment of how simple, spare people lived simple, spare lives. He'd return from sailing invariably refreshed, more content than when he'd set out.

She didn't worry about her marriage. She was mired in it, propelled forward on a kind of automatic pilot of tending.

Elaborate dinners. It was all she could do for him when he came in, tired, at eight o'clock or so each evening, so she cooked dinner each night with a vengeance. Yet to compensate for the little tending he seemed to need, she tended Anita mostly. They drew together, and read together, and swam together. They talked together, and once Anita had said, "I don't feel like I know Dad," and Helen had answered, "He's a plain man. He likes orderliness, good food, solitary times. It's not for everyone, I suppose."

In the months before he left, signs of a less predictable, changing James began to appear. He'd stay inside on the weekends and read. He began reading classics suddenly, *Madame Bovary* and *The Great Gatsby*, and he'd call to Anita and insist he read to her. She was delighted, and they'd begun taking turns reading to each other. Helen thought of getting in on that, of renewing her friendship with James as he was doing with Anita—and pointedly not with her. Then she scolded herself for her selfishness, for not being happier for Anita's sake, for wanting, simply for wanting.

Still prone on the deck, she thought hard about the next thing she would do, trying to pin it down. Classes, home, change clothes, homework . . . *Would an economist agree with this decision?* When had she ever given thought to what an economist would think? That's what she longed to explain to the professor and to the assured, young, certainly unmarried Miss Landers. To Anita. To James.

When? When did I have time to think?

As Anita hit a bad note on the piano, squealing, then groaning in dismay at her musical mishap, Helen remembered.

"Soufflé," she said out loud. "Yes. A cheese soufflé."

She sat with the girls while they ate the soufflé. They couldn't get the show tunes out of their minds and kept bursting into song in between bites. She laughed with them, sipped water, watched. At one point Anita lifted a fork to Helen's lips, offering her some of her own delicate concoction.

"Not now, sweetie. Mom's going to eat later. Don't worry."

"Is Mom?" Anita asked, her voice quick, a snap at her mother. Helen turned, surprised.

"I'm not four years old," Anita said. "You don't need to refer to yourself in the third person. It's absurd." She took the fork to her lips, then put it down. Swallowing, she sputtered forward with, "You always do this."

"What? What do I do?" Helen saw Anita turn a hopeless gaze toward Carolyn who cast her eyes down at her plate of food. Carolyn obviously felt awkward, Helen could see, caught as she was in another family's conflict. Helen lifted her glass of water, but she didn't take a sip. She waited as patiently and politely as Carolyn.

"You're so nice that it's impossible to get mad at you," Anita angrily answered. "But listen, if you don't eat sooner or later you're going to flitter away. That's all I meant. What do you want to do, Mom, flitter away?" Anita helped herself to more food.

Helen didn't want to flitter away, but she wasn't hungry. It was as simple as that. Still, for Anita's sake she helped herself to some soufflé and ate the small piece quickly. The meal finished, the girls went upstairs to Anita's room. Carolyn would be sleeping over.

Later, after Helen had done the dishes and read the newspaper, she wandered toward her bedroom where she'd perform her evening exercise ritual—fifteen minutes of jogging in place, followed by fifty knee bends and fifty sit-ups. The bedroom was surprisingly big. Carpeted in the former owner's green shag, and filled with only her bed, night table, and dresser, it had a barren appearance. *Bertha*, she thought of calling it as she pulled her upper body from the floor. Then she lay on the floor to catch her breath, staring at the ceiling, a remote sky. *Bertha the barren room.* Even when James had been there it had this look, like an indoor open field, only then she associated it with something exotic, an airy grandiosity, a promise of space. Anita liked to use the floor for practicing handstands and cartwheels.

Picking herself up, she changed into her nightgown, used

the bathroom, then slipped underneath the bed's blankets. Even though her feather pillow curved around her head, she pressed her face further into the pillow. She hoped to feel contained, perfectly enclosed, but when she shut her eyes what she could see of herself created a now familiar panic: a forty-four year-old woman, alone in a queen size bed, which, in turn, looked like a tiny island floating on a massive sea of green shag carpet.

Two hours passed and she couldn't sleep. She left the bed, lifted off her nightgown, and grabbed her cardigan sweater. She tiptoed from her room across the living room and down the stairs. She opened the floor-to-ceiling sliding doors and let herself out. Throwing the sweater over her bare shoulders, she began her way down the path, from the deck to the dock at the lake's edge. Her skin broke out in goose bumps as she made her way through the night's coolness. She wasn't worried about not being able to see the path: from so many nights like this, she knew it by heart.

She went to the dock's far end where a ladder provided access into the water. Holding the ladder's rails, she leaned over, staring into the black pool that she could best make out by its reflections of the few stars in the sky. Her wedding band, cooling as it rested against the ladder, also shimmered with a trace of light, and she stared at that too, amazed at how such a slim slice of metal could connect with signals from a source so distant. She dipped her toes in. The water was slightly warmer than the night air.

Tossing off her sweater, she lowered herself. She sighed as the water swirled around her naked body, in and around her legs, over her stomach, across her protruding rib cage, buoying her shrunken, dense breasts. She didn't sink her head underneath the water, but swam forward into the darkness with her neck stiffly holding her head up, as if she were on the lookout.

She straightened her arms before her, then parted them to stroke. She punctuated each stroke not with a breath, but a quiet plea. "James," she said. Then another stroke.

Then, "James."

When she'd swum as far as she could, she flipped on her back, her arms paddling by her hips, but just barely, just enough to allow her to stay afloat, to rest.

She could see more stars now, tiny flickers of light, and she thought she saw a cloud moving, but she couldn't be sure. She could hear only her own breathing. Unlike her mind, the lake was a sea of silence and as she rested against this tender, liquid pillow she finally achieved that longed-for sense of containment.

She dipped her head backward, then felt the satisfying pull of her hair as she lifted her head upright. Arching her back, she thrust her breasts forward. The cool air brushing against them was delightful, sexual. She arched further. She rolled over once, onto her stomach, then her side, emerging again on her back.

Luxurious bath, she thought. Luxurious night.

As she reached to graze her breasts she called again, urgently, "James."

Then silence: in the water, in her mind. Then the recognition once again of that air: crisp, nimble, delicious. Just to have breasts, she thought, alive in the air, the water, the darkness.

A few minutes later, swimming toward shore, she caught herself humming. What was the song? How did she know it?

Oh, yes. Of course. *A Chorus Line.*

The next day, Saturday, she was back on the deck by ten in the morning, rooted to her study spot by another thousand-page legal text, titled, simply, *Property*. She was reading about easements and other rights of way. She was alone and read contentedly for an hour or so. The air had warmed again and she sat comfortably in jeans and a t-shirt. The girls had gotten up early and had taken the canoe out. She could see them in the distance as they paddled aimlessly this way then that. Every so often she thought she heard a familiar melody line.

They were romantic, the two of them, always lost to one

Broadway fantasy or another, and she liked their company so much. Anita and Carolyn made the best of things; they kept the day interesting. She knew they wanted to start dating, that despite the singing in the boat they were as frustrated and frightened as she'd once been—would it ever happen?— how?—and how do I make the time pass until it does? The last time she and Anita talked—and that was so long ago already, before James left—she'd told Anita that the secret to love was to trust herself. You be yourself, she'd said, and someone will surely notice. You can't fail. It isn't possible. And Anita, who'd been crying, her head in her lap, had said a timid, "You sure?" And Helen had answered, patting her head, "Of course I'm sure."

Now they were paddling in. When the canoe hit the dock they leapt out, as if the boat had been cramping their histrionic style. They lifted the canoe onto the dock, then carried it, carefully, the way James had always insisted, up the bank.

"Hey!" they both said, clambering up the deck's steps.

"Good morning." As she looked up to them, lifting her left hand to make a visor over her eyes, the girls came into focus: their rolled pant legs, their untucked t-shirts, their tan arms, and Anita's hand—rising, outstretched, now pointing at her.

"You took it off! Your ring! Mom, it's off!"

Helen held her hand before her eyes. What was Anita talking about?

She pulled her hand down, rubbing the bare finger in disbelief. She checked the pockets of her jeans. She looked around her, slapping the deck's surface, searching, then turned her attention back to her hand.

Last night, in the water?

Anita clapped, as if the loss were a triumph.

Though Anita's face was smack in front of hers, Helen heard her as if she were somewhere in the distance. "Good for you. It's about time you realized." Louder now, her voice registering at last, Anita said, "He's gone. Mom, do you realize he's gone? The only thing I never understood is why you didn't get mad. Mom, are you mad now?" Anita looked hopeful, as if Helen's being mad were the key to some lost treasure.

She sat upright and her words came slowly. "Oh, sweetie," she said, "I don't know. I just don't know. How *would* I know?"

A breeze blew past, ruffling pages of the book in her lap.

"No. I'm not mad." She looked down at a blur of words, then up at a blur of leaves, branches, and two girls' faces.

"I wasn't what he wanted," she said. "Happens all the time."

"Maybe," Anita began. "Then again—" But Helen cut her off.

She breathed in deeply. She brushed Anita's hair out of her eyes. She was certain. She wasn't what he bargained for.

And he—

She couldn't finish the thought.

Anita was shaking her head, but Helen held a finger to her lips. "Shush," she said. "No more. Not now."

Her legs ached, but she didn't lift the book from her lap. Instead, she read on about a phone company's right of way to install its wires on private property. There were so many things to learn, after all, if she were really going to do this, become something new, something else—a lawyer, say. She'd have to practice confidence, to study Anita's and Miss Lander's assurance. One of these days just maybe she'd buy herself a suit.

The girls left her side. When the next breeze swept past, feathery and gentle, she grabbed her sweater, wrapping it tightly around her. Then, because her life depended on it, she turned the page.

Speed Reading
(Carolyn Kahn—Spring 1976)

Carolyn spotted the ad in the county paper's classifieds: *Speed Reading, Six-week course, Mondays, 5:30-7:00. Progress Guaranteed. Better Yourself! Reach Your Goals!*

That first Monday, a cool evening in late February, she walked from her house the half-mile to the elementary school where the class was held. Earlier she'd brushed and brushed her thick auburn hair as if Speed Reading required groomed looks. She'd dropped the soprano recorder she'd been playing—simple beginner's tunes—into her school bag along with an unused notebook. She knew that carrying the recorder would somehow help. After all, wasn't she learning to play it pretty fast?

The class would meet in what had been her sixth-grade room. Now a junior in high school, Carolyn recalled the time when she was an eleven-year-old girl struggling with long division and fractions, with reading and geography, struggling out on recess to run fast, or fast enough, struggling to keep up. Even then she believed she was slow. She'd always been slow, she figured, not so much in reading as in running, but her sense of physical slowness had spread until it settled into that part of her that was at once the closest thing to her and the most amorphous thing about her: her identity.

As she walked into the classroom, tentatively, Ms. Jarrett nodded in recognition, then resumed writing something on the blackboard. Ms. Jarrett, Carolyn's old teacher, was offering Speed Reading for the second time that year. At times she'd been a harsh teacher, Carolyn remembered, but perhaps sixth grade wasn't her strong suit. Perhaps Speed Reading was.

Carolyn sat in a desk near the front, but safely inconspicuous by a wall. She blinked to adjust to the room's fluorescent glow, brighter than the dim evening tones she'd just left behind. Ms. Jarrett still wore her blond hair piled on top of her head, a style that gave her tall frame even more height, and she wore a business suit: a navy blazer with a round gold pin in one lapel, a matching skirt, a striped blouse, and blue pumps. To Carolyn, the look was less prim than frightening.

The twelve others in the room were mostly adults. A cluster of women chatted in the first two rows, their pens, notebooks, and eyeglass cases stacked neatly in front of them. Carolyn was surprised to spot Ted Oberry across the room. He was in her class—a good student, like her, but more self-motivated. He ran track, served on Student Council, captained the chess club, and even played supporting roles in school plays, an act that signaled an unusual inner strength, she thought, for by high school it was clear that masculinity and theatricality didn't mix.

Most recently Ted had become religious. He was into Jesus. Not Jesus as in, say, the Lutheran Jesus or the Catholic Jesus, she heard him once explain. He was into the real Jesus, "the Jesus of love." Carolyn almost liked the idea. She admired Ted's serious pursuit of the serious. But nobody in Wells was into Ted's Jesus except Ted. His new faith set him apart more than ever.

Just the other day during a school-wide assembly about school spirit, Ted, speaking for the Student Council, had managed to get in a word or two about this Jesus. *Here we go*, Carolyn had thought, squirming in her seat, embarrassed for him.

Yet he had a point. The school *was* in crisis. "The spirit of '76," a phrase meant to inspire, was no spirit at all. The administration's line was that 1972 had been the last year that students did their homework with dedication and respected teachers. The next speaker, Mrs. Malin, an English teacher at Wells High since 1954, said so. Since 1972 Mrs. Malin had watched a steady, "horrific" decline. Blue jeans and long hair on boys were "symptomatic." Marijuana, too. Mrs. Malin had a theory.

"The sixties started it," she explained. The Generation Gap, a spillover from the last decade, caused the loss in spirit, Mrs. Malin's "crisis of delinquency." She thought discipline would help.

And Ted thought Jesus would help. Or Ted thought *he* could help by spreading a simple, loving message.

Diana Nicholson had enrolled in Speed Reading too and sat nearby. Glancing her way, Carolyn dimly recalled Diana from first or second grade when Diana had stayed back, a true slow reader. Carolyn took note of her greasy skin and hair, her lumpy, overweight shape, her faded, threadbare dress—a sign of her poverty—and her strong smell, one that suggested sex.

She didn't know for sure if it was sex that she smelled but thought so because she'd recently seen Diana having what seemed like sex in public. She'd been driving through Wells's small downtown area, the nightly hang-out for a group of unkempt boys known at school for their steady supply of dope. One of those boys was with Diana in a dimly-lit phone booth, his car with the jacked-up rear end and oversized tires parked nearby. As she paused at a stop sign, Carolyn witnessed the emergence of Diana's odd, wistful smile, slow to form but once there clearly deeply felt as if she were smiling to herself about a good thought just surfacing in her mind. The boy was pressed up against her in the phone both, concealing exactly what was going on, and Diana leaned into him while looking away from him, out at the street, which was empty except for Carolyn's car passing through. Recalling that scene, Carolyn sniffed, scratched her nose, and tried not to stare at Diana Nicholson's pimply but optimistic face.

Ms. Jarrett cleared her throat, then uttered the word "efficiency." Except for her forehead, wrinkled in expectation, her face was serious, even stern. "That's what Speed Reading is all about. It's just like shopping." She stopped, winked, and her features softened. "No one said you have to *get* everything."

She threw a piece of chalk in the air, then snapped it up, a solid catch. The women in the front nodded, already taken, it seemed, with the practical essence of Speed Reading. Ms. Jarrett pulled a newspaper from her briefcase. "What's the big question in this dense editorial?" she asked, holding the paper high.

She paused briefly, then answered, "Whether the President should pardon the President. Stick to the point and it'll take no time." She turned then to a book on how to cope with problem children and, nodding to the women, said, "This could be useful. But not if it's going to eat up your day, right? Know your purpose, parents. Know your purpose, students." She glanced at Carolyn, Diana, then over at Ted. "And you'll know what's in it for you."

She raised her index finger and told them each to raise theirs. "Once you know your purpose—exactly why you read each thing you read," she said, "then this instrument will get you where you need to go." After several people discussed what they read and why they read, the class practiced skimming an article on coping with insomnia. Based on the number of phrases underlined and circled, Carolyn guessed it was from Ms. Jarrett's personal library.

But Carolyn could barely read it as she'd become acutely aware that she wasn't sure of her purpose for reading—or doing—anything. She went to school because she was growing up. She read novels, occasionally, for pleasure. More often she read homework assignments because she had to. In response to Ms. Jarrett's question about what they read and why, Carolyn had sat still, paralyzed with the fear of drawing attention to herself.

She hadn't realized that Speed Reading required a sense of purpose. She thought she'd just show up for class and follow the program. Becoming faster at reading would somehow make her faster at other things: reaching decisions, having self-confidence, meeting boys, knowing what she wanted to do with her life. Just showing up for Speed Reading would improve herself—and that was enough.

Diana Nicholson was having problems with "subjects," as

she put it, and when Ms. Jarrett said, "Subjects at school?" Diana nodded ardently. "You're in the right place," the teacher told Diana. "Good girl," she added. As if Diana were just a kid, Carolyn thought, but the remark made Diana beam.

"Ms. Jarrett . . . let's see . . . yes, I remember her. Tall. Serious. Thick legs. Right?" Carolyn's mother was at the dining table with the newspaper spread before her. She and Hannah had already eaten. Her father hadn't come home yet. These days he stayed away as much as possible. It was easier that way for them all. In this way Carolyn hadn't had to talk to her father— not really—in years.

"Thick legs. Right." Carolyn stood by the stove, reheating spaghetti for herself. She was sipping Tab and wondering, vaguely, if she'd ever die from saccharine-induced cancer, a risk she'd read about that morning in the newspaper her mother now held.

"She never married." Her mother spoke in a distant tone as if she were reading the line from the paper's obituaries. "Did she, Care?"

"I guess not," Carolyn said. When she was in elementary school *Ms.* Jarrett was *Miss* Jarrett, but her new title created new potential. "She doesn't seem married. She seems busy. Professional. Organized. But not married. She doesn't seem married at all."

"I guess some women don't meet the right man," her mother said. "Or some don't want to marry. Or some aren't attractive, or don't feel attractive, and give up."

Her mother sneezed and asked Carolyn to bring her a tissue. She did, pausing along the way to stir the spaghetti.

"Some women are lesbians," Carolyn added, handing her mother the tissue, knowing this sole additional option would jerk her mother awake. She'd been reading about love-making, heterosexual and homosexual, in *Our Bodies, Ourselves.* She'd also been reading about breast cancer, cervical cancer, pregnancy, motherhood, daughterhood, pap smears, and yeast infections.

118

She might still have been a virgin, but she was certainly a well-informed one, ready for all contingencies should she make it to life's other, more active, side.

"Do you think?" Her mother looked up. Her dark hair, recently cut short, fluffed around her head. The new thought made her blink and blink.

"No. She doesn't seem like a lesbian. She seems busy, that's all." Before Carolyn turned to go, she asked, "Did you think *you'd* marry?"

"Of course I thought I'd marry. We married. That's what we did then." Carolyn knew that "then" referred to the 1950s, The Decade When Young Women And Men Married. Her mother had emphasized this above all else as if it happened in that decade as it hadn't in any before or after.

"Did you know you'd marry *Dad*?"

"Not exactly." Her mother looked up from the paper. Her elbow bent on the table, she leaned her chin into her empty palm. "But he was the person I was dating. And what I felt was safe, or happy, or something. And it was time. That's what we did. That's how it happened."

"Couldn't you have taken more time? Thought it over some?"

"It wouldn't have occurred to me." Her mother seemed startled by her own response. She combed her fingers through her hair and pushed the newspaper aside. "I know that sounds odd, but maybe I was in a hurry. Maybe that's it. I didn't want to stick out. It was time, so I got married. Because if I waited, maybe I wouldn't get married at all. And then what would I do?"

Carolyn paused, then asked, "Well, what are you doing now?"

"Raising you, aren't I?" Her mother began to nod her head, then abruptly stopped. "Carolyn, where's this coming from?"

"It's Ms. Jarrett. She said we should know our purpose."

"Well, I wonder if Ms. Jarrett has a purpose. That's what I wonder."

Then, because her mother sounded hurt, Carolyn said, "I know what you mean."

Carolyn practiced Speed Reading each night that week. After dinner she'd go to her room, pull out her Speed Reading text— a paperback of essays on all kinds of subjects—and click on the stopwatch borrowed from Hannah, an avid collector of sport paraphernalia.

Ted Oberry has a purpose, Carolyn mused, in between articles. It was Friday night. She wasn't going out, as usual, so she figured she might as well speed read. Her mother was upstairs knitting and watching TV, and her father was downstairs reading the newspaper and *Forbes* magazine.

Jesus. Jesus had given Ted a purpose. Or maybe Ted didn't have a purpose but needed a purpose. It still came down to Jesus. Jesus filled Ted's need for a purpose and now *was* his purpose. Ted Oberry had known what to say in response to Ms. Jarrett's question.

Hannah wandered in, flopped on Carolyn's bed, and asked what she was doing.

"Dirty sneakers," Carolyn warned, pointing at her floral print bedspread, then at Hannah's grass-stained Nikes. Hannah wiggled until her feet dangled off the bed's end.

"Hannah," Carolyn said, "what do you think you'll be?" It was a question they used to ask often, sometimes eagerly, sometimes in a matter-of-fact tone, but over the years they'd stopped. Like childhood toys, their early ambitions were put away, though Carolyn couldn't remember when, by whom, where, why, or how.

Hannah rolled on her stomach, leaned over the bed's edge, and stared at the floor. She mumbled something.

"What?" Carolyn asked.

"I can't say what I want to be. I'm too embarrassed."

"Just say it. I won't look at you. I promise." Sensitive truths had always been coaxed out this way.

Carolyn turned from Hannah to the open paperback on her

120

desk. She held the stopwatch in her hand. "I'll time you. I'll tell you how long it took you to say what you want to be."

This made Hannah laugh. Carolyn heard her sister take a deep sigh. Then she gushed forth with, "I wanted to be in the Olympics when I was little, you know, ice skating, and I wanted to be a teacher, every year I wanted to be a teacher of whatever grade I was in, and a musician, I always wanted to be a musician, especially a singer, I know, I don't really have a voice, it'll have to be piano, but I wanted to." She stopped to breathe. "And maybe a composer too!"

"Hannah!" Carolyn exclaimed. "You really want a lot!"

Carolyn turned to face Hannah. The stopwatch in her hand was on and ticking.

"Not want. *Wanted*," Hannah insisted, still on her stomach, face down. She turned her head toward Carolyn's pillow and mumbled, "It's not like I think I'm something."

"Okay," she quickly assured her, identifying with Hannah's resistance. *Ambition*. The idea seemed foreign, masculine, like *trigonometry*. She said, "Don't feel funny. Hannah, I know you're not something."

Then, because Hannah's answer hadn't really been an answer—want*ed* but not want*ing*—Carolyn didn't click the stopwatch off. Instead, she let it roll from her hand, dropping it to dangle by the rope it was attached to, her eyes following its motion, her ears pricked to its count of seconds, one after another, on and on.

She decided she'd speed read Leon Uris's *Exodus*. The thick paperback was lying around, shelved with other books that involved the "Jewish struggle," as her entire extended family referred to their heritage. She'd seen the movie on TV and knew she'd like the story. The book was full of danger and intrigue, bravery and self-sacrifice, romance and a little sex. Mostly, though, it was full of purpose. The settling of Israel was vital to the characters; they were being annihilated in Europe and needed this safe haven. Carolyn didn't have to use her index finger to speed read; once she discovered the book's sense of purpose, she couldn't put it down.

When she was through, she was even more convinced that purpose was the essential ingredient missing in her life. At night in bed she longed, guiltily, for some dramatic circumstance to arise, like a war, a dictatorship, even a fire, that would alleviate her self-doubt and provide her with clear and worthy objectives. Her parents' divorce would be nice; then she could live with Hannah and her mother the way Anita lived, so perfectly, with just her mother. But that was like wishing for snow in July. As distant as her parents were, the big event just wouldn't happen. If only her mother could miraculously lose her wedding ring, she once mused, like Anita's mother had that fall. One night she dreamed about the death of one of her parents—she couldn't go so far as to visualize which one—and saw herself redeemed by the grieving process, holding the shattered pieces of her life together, taking care of Hannah and the remaining parent, the death imbuing her life with the focus it now lacked.

Waking brought her back to her own life where nothing dramatic occurred: no deaths, no sicknesses, no obvious worthy cause to champion. Even her parents' marital tension was nothing to talk about. Not really. Hadn't they adjusted to it long ago? What difference did it really make? Purpose, she concluded, happened in another time, or on other continents. Life in Wells was quiet, comfortable, dull. The only debate was how to finance a town-wide sewer system. That, and the problem of the high school students' spirits, that "noxious Generation Gap" as Mrs. Malin, not without a certain amount of verve, referred to it.

She read about 115 words per minute, a pace Ms. Jarrett told her was good. "You're on track," Ms. Jarrett said, hovering over Carolyn for a minute during the next Speed Reading class, a long minute in which she breathed in her heavy perfume and squirmed under the pressure of being watched by this intimidating woman.

Diana Nicholson, who regularly sat by Carolyn, read well below 100 words per minute. Ms. Jarrett spent even longer near Diana, quizzing her on the assignment, an article about stress reduction and yoga. Carolyn was surprised to hear Ms. Jarrett tell Diana to slow down. "Don't go too fast. Make sure you take in all the important words," she advised.

Diana, concerned about her performance, had sweated through the armpits of her faded dress. And she radiated that odd, sexual smell as she looked anxiously from Ms. Jarrett's face to her reader, trying to grasp both the words and teacher's messages simultaneously.

"Take it easy," Ms. Jarrett said. "Don't expect too much too fast."

At that Diana relaxed. She nodded her head and sat more comfortably in her chair. "Am I improving?" she asked.

"Yes," Ms. Jarrett said. "You can't help but improve."

Diana's face was flushed with pleasure even though the words, to Carolyn, comprised a mixed message. Diana smiled over at Carolyn who hated herself for the envious impulse she felt, watching them. Diana's circumstances were much less fortunate than her own; her reading abilities were much poorer too, but Carolyn couldn't deny it: she wished Ms. Jarrett would pay *her* that extra attention, telling her with even greater specificity exactly what to do to improve, to better herself, to reach her goals—despite the fact that when pressed she couldn't even say what those goals were.

At Ted Oberry's suggestion, Carolyn walked home with him after class. Tall, with curly brown hair that fell into his eyes, Ted wore basketball sneakers and two double-insulated sweatshirts. Once outside in the cool night air, he put a baseball cap on his head. They walked out of the schoolyard and onto Main.

Carolyn, though tall herself, rushed to keep in step. Ted was talking about Speed Reading, how many words per minute— "WPMs" he called them—he was up to, and then about getting in shape for track. She listened. He got in shape for track, preseason, by running each morning around the lake. It was six miles around and he could do it in about forty-five minutes. "I wear a watch," he said, "for pacing."

She nodded as she huffed beside him, her breath creating clouds of condensation. They were passing the post office now, and she had to step aside as a car pulled over and opened the passenger-side door, blocking her way. Ted waited for her to catch up.

"It would take me an hour and forty-five minutes!" She laughed.

"Don't underestimate yourself," he said. She was looking up at him, and he looked over and smiled, then pretended to throw a basketball through a hoop. He stared at the bare branches of the maple he'd aimed toward, just visible in the fading light. "It takes faith, that's all."

She raised her eyebrows, thinking she was about to hear a lecture on Jesus, but Ted only said, "Yup, a little faith. And you'd be surprised at what you can accomplish."

The Leon Uris novels had given her some faith. She'd moved from *Exodus* to *Mila 18* to *QB VII*, blazing through each in a natural speed read. Zionism began to hold an abstract appeal. It was an aspect of Judaism she'd never considered before, and seemed separate and clear of the tangled family dynamics she associated with the two holidays, Passover and the New Year, which the family still celebrated. She'd never thought of farming before, but the idea of living on a kibbutz, settling the land of Israel, now occupied her mind. The only catch, she knew, was that when push came to shove she wasn't a traveler or an adventurer. She was slow. She'd always been slow. The two ideas—Carolyn and Zionism—didn't work together.

Despite her new faith she had another idea, more immediately possible. She wanted to go on a date with Ted Oberry. Quite literally she woke up to the desire; it came to her the next Thursday morning, the second Thursday in March. Rolling her head back and forth across her pillow, she strove to dismiss the contradiction between her budding Jewish zeal and Ted's for Jesus.

This wasn't about religion, she figured. This was about romance, maybe sex.

"Should I ask him?" she said to Hannah at breakfast.

Hannah responded with a resounding affirmation. Then, as she was in the habit of doing, she burst into song, this time Helen Reddy's "I Am Woman." They'd been taken with it, this song that was both top-forty and feminist, an original combination.

"Okay, woman." Carolyn urged her tentative voice to carry some authority. A fleeting image of her mother gave way to Ms. Jarrett, whose voice gave her a hint of what to shoot for.

She approached him during their next walk home. Spring was only weeks away and the air had warmed some, though it gained in breeziness what it had lost in coldness. As they passed the post office Carolyn stopped to tighten her shoelace, a premise for laying low and breathing, for buying time. She stood up. She cleared her throat. She thought she felt a sneeze coming on. Or maybe she didn't. She noticed Ted staring at her, confused.

"How about a movie Saturday night?" she blurted. "I'll drive. Unless you want to. Not that I'm assuming you want to go. Really, I'm not. But—"

Before she knew it, the wind carried Ted's "sure" her way. Ambling beside her, he began to hum.

She was elated, lifted by both the word and the gust that sent it. Keeping pace with Ted, she hummed too, swinging her arms freely in rhythm with her tune. When the next gust blew, she turned her face into it, letting the breeze drop over her like a wave. She was strong; she was invincible; she was—

She noticed Ted's song wasn't the same as hers. Glancing his way, she stopped singing.

When he turned and said, "What is it?" she said, "Sorry."

When he said, "What for?" she said, "I was interrupting, I think."

When he said, "Hey, no problem. I didn't even hear," she said nothing, relieved.

The night of her date she changed outfits seven times. Her oldest jeans looked ragged. Her newest jeans looked stiff. She looked "fat" or "ridiculous" in several skirts. She returned to the oldest jeans and wore them with a green wool sweater.

"Is it me?" she asked Hannah. Then she spun around, too impatient to wait for her sister's answer.

To avoid running into anyone she knew, she chose a theater thirty miles from Wells. Self-conscious with Ted beside her, she awkwardly parked the car in the movie theater's lot, straddling the yellow line. Inside, she and Ted each paid for a ticket and a bag of popcorn. She hoped Ted would offer to pay for something—a sign of interest, or, better, a sign that he knew he was on a date and, once he showed her that he knew this, she would know too.

But when they sat down he crossed his arms over his chest and began describing "runner's high"—a condition he called "true, pure, essential, like meditation, TM"—and Carolyn crossed her legs and appeared to listen, though in truth it didn't interest her much. Her focus was simple: did he like her, or what?

"Yes!" Ted said, turning to her halfway through *Rocky*. Rocky was getting into shape for a boxing match, eating a raw egg, jogging at dawn, and clambering up a mountain of stairs. As he climbed, the music swelled, and Ted, leaning forward in his seat, repeated, "Yes, yes."

"Yes," she silently agreed when later in the movie Rocky's homely girlfriend began to show signs of life—a new haircut, stylish glasses, sex appeal.

After the movie, at McDonald's, Ted still didn't offer to buy her french fries or a Coke, but he did offer his opinion. "Radical," he said. "I can totally relate. You know, to live your dream, create your destiny. That's what I'm after."

She wanted to say "me too," but she feared that Ted might

ask her to explain herself and then what would she say? When it came to her life's purpose, she still had no specifics. She sipped her diet Coke, listened. Before dropping him off—mildly tired of the way he'd gone on and on—she turned to him, admiring through the darkness his earnest expression. She leaned in his direction, enough so he could kiss her if he wanted to but not enough so it looked like she wanted that. But he didn't. He smiled more broadly and said, "Rocky!" Then he punched her arm lightly, a quick one-two.

Home again, Hannah hounded her for the details, and Carolyn summed up the evening by declaring that she wasn't even sure she could call it a date.

"Jesus," Hannah said sadly.

The remark made Carolyn think of Ted. "Jesus," she agreed as she patted her floral bedspread, inviting Hannah to come sit with her for a while, for company.

"It's all in the movement of the eye."

Ms. Jarrett began the next Speed Reading class by discussing the problem of regression. She explained how, when reading, the eye paused to take in words like a camera snapping a picture. Then it moved along. But sometimes the eye moved backwards to re-read the words before, the ones it didn't really see the first time. That was "regression," Ms. Jarrett told Diana, in particular, who did it too much. It slowed her down.

"It's like I said on Day One. When you read you don't have to *get* everything."

By then Carolyn figured she'd gotten all she could from Leon Uris–a purposeful high while reading, only to be followed by an abrupt sense of despair over her own life once each book was done.

But there was still hope in Ted. He'd passed her a note in class. At first she couldn't believe her eyes, but when she re-read the words there was no denying their meaning. *Tomorrow night?* he began. *A movie? Don't worry, I'll drive.*

He wanted to see *Rocky* again.

"Again?" She looked ahead at the stretch of highway. They day's light was dim, but not yet dark. The glow from the oncoming cars' lights didn't cause her to blink. They were going to catch the 7:30 show.

"Honest to God, Carolyn, I loved it. I mean, why not see it again? We could take our chances on something new, something, maybe, well, crappy, or we could see something really great again. What do you think?"

"I never thought about it like that," she said, crossing her legs and turning to stare out her side window. Either we see something crappy or we see *Rocky* again? Is that what he said? "Well, all right. I guess that makes sense."

Inside the theater, they chose seats by an aisle. They settled in, Ted standing aside while he let Carolyn sit first. This is lovely, she thought, recalling the moment before when he'd bought the tickets and then the popcorn. And now this. This politeness. It was proof. More proof. She was definitely on a date. And when their hands touched while they reached for popcorn and he didn't instantly pull away, wasn't that proof too?

End, end, end, she intoned throughout the film. Ted was at his seat's edge again, nodding and staring forward with such intensity she thought he was practicing his TM. There were no further touches. Nor were there glances her way, not even at the love scenes, especially not at the loves scenes, she noticed, when Ted edged even further forward. Still, *hurry, hurry, hurry,* she thought, daring to fantasize about their drive home, how he'd take a detour when they hit Wells, drive around the lake, say, find a quiet spot, park. They'd stare in the darkness and Ted would hold her hand, touch her face . . .

And he did. He steered the car toward the lake, without saying anything, but she knew. Now they sat side by side. The stars blinked overhead. The lapping waves made quiet splashing sounds. They'd each cracked a window to let some cool, fresh air in. Since they'd left the theater, Ted had been talking relentlessly. He wasn't into contact sports, no he wasn't, and boxing was the worst of them, it was violence plain and simple, it was insane, maybe it should be illegal, but it was the idea of the movie that mattered, that drive to reach your dreams, no, he'd had bad experiences with contact sports, he hated contact sports, he liked solitary sports, like running, like he was telling her before . . .

He was talking and talking, and she was nodding and nodding, waiting and waiting, and finally he reached for her hand. Finally he grew quiet, leaned toward her. Finally she could see the details of his face: the eager eyes grown wide, the narrow nose, the faintly freckled cheeks, the lips slightly parted. Hers were just parting too, yet as their faces neared she sensed something old and familiar, a kind of male body smell that she recalled from years back when she got angry at her father, when he droned on and on each evening just like this, when he'd talk down to them, Mr. Authority, when she pushed him away, all that leading to that day when he'd hit her and for all intents and purposes they'd stopped talking.

She jerked back, choking at the crowd of feelings—anger, panic, and an intense, uncomfortable vulnerability—suddenly clogging her throat. Gasping, she cranked open the window. For the first time that night she didn't care how she looked; she let her head hang the way it would, limply out the car. In this position, squashed against the car door's armrest, she felt a little less tiny, a little more in control.

"Huh?" she heard Ted ask. He seemed very far away.

"I've got to go," she mumbled. "Don't feel good. I'm really dizzy."

"Yeah, sure, okay," he said, his voice louder now as she pulled her head back in. She watched as Ted fumbled for his keys. Leaning forward, he jabbed with the key until he found the ignition. Driving again, he didn't look pleased, but she was grateful for the silence, thick though it was with disappointment, confusion, and, for her, a new fear. Would she ever be kissed? Could she ever let herself be?

Inside, she bolted for her room, rushing past her father, reading in his downstairs study, then slipping past her mother, in her bedroom, clipping coupons from the paper while watching TV. When she reached her own room, she shut and locked her door.

At her desk she pulled from a drawer a pad of lined paper. She sharpened a pencil. She'd make a list, figure it out, regain control, pronto. And she didn't really want Ted Oberry, she assured herself, that much was clear. It wasn't meant to be. It wasn't like *Rocky*. And it wasn't the romance in *Rocky* that was important anyway. It was the dream, the purpose. That's what Ted had been saying all along, wasn't it? And now that she knew one thing she didn't want, now that she was definitely, absolutely clear on that—she took a deep breath—maybe she could know one thing she did want.

She grabbed the stopwatch lying on the desk and clicked it on, its soft yet insistent ticking urging her to proceed.

She wrote: *What I Can Be.*

The words came slowly at first but soon the pace picked up. *School teacher (high school social studies preferred); entrepreneur specializing in girls' sporting goods (Hannah in business with me); bookstore owner (with section of books with purpose!); publisher; news broadcaster; movie critic; movie director; movie producer; movie theater owner (with homemade treats for sale); movie actress; famous movie actress; dramatic, serious movie actress!; Speed Reading instructor; Orthodox Jew; non-Orthodox Jew who goes to Israel to settle; non-Orthodox Jew who stays in U.S. and raises funds for Israel; fundraiser for underprivileged girls who need help in reading and sex education (Diana N.); counselor for the above kind of girl; counselor for middle-aged mothers who never had a separate purpose; counselor for daughters of above kind of mother; counselor for teenage girls who feel funny about wanting (Hannah . . .); college professor (Who? Me?); president (Ha!).*

She turned to a new page. The stopwatch ticked on: seven minutes thirty-five seconds. She wrote more, imagining possibilities she'd never conceived of. *Doctor, chiropractor, nurse-midwife (like in* Our Bodies, Ourselves*)*. By the third page, exhausted, she sat back and said to herself, smiling, relaxing some, "This is radical."

She re-read the list, refining it some, crossing off some options, then erasing her cross-outs and re-writing the very same words. She sat at the edge of her chair, sweating some behind the neck and under the armpits as if she'd been outside jogging. But the more she read the less excited she felt. Her list overwhelmed her. Sweating the way she'd seen Diana Nicholson sweat in Speed Reading—a nervous, clammy, smelly sweat—she realized it wasn't sex but panic that had made Diana reek.

Every option sounded good. She struggled to choose a few, to narrow the list, to find a sensible range of options, to make it all right, definitely, absolutely, but all that came to mind were more ideas. *Coffee shop owner, offering 4:00 tea plus classical music (every Wednesday, music for recorders only).*

In less than one minute, another half-page!

With pad and pencil in hand, she collapsed on her bed. She lay on her back, holding the pad above her as she read it over, so hastily the words blurred. *Organizer of public, cultural events (is there a name for this??).* Her heart was pounding and she felt sick again, almost nauseated, as if the pencil's lead, the smell of which she couldn't get out of her nose, had infected her brain.

Her mother's voice came to mind: some women don't meet the right man, some don't want to marry, or some aren't attractive . . . *Wife and mother*, Carolyn hastily scrawled. *Of course.* Then, feeling the old panic rising, she crossed the line out, then re-wrote it, then, thinking of Ted, thinking of her father, feeling angry, confused, and vulnerable all at once, she erased it completely.

She dropped the pad on the floor and closed her eyes, yet still she smelled the crowd of words and saw in her mind's eye the endless list, the possibilities of what she could be, if she only could choose, only knew how to choose, only felt sure and steady enough to choose.

She raised her hands over her face as if protecting herself

from the flood she'd created. She stamped her feet on her soft bedspread. But she couldn't stop her mind from naming the options over and over, while the stopwatch she'd left on her desk grew louder, each tick marking another moment of indecisiveness, entangling her further in the race she'd just entered, her own journey toward what felt then, at its inception, like a kind of oblivion.

A Crack in the Ice
(Hannah Kahn—Winter 1978)

"You think she'll like it?" Francine asked. She sat in the passenger seat beside Hannah.

"Peggy said she wasn't exactly into cello and piano—" Hannah began to laugh. "But still she wanted to come," she added. A moment later when Francine joined her laughing a moment later, tapping her clogs against the car's tinny floor, Hannah eased back, settling into the comfort this friendship always brought. She and Francine were forever in sync. She felt certain that Francine knew what she was thinking about Peggy Hardley's insistence that she, too, be there tonight—Peggy's first university concert, and her first of classical music. How the event was exactly as interesting to Francine, in the same potentially comic way, as it was to Hannah.

Exactly. That was the miracle of their five-year friendship.

As Peggy raced from her house to the car's back seat, struggling the whole time to force her wiry frame into her white polyester parka, Hannah and Francine exchanged knowing looks.

She's overdressed, Francine's raised eyebrows told Hannah, who, by frowning, relayed back to Francine, *Panty hose? To a college scene? And what do you make of that perm?*

Despite Peggy's claim that she wasn't really into cello and piano duets, once inside the dim concert hall an expectant flush colored her usually pale face, and her left leg jiggled—nervously, excitedly, incessantly, Hannah finally decided. She couldn't help but dwell on Peggy's unsuitable appearance, her stiff pleated skirt, her staid panty hose. Hannah and Francine had been going to these concerts at U-Conn since Hannah had gotten her driver's license a half-year ago, but even before then, Hannah realized, they'd known about college dress: ragged jeans and your loosest sweater.

The two musicians bowed, tuned up, and began. The first piece was a Beethoven sonata, and all was going well until the musicians paused at the close of the first movement.

Then Peggy clapped, an elated, loud burst.

As the solitary sound echoed, eyes—from below, behind, on each side—even the musicians' eyes—turned toward the girls, and Hannah and Francine began to sink, in sync, in their chairs.

Hannah raised her hand to still Peggy's. "It's not over yet," she whispered. "You only clap when the whole piece is over." She gave Peggy a knowing look.

As Peggy slid down with them, her cheeks reddened. But when the cellist smiled their way, Peggy shot upright, instantly redeemed. Hannah watched Peggy, balanced on her seat's edge, and her heart warmed. It was good that Peggy was here, she thought. After all, Peggy's parents weren't well-educated and the most outrageous thing she'd ever done was join the regional association of the Girl Scouts. *Big whoop*, Hannah thought. She'd tell Francine this later: *The problem with poor Peggy is she's hardly lived at all.*

To Hannah's surprise, during the ride home it was Peggy who proffered all-knowing looks.

"It's time," Peggy said. Hannah had already dropped Francine off and now was en route to Peggy's house. The road, an unlit one on the outskirts of town, took a sharp turn, causing her to lean slightly toward Peggy. There wasn't a house for miles and every so often Hannah passed a plowed entrance into the state forest, the black density on both sides of them. It was mid-January and out here, cold, still, quiet. Earlier, when returning to the car after the concert, Peggy had taken the front seat—presumptuously, Hannah thought. Wasn't there an unspoken hierarchy of friendship with the driver that determined absolutely who went where? In the end Hannah had shrugged and Francine had shrugged and they'd settled peacefully inside the car, traveling to the tunes of a top forty station—Peggy's choice—in silence. The evening wasn't so funny after all. It was tiring. Now Peggy sat forward and fidgeted with the radio's tuning dial, the reception having gone bad as they'd gotten further from town.

Peggy said, "You've been seeing him for what? A year?"

"He's shy. So what. Jackie cares, Peggy. That's what matters." Hannah flicked off the radio and Peggy sat back.

"Wait until you do it. Then you'll know what matters." When Hannah turned, she saw Peggy clutching herself, wrapping her arms, which in her parka looked like cloudy puffs of white, around her body. She puckered her lips, then pronounced the word *intercourse* as slowly as possible.

Hannah looked straight ahead. "Intercourse," she echoed, briskly and lightly. She might have been saying "summertime." A moment later she glanced in the rear-view mirror to check Francine's reaction, forgetting she'd already been dropped off. She only saw herself: her gray eyes open wide, her front teeth hanging over her bottom lip, biting it.

"Intercourse," she repeated, appalled when the word came out in sync this time with Peggy. With forced composure, she added, "In my book, Peggy, I just say *sex*."

Sex was in everybody's book. She knew that, never doubted that. But it seemed especially prominent in the books of her high school junior class. That year, 1978, sex was the very page they were turned to, and weren't they all writing it in vibrant italicized print?

Still, she hadn't believed anyone was actually doing it—not anyone she knew well, that is. Certainly not Peggy Hardley, that grade-school friend with the invariable perm and that whiny voice and that grating tendency to pronounce the letter "s" with a slight whistle. The news was astounding. Once Hannah arrived home, she unlaced her Wallabies and skated in her wool socks the kitchen's short length.

Peggy hadn't gone into the physical details, just its general sense: "It feels *so good*. You hear it hurts. You do. But don't buy that. I went for it, and am I ever glad." Occasionally Hannah slid to a stop at the counter by the cookie jar and popped an Oreo or two into her mouth. Her appetite was suddenly limitless.

Of course it was bound to happen—someone she knew would lose her virginity—but she hadn't thought in terms of specifics. Who? When? Where? With whom? She sucked the sweetness in her mouth for comfort and distraction. She shoved off, center-kitchen, and began to spin.

As far as she knew, Carolyn, now at college and more interested in a career, it seemed, than anything else, hadn't lost it. And certainly not Francine, yet to have a boyfriend. What bothered her was Peggy's assurance. How could Peggy know it was her time? What did she see in her face that she didn't recognize in herself? And, if it were true, if it *was* time, how could her time come before Carolyn's time? Worst of all, how could her time come before Jackie's?

She opened the fridge.

She'd always chalked it up to shyness, Jackie's and hers, to explain their creeping sexual progress. Carolyn had once asked her if they'd done it, urging her if so to use birth control and read *Our Bodies, Ourselves*. But Hannah had shrugged. She and Jackie were more into playing guitar and piano duets, romping outside in the snow, skating on Friday nights, going to movies with friends. They explored each other thoroughly above the waist but somehow, without talking about it, their waists had become boundary lines and everything below them elements of a jointly shared safety zone. If Jackie was ever interested in more he never mentioned it. And whenever she was interested in more she'd decided it was better not to push it, better to wait until it was clear he wanted what she wanted.

Differences like that were dangerous, after all. Weren't differences—all kinds of differences—the cause of that unbridgeable chasm of silence that lay between her parents? Even now, 10:30 Saturday night, both parents home, and she'd never know it but for their respective cars resting icily in the driveway. She'd stopped listening to that silence a long time ago.

But there was Peggy Hardley—so glad she'd done it because it felt *so good!*—throwing caution to the wind, yelling *intercourse!* out the car window.

And getting what she wanted, to boot. She was having sex regularly, she informed Hannah the next week. Friday nights, after skating. And every other Sunday before the Girl Scouts met for their bi-weekly pot-luck.

They were walking down the hall at school and Hannah, envious, stunned, stopped to stare at Peggy. "It's something you can count on?"

Peggy breezed past her. "Sure is."

"It gets better," Peggy insisted later at lunch. Hannah was now with Francine, who pretended to be reading. Peggy clutched herself as if she were her own prized possession. "Hannah, I'm telling you, you don't know what you're missing."

"Maybe she does know." Francine's small eyes widened with indignation and her index finger pointed to the paragraph in her history text where she'd left off. "Maybe she believes in *restraint.*" When she snapped her head to glare at Peggy, her braid, usually a neat line down her back, flipped over one shoulder—suddenly a live snake.

"Maybe," Hannah said, sitting between the two. She tried to sound agreeable and happy, appeasing both the virgin to her right and the non-virgin to her left. "Maybe."

The next Saturday night Jackie was playing James Taylor's "Fire and Rain" on his guitar. They were at his house, in his room. Sheets of tracing paper covered his desk which was next to the bed where the two of them sat. He was going to be a builder, maybe an architect, and he spent his free time tracing and re-sketching complicated architectural drawings. For weeks he'd been working on the Parthenon.

"It's the symmetry," he'd explained earlier that evening. "It's the perfection. It gets to me."

"All those pillars." Hannah teased him as she scanned the detailed pencilled drawings. Though the Parthenon didn't reflect her own tastes, she didn't dwell on that difference. What she liked was how the Parthenon got to him. That it *could* get to him, that it moved him to take such care, exhilarated her. Each line was executed in a thin, controlled stroke. The pencils that had done the work were sharpened to a crisp point and arranged in a neat line. "I don't know," she continued, still teasing. "There's nothing like a simple country house. That's what I say."

"Maybe I'll build one." He flashed her a guarded smile. She liked how they did this, played house together, but he'd never gone so far as to say he'd design *her* a country home, just that he'd design *a* country home, as if maybe if she were lucky she'd chance upon it.

He finished the song and she cuddled up to him. He was built solidly and compactly, his body, like his face, more broad than tall. He had nearly black hair, straight, and cut short. She liked the feel of it, softer than her shoulder-length frizz. When he stood up to put the guitar in its case, she stood up too, her left leg suddenly jiggling just like Peggy's: nervously, excitedly, incessantly. After he'd closed the guitar case she threw her arms around him—they were exactly the same height—and began kissing him. She was disappointed when just as she was warming up and she thought he was too, he pulled back. The smell of his herbal shampoo lingered in her nose.

"We're going to be late," he said.

"For what?" She quickly backed off, her legs bumping against the bed's side. His compact room, usually cozy, now felt cramped.

"Skating." He turned from her, and for some reason wouldn't look her way.

When he turned back, she saw that his face was a bothered, beet red.

"Is something wrong?" She crossed her arms and spoke quietly, carefully.

"No." He looked down.

"Is it me?" She stepped back.

"No." He dropped his hands into his pockets.

"Do you care for me?" She turned her back to him.

They'd had this conversation before. No matter how many times he said *yes,* she was always compelled to see if he still cared. You never knew, she thought, suddenly and inadvertently recalling the roar of silence that filled her home.

When she heard him kick impatiently at the floor, she reacted with a dazed, silly grin. Grabbing his arm, afraid to struggle more, she said, "Come on, Jackie. Let's get out of here."

Like most Friday nights that winter they skated at William's Pond on the outskirts of town. Jackie played hockey while Hannah watched, practiced spins and back cross-overs, or sipped beer and talked with whomever she knew—which was often only Peggy Hardley. Francine came with them some-times, and then it was more fun, but she hadn't come tonight.

When they arrived, the hockey game was in full force and Jackie patted Hannah's head and said, "Be back soon."

"Soon," she hummed after him. She pushed out on the ice, away from the hockey game and the crowd that circled the rest of the pond's smoothest area. She went beyond the glow of the street lights and the bonfire to where ice had formed around thick patches of tall reeds. Because of the reeds she had to skate slowly, which she didn't mind as she was in a reverie, dreaming of herself and Jackie skating arm in arm, their smooth-as-ice back cross-overs in rhythm with James Taylor's "You've Got a Friend." It was a kind of Fred Astair-Ginger Rogers act, only performed on skates to a contemporary folk song on the outskirts of a small, semi-rural town. It was her picture of perfection. She'd mentioned it once to Francine and the two of them had burst into the melody, agreeing, instantly, it was some kind of perfection.

Peggy pulled her hat off.

"Hey!" Hannah was startled at the rush of cold air.

"What are you singing?" Peggy wore her white parka with fake fur around the collar and no hat. Her hair was still full with a perm, her curls dutifully bouncing with each move, even small gestures like handing back Hannah's hat. Specks of ice dotted Peggy's thick, red mittens.

"Did you fall?" Hannah pointed to the mittens.

"I always fall." Peggy turned to stare at the boys playing hockey. "See Stuart?"

"Yeah, I see him."

"I see Jackie."

"Yeah, I see him too." Hannah dug her points into the ice, chipping at it impatiently.

"Want to come with us after the game?" Peggy was giving her that knowing look.

"Don't think so." Hannah turned toward the darkest part of the pond, staring intently as if it were a blank movie screen. If she stared at it long enough maybe her dreamy mood would resurface, her fantasy reappear.

"Hannah, I'm telling you. You're ready."

Hannah faced Peggy. "No," she said, inching back some. Ever since she'd found out Peggy had been having sex, Hannah found her slight presence dismaying. "It isn't like that with us," she added. "Please don't tell me you think we're ready."

"Okay. You can stop yanking weeds. But when you are ready, just remember." Peggy patted Hannah's back, then began to skate around her. "Maybe I can help."

They glided through the grassy area of the pond, Hannah leading and Peggy annoying Hannah with her ongoing comments about the hockey game's progress. The game created a certain amount of racket, the clap of hockey sticks hitting the puck, the shouts between players echoing in the night. But Hannah stopped, turned, and collided into Peggy when she heard a sharp scream.

She heard Jackie's name mentioned but she couldn't see him. Peggy was the one to grasp it first. "He's fallen in!" she said, pointing toward the far edge.

By the time Hannah reached him, he was already out. But the jagged hole was there, near another grassy section of ice, and Jackie was beside the hole, drenched to his hips and surrounded by a herd of sweaty boys. His face was grim except for his eyes which bulged in shock. The wet part of his sweater and his dripping jeans clung to his body.

A minute later they were skating hand in hand as if a part of her dream *had* come true. But their words lacked the romance she'd envisioned. She leaned her head toward Jackie's, repeating the only thing she could think of, "Hang in there," while Jackie's mantra was, "Let's get the hell out of here. Hannah, I'm fucking cold."

When she pulled his car into the dirt drive to his house, he said, "I never thought that'd happen. It scared the hell out of me." He was shivering despite the hot air that had been blasting. She nodded. She hadn't realized he'd been as scared as he was. William's Pond wasn't deep, after all, and Jackie wasn't the kind to be taken by surprise at anything; unlike her, he was always prepared. She'd never seen him flustered, had never seen him make a careless gesture. What he lacked in spontaneity, she figured, he made up for in constancy and practical sense.

And she depended on that.

He told her to wait in the kitchen while he changed. But before he left, he turned to her. "Let's just say it and get it out."

Leaning his back against the refrigerator, he stood balanced on one foot. His mouth was tense and his dark eyes were focused on some spot just over her face.

A part of her heart began to sink. "It" had to be bad news, didn't it? "It" had to be that he didn't really want her, she instantly decided. Had she gone too far earlier that evening? Their relationship had been on for a solid year, and though she didn't talk about it to Jackie, its durability surprised her. She sensed, always, that she was riding a wave over an undercurrent of unpredictability. That's how life felt; that's how love felt. That's how the silence at home felt, but no, she didn't listen to it anymore.

You never know when the bond between two people will snap, she thought, will leave a space between them, like a crack in the ice, wide open.

"I'll go," she said, quietly.

"Why?" She saw him scratch his head, but otherwise he stood perfectly still.

"To make it easier." She pushed her chair back. "Just tell me this. If you knew you didn't want me, why didn't you say so before?" She walked toward the door.

"Hannah!"

"What?"

He no longer leaned on the refrigerator; when she pivoted around she saw that he'd sprung upright and now stood in the middle of the room, awkwardly, nodding his head. His expression was still serious. "I *love* you."

She was only just beginning to register his words when she heard him rushing, two steps at a time, upstairs.

It took him only a few minutes to shower and change clothes, during which time she wondered what made him feel he had to say what he'd just said. The falling in, she decided. The being scared.

"Where are we going?" she said. They were walking to his car. He wore a different pair of jeans, two sweaters, a hat, and a plaid scarf. He's beautiful, she thought.

"I don't know."

To her surprise he sat in the passenger's side. He threw her the keys. The falling in, she repeated to herself. The being scared. It's made him need me like this.

She drove through the downtown, empty and silent, then past her house. They didn't talk and every so often she turned for a sign of what he was thinking, but he only stared ahead, serious and alert. Even though he faced out the window, he gripped her free hand and she liked that.

"There," he said, pointing to a barely visible dirt road that led into the state forest. They were half-way around Lake Topaqua. She'd been past this dirt road before but had never taken it. She turned off it when he said to, then parked in a clearing surrounded by trees.

When the silence between them bloomed, she felt slightly faint. He shivered and she motioned toward the heater but he shook his head. He leaned toward her and she thought she still smelled the mud of William's Pond or maybe it was the smell of wet wool, but he was dry now and his two sweaters, when she got up next to them, smelled like laundry detergent. He slid his hands beneath her wool pea coat. Then she began to sink down onto the car's seat and he followed. His hands were warm underneath her sweater. He stroked her breasts, slowly and methodically, and she leaned her head back, enjoying his touch, relaxing some. After a while she slipped her hands under the t-shirt she found beneath his sweaters and felt his back, its mixture of muscles and bones, its soft skin.

"You feel good," she whispered.

He didn't move, which made her nervous, and she kept running her hands up and down his back. Still, it was comfortable inside the car, stretched out along the front seat, with Jackie as her blanket. She tried to calm down. The night was dark, though she could make out the pillar shape of tree trunks and the random shape of branches as they twisted and turned on their journey toward light. She could just hear the grumble of cars and trucks that occasionally traveled on the main road they'd left.

"This is nice," she maintained, hoping to trigger a response, but when she hugged him tighter he pulled away, bumping his head on the steering wheel.

"Nervous?" he mumbled from somewhere above her. In the dark she couldn't make out his face.

"A little." She loosened her grip on him.

"Hmm," he said, then eased back down, nestling his face against hers. She didn't dare move. She held her breath, waited. What were the words to get past this point?

Several moments of silence passed before he whispered, "Say something cute."

"What?"

"You know. The way you do."

She pinched his back. She was as insulted as she was relieved, and the pinch captured both feelings.

"Easy, Hannah. What is it? Is cute bad?"

For once she dared to disagree, couldn't help it. "Aren't I a little more than *cute*?"

Silence, dense, heavier than Jackie. She began to doubt her small bout of assertiveness.

"You're not *only* cute. There's funny, there's kind. And every so often—" He buried his face beside hers and in a voice she could barely hear, he said, "there's brave."

The falling in, she knew. The being scared. She finally exhaled. Now it made sense.

Her head was buzzing when she arrived home at two in the morning. Her parents were asleep, and she made her way quietly through the unlit house.

Studying her face in the bathroom mirror, she wondered, How can it still look like me? When she sat on the toilet she had trouble peeing. The area from her left inner thigh, up to her navel, then down to her right inner thigh throbbed. She felt like she had no legs, that she was reduced to the area throbbing between her legs, and when she finally managed to pee a few drops her muscles tensed and she had to wait, relax, then to go through the process of peeing, tensing, and relaxing several times more. She noticed specks of blood in the toilet bowl. Before she flushed, she stared at them in awe.

In bed she rolled back and forth, reliving in her mind each moment of the evening. Jackie's soft back, Jackie's unzipping her jeans—then having to push him away to actually get them off. By the time that happened the mood between them had changed. Worrying and kissing him hard to get it back. Then Jackie sitting up, squirming and saying, *shit*, then laughing, not without embarrassment, as he decided he didn't need to take off his pants, anyway. What were flies for? Then thinking again. More embarrassment.

It hadn't felt exactly good, she decided. It felt *wonderful*, thinking of the word in its most literal sense—wonderful as in strange, totally absorbing, physically pleasing, physically painful, confusing too, as in how much was she supposed to feel, anyway? Intercourse, as Peggy would call it, was no simple matter. At the time, she'd wanted to laugh at their first tentative attempts, but this was *sex*, she told herself, this was *the night,* and she didn't want to ruin it by cracking up. Later, each time he pushed, she'd say, *a little easier, please?* and once he was in she'd lied, telling him it felt *so good!* when in truth she felt only a raw burning sensation, and within minutes she could barely feel him or herself aside from the throbbing she still felt now, two hours later, as she lay, restless and turning, alone in her bed.

They tried to pace themselves, to not get carried away as Jackie suggested and she agreed, but each Friday night they headed out earlier to their spot in the state forest. Jackie's front seat became for her a kind of sentimental love nest— "who needs the Parthenon?" she once quipped—and she began to marvel for the first time ever at the remarkable design of cars, how each make was built to accommodate love making.

"We don't have a whole front seat," Peggy explained. She and Hannah were at William's Pond, skating around the reeds. Their heads were nearly joined, talking. "We have bucket seats. But the passenger seat reclines. It's easy. My sister and her boyfriend do it in a hatchback—back seat down."

Unbelievable, she thought. I know the secret purpose of cars! And she felt as privileged at being let in on what felt like a great, universal truth as she did shocked at her old self, last month's self, a person to whom this truth was beyond the range of being grasped.

She felt she knew the secret purpose of life, really, and she felt worldly, earthy, part of things, things bigger than her own life. Friday nights became central to her thoughts when she'd have her next go-round at love making, which, because it was more comfortable each time, because they were learning better what to do with themselves and each other, was always as wondrous as their first time. She'd be having orgasms soon, she knew. Perhaps this Friday. Perhaps the next.

Three weeks later, in English class, Francine passed her a note.

What's with you? I never see you anymore You always seem so zonked out—spacy. H., what's happened?

She wrote back: *SEX!!*

After class, Francine grabbed her arm, pulling her from the stream of students making their way down the hall. Her thin face looked strained.

"Sex?"

"Sexual intercourse. Francine, I'm in love with cars!"

She saw Francine's bewilderment. "When?" Francine whispered.

"For more than a month already."

She wanted to tell her everything, how exciting it was, what birth control they were using, how sweet Jackie had been once he got going, how it began that night after he'd fallen in the pond and been scared out of his mind. "It's amazing how much love has to do with vulnerability," she wanted to tell Francine, but she didn't say anything because Francine looked dejected. Her shoulders drooped, her jaw sagged, her mouth hung in a frown. *The Grapes of Wrath* dropped from her arms to the floor. Hannah's and Francine's hands touched, briefly, as they both bent to pick up the book.

"What is it?" Hannah asked.

"It's just that I didn't know. I had no idea. No idea at all."

With that Francine stood straight, her book in her hand. She sighed and re-entered the stream of students. The current carried her sagging frame. Hannah felt deflated too. She re-entered the flow, several paces behind Francine, unable to muster the drive to catch up, much less pull her friend along.

That weekend, Peggy and Stuart and Hannah and Jackie double-dated. They went back to U-Conn, to a modern dance performance, a group of two men and three women, all dressed in different colored leotards and tights. Their costumes were plain, the stage was plain, even the lighting was plain.

"I can't get enough of this plainness!" Hannah whispered to Jackie. "It's gorgeous!" She turned to catch his expression but was dismayed when his raised eyebrows signaled he wasn't with her on this.

She watched the dancers' bodies twist and leap, stretch and collapse. They danced together and apart, bending and folding into and around each other. She punched Jackie's arm each time a dancer made a move she couldn't believe—a spontaneous punch of rapture—until he muttered, "Hannah. Knock it off."

More disappointment came later when both Peggy and Stuart called the dance only "Okay."

"Weird!" Peggy said. "But good weird. You know?"

They were at McDonald's, post-show. Whether they went to a movie, a concert, or just for a drive out of town, they ultimately went to McDonald's. She was bored with the routine.

"I thought it was beautiful," she said. "I thought their bodies made the music come alive. I thought I saw the music *in* their bodies. I thought—"

Three faces stared at her. No one said anything. She popped a salty french fry into her mouth. She looked to Stuart, munching down a Big Mac, who seemed as bored with her comments as she was with McDonald's ambiance. Jackie sipped a shake.

"Not even you?" she asked.

"You know me. Classical, all the way."

"Old-fashioned!" she snapped, but she quickly regretted the phrase mainly because she believed it and that scared her. Their differences in taste used to be simple to handle, a small matter, easily ignored. Now she was desperate for him to have liked the performance exactly as she had. She wanted that extraordinary closeness she felt in his front seat, occasionally after they'd make love but always right before, just when they were about to sink down, to begin, and he'd glance at her and she'd glance back, shyly, as if they'd just met. She didn't want to feel this gap surfacing between them, the one that even sex hadn't fully bridged, though she longed for it to, kept returning to it hoping for a sustained union the experience refused to yield.

Peggy said, "You've seen one university show, you've seen them all." She giggled. "But I liked it okay. Hey! Hannah, you look like you're about to puke!" Then she nodded Hannah's way. "I get it," she said, offering that old, knowing look. "I see what's happening. Burger not cooked through?"

The next week it was Hannah who passed Francine a note. *Want to go to a concert—Indian sitar? I've no idea what it's like.*

Francine replied: *Yes!*

In the car after the concert, Hannah laughed at Francine's imitation of the sitar's melodies. Even Hannah conceded that this concert wasn't like anything she'd heard before, but she'd liked it so much, and she wasn't surprised when Francine nodded and said, "Me too."

Francine said, "It was like a buzz at first, an insect's buzz, that barely changed in tone. But once I got used to it I could really hear the notes. Up, down, all over the place. A zillion notes!"

"Yes!" Hannah agreed. She leaned back against the car seat, sighing, happy to be exactly where she was, in sync once again with Francine.

Later, after they walked through the silent house to Hannah's bedroom, they sprawled on her floor. Hannah had reserved the whole Saturday night for Francine. They'd broken in a new deck of cards, starting with their favorite game, Gin Rummy.

"Me too," Francine blurted, as if the comment were part of a conversation already going on in her mind. She sat on the floor cross-legged, her back straight, her thin head lifted slightly, her small eyes focused on her cards.

"Me too what?" Hannah asked.

"Me too sex."

Francine spoke the words slowly, as slowly as Hannah remembered Peggy first pronouncing *intercourse*. "You wouldn't know him. He's a friend of my older brother. He's not a boyfriend, really. But we went on a date and it just happened. It just happened to happen, you know?"

Francine was now gazing toward the Alice in Wonderland poster on Hannah's wall, but Hannah could see she wasn't concentrating.

Francine continued, "He's a bit screwed up. Physically, I mean. He's a paraplegic." She paused. "Semi. Some parts work."

For Francine's sake, Hannah tried to keep her face expressionless, but her mouth was opening, she knew, more than just a little. Several tense moments followed and the whole time Hannah didn't dare look at Francine. Finally she whispered, "How?"

"He came back from Vietnam that way."

Hannah's back straightened as she breathed in, slowly. Here it was again, life or love, she didn't know which, but she recognized the dizzying, unpredictable feel of the rupture that had just opened in her room. She sat still, frozen, at the edge of sadness.

After a long pause she asked, "Why did you?"

"Why did *you*?"

"I wanted to."

"Me too." The accusing tone in Francine's voice was gone. "I did it because it was exactly what I wanted to do."

Exactly, Hannah repeated to herself. She swallowed, stared at the ceiling, then at Francine, her thin, forlorn face, her neat braid lying limply on her back. Francine was looking at the floor. Still, she kept realigning her cards.

Hannah reached across the pile of cards and stroked her braid. "Was it okay?"

"Yeah, okay. A beginning, anyway."

"A beginning," Hannah echoed quietly. She picked up the cards, reached for Francine's, and shuffled the deck. She dealt them each new hands. For the rest of the evening, until Francine went home, they barely talked. Instead they played rounds and rounds of what Hannah called "the easy games," the kind they played when they were just girls: Go Fish, Crazy Eights, Old Maid.

Part III

Breathing

Swimming Like an Eel
(Hannah Kahn—Summer 1979)

When my grandmother–my father's mother—talks, she comes down hard on her nouns. "We ate a good *meal*," she might say. Or, "I have a Goddamn *backache*." Speaking this way, no matter what the subject, talking loudly and forcing her views on us all—her family—her tone is one of conviction. This evening, she noticed my hair.

"My God," she said. "Hannah, have you done something with it?"

"What's wrong?" I asked. I knew she didn't mean to give me a compliment.

"Why, it's as wild as mine. But no matter, no matter. What I mean is, you have one good head of *hair*." She leaned forward in her armchair and I waited for her to make her point.

"Be thankful, Hannah, and for God's sake take care of it." She leaned back. Her point, as always, was short.

I was thankful for my hair, which was a thick, wavy auburn, and I tried to take care of it. But I lacked my grandmother's intimidating beauty. Even at seventy-four she was magnificent to look at. With barely a wrinkle showing on her face, her skin, slightly tanned, glowed. She kept her own hair meticulously cared for, dying it its original shade—the same rusty tone as mine—brushing it tightly back from her forehead, and teasing it each morning until it stood high, an invincible mass on her head.

"Why don't you push those bangs out of your eyes?" she asked as she scrutinized my face. "It's not becoming, Hannah. Not becoming."

It was early evening, and we sat in the living room of her house, a two-story, six-room cottage with floors warped from

153

the moisture of the sea air. In the last year, she had moved from Worcester, where she'd lived her whole life, to Stonington, Connecticut, where she'd finally found her "dream" house by the shore. "It's been a hell of a long life. A long *wait*, I mean," she had said upon my arrival as she'd briskly but happily showed me around. The cottage was decorated with her old Worcester furniture made of thick, wooden frames that by now had settled comfortably into the wavy grooves of the Stonington floors. "I deserve a little dream come true. Yes," she'd said, "I do."

What she meant by that, I figured, was that she'd done plenty for others, so why not a little for herself? I was seventeen, in between my junior and senior years in high school, and spending the summer with her. We didn't plan to live together that summer, but when my parents separated in May, my mother going off with her friend, Candice Eastman, on an "open-ended vacation," I still hadn't gotten around to finding myself a summer job. My grandmother knew this and began to place frantic phone calls to me when it seemed like I might let the summer go without earning a buck. Besides, my grandfather had died recently, and since she was still not used to being alone, she made me an offer.

"You can teach swimming here. At the shore," she said. "God knows you're qualified. Though I wish you'd take a job at a *bank*."

I applied and on the spot got a job teaching at the beach. My mother had already returned by then, but I still wanted to go. The job suited me. I was experienced, having taught swimming to children at the Y.M.C.A. every summer since I was fourteen. Mrs. Gilgrist, Director of Water, told me that nobody could teach the butterfly like I could. "Pretend you're an eel," I'd order my nine-year-old students. "Hold those arms out in front and swim like an eel to the other side." I'd start them on the kick only.

Mrs. Gilgrist liked my approach. She said that from the very beginning I knew how to make a hard thing simple. I had

154

a talent, she said. An innate talent. By the next summer, I was teaching the beginner's class for older kids, twelve- and thirteen-year-olds who had never learned to swim. They were the hardest group to teach because they were stiff as boards in water. They'd stand in the shallow end of the pool waiting for me to tell them what to do, shivering as their eyes popped out in anxiety the way Teddy my cat's did when we'd put him in the car for a ride. Even when I had them do simple flutter kicks while holding on to the side of the pool, they'd arch their backs in an effort to keep their faces out of the water.

"You don't have to hold on so tight," I'd tell them. "Pretend you're a piece of seaweed swaying in the tide."

Though by the end of a four-week session I'd only have taught the older kids the rudiments of rotary breathing, Mrs. Gilgrist kept me on her staff. "You've taught them more than you know," she'd assure me. Innately, she explained, I'd known how to teach them to relax. I was always glad to hear that innately I knew what I was doing. I was fifteen then, and the side of a swimming pool was the only place where I felt in control of anything.

As on most of our evenings at the beach, my grandmother and I were knitting. It had been my idea to knit each night. I'd taken up my grandmother's offer for the summer, but not without certain trepidation. She had a strictness to her, and when push came to shove, she had a temper too, more volatile and frightening than my father's. I thought the knitting would help.

I knew she wasn't a knitter herself, but explaining the stitch work would give us something to talk about. We'd have a project, we'd have conversation, and maybe, if she found it interesting enough, knitting would keep her at bay.

"Am I getting it?" she asked. "Hannah, what do you think of this?" Leaning forward in the armchair, she held up what was to be ribbing for a cardigan sweater.

"Yes, you're getting it." I said. "See how your stitches are evening out?"

My grandmother smiled. "Looky here, I'm going to knit me a sweater. In the heat of summer, I'm knitting a goddamn sweater." She laughed and leaned her head against the soft upholstery.

Sighing, she put down her ribbing. "I'll tell you, I just feel like myself here at the shore." Apparently, holding the yarn had put her into a talking mood.

"Oh, I loved the old house in Worcester. God knows, your grandfather and I had good years there. Tough years, though. Raising our boys. Trying to keep them in line, to be good people. And do you know what?" She looked up to the light on the ceiling.

"They are good people." My grandmother sounded truly relieved. Her needles clacked as she picked up the pace of her stitch work.

"My sons are fine people. You don't know how lucky you are not to have to cherish each penny in your pocket. You owe that comfort to your Daddy's hard work, Hannah." The clacking stopped as she put her knitting on her lap. She placed her feet firmly on the floor and I sensed she was about to make another point.

"Now, I warned my boys not to fool around and have too many children—too many children, too many mouths to feed. I told them, before you have children think *twice*."

She raised her eyebrows and she raised an index finger. "And when the time comes for you, I hope you'll remember your old Gram's advice. Think twice," she said, her voice grave. "Hannah, at least twice."

A breeze wandered in through an open window, and she took to her needles once again. She sat silent for a moment until, with a noticeably lighter timbre, she sighed.

"You know, it's only here at the beach that I feel, oh, that I can take a deep breath. Yes, that's it. You know what I mean? Hannah, don't you feel you can breathe?"

Yes, I felt I could breathe. I missed being close to my boyfriend, Jackie, but otherwise I was content. My swimming lessons were going well. I taught two classes each morning, one to four- and five-year-olds, and one to kids around the age of eight. I had my preschoolers crouch on the shore by the edge of the water. I told them to make believe they were rocket ships and together we'd count down from ten. At blast-off they'd shoot into the salt water, pushing themselves off with a burst, their arms stretching as if they were on a direct course for the moon.

I had my eight-year-olds tackle the backstroke. I'd hold them under the smalls of their backs and talk to them as they'd float. "Do you see the gulls?" I'd ask. "Do you think gulls have to be taught the backstroke?" Over time I'd ease up on my grip. "Do you think penguins have to be taught the backstroke?" I'd pull my hand away, but never too far. A child who noticed that I'd let go was apt to look for me and, in lifting his head, would buckle at the waist. By leaving my hand nearby I could slip it back for instant reassurance, pushing up a sinking middle, pointing a chin toward the morning sky.

I turned to my grandmother as I put my own knitting down. "Gram, it's been two weeks since I've been here. Would you mind if I gave Mom a call?"

She'd picked up her ribbing and was just about to start a new row. She'd slipped one bare needle under another needle looped in stitches. When I spoke, she was pulling a loop onto the bare needle but she lost it before it was a secured stitch.

"Dammit."

"Gram, did you lose it?"

"Yes. I lost that goddamn *stitch*."

"Hang on. Maybe I can help you." I reached to take the needles out of her hands.

"No!" she said. She threw the yarn down on the wooden coffee table before us. Rings of stains were intertwined on the surface of the wood. "No, you can't call your mother. At least, not from my home!"

I looked at her grim face, then to the knitting in my lap. I was making a blue cotton sweater, a pullover with a raglan sleeve. I was trying to change my wardrobe and had this idea that the raglan looked adult.

"Hannah, I know you want to call your mother," she said. She spoke almost quietly now, but I was still on the alert, my anxiety mounting as she slapped a knitting needle across one knee. I kept staring at the ball of yarn in my lap, noticing the way in which a single strand was comprised of several smaller strands twisted together. "But it hurts me too much to think of your mother. Your Daddy's my son. We're a *family*. We're one *thing*. And your mother, she thinks she wants to leave him—to break up the family. Do you hear what I'm saying?"

I could hear her clear enough. Her voice had risen with each word.

"Go, go on. Call your mother. I'm not going to stop you from calling your mother. But go to the pay phone up the street." She yelled, "I know I can't stop you from calling your mother! But I won't have it in my *home!*"

I began to walk upstairs toward my room. I felt sick, intimidated by her tone.

"Well, are you going to call your mother?" she asked.

"I don't know," I mumbled.

"What?"

"I don't know," I said. "I don't know what phone you're talking about."

"Oh." She stood up too, causing her knitting needles to drop to the floor.

"Maybe I'll look for it in the morning. Then I can call her tomorrow night."

"Yes, why don't you do that," she said. Her voice calmed. She patted her mass of unruffled, teased hair. "Think about it again, Hannah, and if you still want to, go to the pay phone tomorrow night."

That last year, especially during the spring, I began to spend more and more time alone. Jackie had taken a landscaping job to earn money for college and Saturday nights became our only

158

time together. Carolyn had been away all year at college; my father worked later and later; and my mother, who didn't yet work, had been in the habit for some time of filling her free afternoons with adult ed, chores, and, most recently, a slew of committees. She even chaired the garden club despite the fact that her own garden consisted of only a single bed of marigolds; the rest of the landscaping was left to the easy magic of shrubs. On Thursdays she met with Wells's new Coalition for a Cleaner Environment.

My mother learned about the Coalition after Carolyn, the year before, had brought home a petition she'd composed in social studies class to pass a town ordinance banning motor-boats from Lake Topaqua.

"Carolyn!" my mother exclaimed the first time she read the petition. She stood in our living room, holding the sheets of paper. "It's a wonderful idea. A meaningful idea. The noise pollution, the water pollution . . . Why, we've been taking the lake for granted."

Carolyn thanked her and insisted it was no big deal, just a natural concern for the environment. There was so much the average citizen could do, Carolyn suggested. Pollution was going to eat us alive, she added.

"Really?" my mother asked. She'd lifted the petition and held it just above eye level, as if it were a photographic slide and she wanted the light to reveal all the steps an average citizen could take.

"If there's so much to do, maybe I could get involved. What do you think, Carolyn? Could I help?"

My father, who stood in the doorway, looked toward my mother. His thick eyebrows were knotted and his expression showed dismay, even disapproval.

"Mom, you can do whatever you want," Carolyn told her. It might take some time to get something concrete accomplished, she warned, but taking action was within her grasp.

"All right then. Maybe I'll fight pollution too."

My father grumbled, then frowned. My mother clutched the

petition. She turned her back to him.

"Or something else," Carolyn said. "Mom, what is it you really want to change?"

My mother looked to Carolyn and her eyes asked her a question.

"Yes," Carolyn said gently. "Mom, you can fight pollution too."

I was alone—without my family—but I was busy. I had my school work and I had my swim team which gave me reason to head to the Y.M.C.A. every afternoon for team practice. I had my swimming lessons to teach as well. In April Mrs. Gilgrist had offered me a job on Saturday mornings teaching two groups of five-year-olds.

"Hold on to the side of the pool and bob," I'd tell them. If the little ones didn't keep moving they'd get cold and whine to get out. "Blow bubbles, kick and blow bubbles. Pretend you're a motor on a speedboat and blow bubbles." A few children would always get excited about that. They'd drop their faces into the water, heaving air out of their mouths as hard as they could, lifting their heads when their air supply left them. They'd gulp another breath as big as the first, then sink their faces into the water. In that split second before their faces hit water, they'd glance up to me standing at the pool's side. I knew this and I kept my head nodding so they could see my approval without losing precious speedboat time.

After swim team practice, in the late afternoons, I'd usually lie on my bed and think. I'd think of games for the kids I taught, I'd think of my homework, which I didn't want to do, I'd think of Jackie and thank God he still loved me, and I'd think of my mother and my father and try to guess why they were still together.

Mostly, I'd think of my mother. She was more a friend to me than a mother. Since Carolyn had left we'd developed a nightly routine that began at suppertime when she'd get home from whichever committee she'd been with that day. We'd clatter about the kitchen as we prepared a quick meal, load it onto a tray, then carry it upstairs to her bedroom. There, as we watched TV, we'd eat lounging on my parents' double bed. After we were through we'd pull out our knitting. Projects. The two of us always had projects.

We'd chatter and knit and sometimes cry if a TV show moved us. I tended to cry even at commercials, at least the ones by McDonald's and Coke that showed grown children coming home after long absences, rushing into the arms of extended family members, mothers and uncles and grandmas and brothers who happened to be outside milling about the front yard of some perfect country home.

Eventually my father would arrive. He'd walk in the door downstairs and dump his suit jacket over the banister. At the bottom of the stairs, he'd yell up that he was home. My mother would hesitate, then yell hello back down, quickly telling him what was on the stove in the kitchen, secretly waiting, I thought, for my father to retreat. Inevitably, though, he'd make it up to the bedroom. He'd thud, step by step, as he carried his tall frame up the stairs. He'd walk in on us in the middle of a show.

"What are you doing?" he'd say.

"Watching TV," we'd answer.

He'd stand awkwardly in the doorway and look at the television set. Though the TV was on and a plot was unfolding, we three were frozen in silence.

"What did you do today?" Another question.

"Chores, committee work, you know," my mother would say. They would never look at each other, but would stare only at the TV.

"Hmm," my father would say. "Hmm." Then, until bedtime, he'd stay away.

Each Sunday when Carolyn and I were school children, my father would take us to visit our grandparents in Worcester. My mother always chose to stay home. She took the visits to be an opportunity to get some time off—some time alone.

"Time alone? You get some of that every day," my father once scolded. "What about your family? Don't you want time with your family?"

"I get that every day," my mother had said.

We'd arrive just as my grandmother was draining peas, or mashing potatoes, or poking a meatloaf to make sure it was done. After lunch, my father and grandfather would wander off to talk business and nap. My grandmother would clear the table and go to the cabinet to get out the checkerboard. Then she, Carolyn, and I would begin our weekly matches of checkers.

My grandmother was an ace at checkers. Her pretty cheeks would flush as she'd hoot at a double or triple jump, and the commotion she caused would lure my grandfather and father back to the kitchen where we sat. The reunion would be her cue to fetch from the refrigerator our weekly helping of thick rice pudding with raisins floating in it.

But her frivolity always came with a price. At some point during our game my grandmother would slap her stack of checkers on the table and stare across at Carolyn and me, her eyebrows drawn closely together, her lips pursed tightly into a ball.

"Are you doing well in school?" she'd ask, placing her hands palm-side down on the table. Then she'd lift an index finger and take turns pointing it at each of us as she put to us the inevitable question.

"What were your test scores this week? Did you make any A's? It's your job, you know, to be good students."

She would offer fifty cents for every A. Her change purse jingled as she'd hunt for quarters; then, as she'd hand us our money, she'd order us to put it quickly into the bank. Before we left, in her presence, we'd hand our change over to my father.

"I have good kids," he'd tell her as he'd squeeze my shoulder and slap Carolyn's back.

Though I believed that my father and my grandmother loved me, I never, ever, dared get too low a score.

It was a Thursday, the day I learned about my mother's affair. She and I were in the kitchen, preparing a salad for supper. The room was filled with the smell of tomato sauce and spices. The sauce accompanied some meatballs rolled in cabbage that my mother had placed in a pot on the stove. My father would re-heat the food for himself when he got home. My father still ate heavy, the old way, but we now ate light.

"One meatball!" My mother's voice sang the words. She sang the line every time we had meatballs, even though she could never remember a word beyond this song's opening phrase.

"One meatball!" I joined in and we laughed. I'd grown fond of this tune.

"Mom," I said, interrupting the concert. "Guess what happened at practice today!" She'd walked to the sink to tear lettuce leaves. The last of the day's sunlight streamed in from the window above the sink and caught seldom seen highlights in her hair. Her hair looked different, more textured.

"Coach said I could swim the I.M. at the next meet." I'd always wanted to swim the individual medley, which I took to be the hardest event the swim meets offered. In it each swimmer would complete two laps of the four racing strokes: first the difficult butterfly, then the smoother backstroke, next the awkward breaststroke, and, finally, release! Freestyle!

"Mom, he said if my time is under two and a half minutes, he'll think about letting me do the I.M. regularly. I'll be a regular I.M.'er."

She smiled as she turned from the sink and headed toward the door to the living room. "Great. Hannah, could you chop this cucumber and tomato? And put a note on the fridge for your Dad to heat up the meatballs?"

She was out the door and headed upstairs. "Be right back," she yelled. "Nature's calling!"

I chopped the cucumber and sliced the tomato; I wrote my father a short note: "Meatballs on the stove—delicious when not overheated and burned." I sat down on a stool that was by the kitchen counter where the telephone was placed. I waited for her to return.

A few minutes passed. I picked up a pen by the phone and doodled on a message pad lying on the counter.

Part of me told me not to do it, but I reached for the phone to see if that's what was keeping her from returning.

I heard a deep voice, though I didn't hear any particular words.

There was a pause in the conversation. Then I heard my mother's voice.

"Tomorrow afternoon, then, say two o'clock?"

Another pause.

"I'll be there; can't wait to see you," a man answered.

"Me too. God, I hope the weather's not shitty."

"It'll be great. I'll make sure," I heard the man say.

I hung up the phone as quietly as I could. I was confused— my mother never swore. She'd tried once, when she'd burned her finger one day on the tea kettle, but the words had come out too tentatively to be called real swearing.

"Oh," she'd said at the time. "Damn."

As soon as the word was out she'd looked at me. Her eyes were as guilt-ridden as our cat's the time he peed outside his lit-ter box.

"It's okay, Mom," I told her. "Did you hurt yourself?"

She nodded and cradled her finger in her other hand.

"Do you need some help? Is there anything I can do?"

She just stood there in pain. For the longest time she didn't move.

"Come to the sink and we'll put some water on it." I guided her to the sink and held her hand under the faucet.

"This should make it better," I said then, grateful to know how to care for her, what to do. "Mom, this cold water will help."

At my grandmother's cottage the next morning, I didn't bother to find the pay phone she'd mentioned the night before. Instead, I ate a quick breakfast, and, a little earlier than necessary for my morning classes, I went down to the beach.

A haze had already settled in over the water. The water was calm almost to the point of stillness, yet as tiny waves tickled the shore, creeping up, I felt a breeze beginning to stir.

This morning we would do the hokey poky. It was a good way to get the preschoolers wet. We'd put our left foot in, we'd take our left foot out. Eventually, we'd put our whole selves in and we'd shake them all about. I stood by the water's edge and waited for the children to gather for class.

"Hannah!" I heard my grandmother's shout in the distance. "Hannah! Come here!"

I didn't turn around. From the sound of her voice, I knew she was shouting from her porch, which was only a hundred or so yards from where I stood. "Hannah!" Her voice was louder this time. "Hannah!" She was on the beach.

"What do you mean to do? Make an old lady walk to get you?" She was in a flowered housecoat and faded pink slippers. Her hair, usually a starched mass, was loose and curling about her face. The style made the woman look gentler, the bitterness less severe.

"Your mother called," she said. Her eyes were bulging with anger. "Your mother called my *house!*"

"Did you talk to her? Did you tell her why I didn't call yet?"

"What do you mean—why you didn't call yet? Of course I didn't talk to her."

"What did she say, then? Did she leave me a message?"

"I don't know what she said, Hannah. Honest, I don't." My grandmother was shaking. Her cheeks were burning red.

"I don't know what to do." She looked at me and raised her hands toward her face. "I don't know what to do, what to do." Her voice wavered. "My Daniel, your mother hurt my Daniel. Hannah, tell me. What kind of woman goes to parties with her husband and spends the whole time talking to other men? Other men! I know. I used to see this." She shook her head from side to side.

"And, and, she couldn't speak up for herself ever. Oh, I tried to talk to her. It's like she didn't know her own mind, what to think, what to say. What kind of woman is this, Hannah? It's not my fault! It's not my fault!"

A breeze, catching wisps of her hair, blew strands about her face.

"You could have been nicer to her, Gram," I said. "Sometimes you say things and they're just plain mean."

"Mean!" She shot me a furious glance. "I'm cursed with an opinion, that's all."

I hadn't noticed it before, but as she spoke she'd kept coming at me, and in response I must have been on the retreat. We both stood now with our feet in the water—my grandmother with her pink slippers on and all.

"It's not your fault." My legs felt wobbly and my stomach empty. Part of me wanted to run from her and part to kick salt water into her burning eyes. I didn't do anything, though, except to stop my retreat in the water.

"It's not your fault, but you didn't help to make a hard thing simple," I said. "You don't understand her. You're just like Dad. You're all one thing, all you Worcester relatives. All one thing. But it doesn't matter now, Gram. The marriage is over."

"Shut your mouth, Hannah. Don't say it's over till it's over."

She tugged at one sleeve of her housecoat. "The pain, the pain. It's not over," she wailed. "I don't know what to do. Hannah, the pain has just begun."

I didn't know what to do either. I didn't have an answer to give my grandmother, and I didn't, I couldn't, try to find one.

We stood in the water, both of us looking out toward Block Island, which had become barely visible on the horizon through the haze.

After some time my grandmother said: "Oh, shit. *Shit!* I've ruined my slippers."

I laughed, more at her words than her predicament.

"Your hair, it looks pretty, Gram. You should wear it this way more often." I took a deep breath of salt air.

"You think so?" She tapped her hair above her forehead as she pulled her wet slippers out of the sea.

I said, "I'm going to run up to the house and give Mom a quick call." My voice didn't waiver and my feet were already on the move. I didn't even turn to look back.

It wasn't until after the summer, when I left my grandmother's and returned home, that I finally told my mother I knew about her affair. Though my parents were living together again—no more "vacations"—as before, they weren't together much. It wasn't so much that they'd reconciled as that they just weren't divorcing. They were doing nothing as far as I could tell.

We were in the car and my mother was giving me a ride to the Y. It was early in the morning—not the regular time for practice—but I was working out now on my own twice a week before school. I still wanted to be an I.M.'er.

"I don't know which came first," she confessed. "That I was unhappy and noticed other men, or that I noticed other men and realized I was unhappy."

We were rounding the corner of the street where the Y was located. She steered the car to the side of the road as we approached the plain brick building.

"I didn't plan it to be like this," she said as I leaned forward in my seat to pick up my swimming bag. "Hannah, I've felt like I'm trapped. I need to breathe. Do you know what I'm saying?"

Yes, I knew what she was saying. I felt I'd been in her cage. "I know. I know what you've been feeling."

"Do you think I should divorce, then? Hannah, do you think I should do it?" Her eyes looked up to me as she asked me the question.

It wasn't mine to answer but I'd wanted to say it, to make it happen, since I was fifteen.

I opened the car door and had one foot on the sidewalk.

"Yeah, I think you should do it." I was about to close the door, but before I did I said, "Mom, get a divorce."

Mrs. Gilgrist was the one who gave me the key to the pool that was otherwise locked until nine a.m. Without thinking, like the way my mother and I floated upstairs each night, I changed into my suit, unlocked the door, and dove into the pool.

I slid under the water and stretched my arms out in front of me, kicking my feet together—a dolphin kick—gliding through the water like an eel. At the other end of the pool I climbed out. I was glad to be alone this morning. I took two steps up onto a starting block and crouched into a racer's position, my head hanging loosely below my shoulders, my weight perched precariously on the balls of my feet, my mind waiting calmly for the gun. This morning I would pretend I was a rocket ship. I counted down from ten until blast off. When I let myself go, I flew.

Hog-tied
(Carolyn Kahn—Summer 1979)

Carolyn's father was doing something strange. He was working out. When she arrived home, he was there, plodding around the corner of Route 27 and Main, jogging. Passing him in the car, she waved a mindless, mechanical wave. Though a part of her brain had recognized him and had instantly responded, it took a moment for the scene to consciously register. *Dad's jogging. Dad's wearing blue nylon running shorts and panting as he lumbers up a small hill. Is that possible?*

"Is that—" Carolyn turned to her mother in surprise.

"That is," her mother dryly answered. She slowed the car as they approached their driveway.

"Weird!" Carolyn shrieked. "Blue nylon shorts. And his

168

pale legs. It's practically a statement!"

"Different," her mother agreed. "But not new. He's been at that for over a year now. You just never come home, that's all."

"You never mentioned it either." Carolyn snapped her head back and forth between her mother and her father.

"You know what they say. No news is good news." Her mother turned off the ignition, and the car coughed once before settling into silence.

"No news is good news? What does that mean?"

"What can I say?" Her mother now stood by the car, feebly leaning on it, rounding her body over the warm metal. "That's what it means." She smiled sadly as she pulled herself upright. Grabbing Carolyn's suitcase, she dashed inside.

Watching her mother flee, Carolyn heaved a sigh. She glanced around at the groomed lawn, the grass green and mowed, the leaves on their many oaks billowing in the light August breeze. If it was pretty, she didn't see it as such. The yard brimmed with fragility, vulnerability. The fluttering leaves held to the branches by lines indiscernibly thin. Even their house, a sturdy, massive thing painted a warm brown-red, looked tired and grim, the trees' shade cloaking the house in a dim purple veneer, the color of bruises.

"Hey, Carolyn!"

She shuddered at the sound of her father's voice, loud and commanding, even though he was just at the driveway's entrance, a good twenty yards away. When he reached the car he yanked her into a tight hug.

He was still breathing heavily and smelled of his salty sweat. She jerked herself free.

"Sorry," he said, letting go. He stood for a moment, a tall, lithe figure, staring at the swaying leaves and purplish house as if he were the one who'd been away for the last year. His forehead was crinkled with lines, expressing worry or bewilderment. She couldn't tell which. She stood by him, stiffly, her body transformed into a kind of mannequin or mummy, something not quite alive. Only her eyes moved as she watched with utter vigilance.

"Hey, what do you think?" He patted his flat stomach, then flexed the muscles in both arms. Smiling, he leaned over, folding his body easily into a hamstring stretch.

"Superman?" she mumbled. Quickly, she refocused her attention on her nylon carry-on bag, which she hauled from the back seat.

"Ah, what the hell. Something to do. You know? How've you been, anyway?"

Her father snatched the bag from her and they walked inside, she a step ahead of him, rushing. She'd been hoping he wouldn't be home when she arrived, that she and her mother and Hannah could have an easy dinner, just the three of them, no tension. Earlier that summer her parents had separated for almost a month, but now they were back together, her mother having come home, finally, from "vacation."

"I made a lot of money this summer," she said, feeling obliged to say something.

"That's always good," he called cheerily.

"Hmm," she mumbled.

"Anything else new?" The eagerness of his question, a kind of optimistic impatience, cornered her as much as his hug had a moment ago.

"Nope." She spoke now with a curt edge.

"Miami hot as the Dickens?"

She stifled her next thought: *Is the Dickens hot?* "Air conditioners," she finally blurted. "You stay inside."

"I figured."

She grabbed her bag from his hand. "Thanks. I need to unpack. See you at dinner."

She left him standing in the middle of their living room, as dazed as he'd been outside.

"Supper, yeah sure," he called. "See you then. I've got sit-ups to do between now and then. So, yeah, what can I say? See you then."

* * *

She spilled the contents of her suitcase onto her bed. One week, she told herself as she sorted through the pile. I'll only be here one week and then I go back to Miami and start my junior year and I'm all set for at least another four months.

August 28 through September 3, 1979. Precisely one week. And nothing that happens this week matters, she told herself. I live in Miami. I don't live here. I don't have a headache. No, I don't.

But she did. Already she felt ill, sickened in part by her frosty reaction to her father. She hated him immediately. Well, maybe not. There had been that moment when she'd waved at the jogging man whom she related to in an unknowing kind of way. But it only took grasping who he was for her body to become rigid, her waving hand to fall to her side, her throat muscles to involuntarily constrict as though they were a fabric's shrinking threads.

It was hopeless, she told herself. She'd never change. She'd always hate him this way, this instantly. She was forever angry with him. Angry at how he behaved toward her mother: controlling, unhelpful, condescending. Her eyes were her mother's eyes. There was no difference between their view of him. That distinction had been obliterated years ago by her empathy toward her mother, an empathy stretched wide by her mother's confessions of unhappiness.

She'd never let a man treat her like he'd treated her mother. No one would control her. No one would put her down. No one would make her feel small and stupid. No one would yell and bully. No one would hurt her. And going to school in Miami helped. No one knew her there. She could start over from scratch.

U-Miami was as close to the opposite of Wells as she could imagine. And that was the point. In terms of weather, its hierarchy of seasons—a bad summer, a good winter—was topsy-turvy to Wells's pattern. And Miami was urban, populous, crowded. And lots of people meant she could be anonymous as

171

she could never be in Wells. Breathing space. No pressure. No obligatory hellos, how-are-yous. No staring. No Mr. Flint, Wells's pharmacist, calling out to her each time she entered his drugstore, "Carolyn! Honor roll again! Read it in the paper. Just what I expected from you. You're not like the other girls. Not one bit like them. What do you make of that?"

The compliment alienated her, convinced her further that the key to her success was getting out, finding someplace where a girl who made honor roll was still, well, *a girl*. He thought she'd go far. That's what he meant, he'd always say.

And she'd done just that. She'd gone as far as Miami. Where you could be anyone, she figured. You could be Caribbean. You could be Afro-American. You could be Spanish, Anglo, Jewish. And people were.

You could be unique in a multitude of ways without being different. And you could walk the city streets amidst this fusion of people who looked different from each other and who accepted you unquestioningly as belonging there, belonging there even though you came from someplace as utterly foreign as foreign could be. And you could go into restaurants alone. You could wear sunglasses and light, breezy scarves and no one thought you had airs, no one wondered why you'd changed out of your plaid flannel shirt and blue jeans. No one said, "Hey, Carolyn, what's the occasion, you know?"

You could buy leather sandals with straps that crisscrossed your calves, a kind of modern-ancient style. You could hop a bus and get wherever you needed, instantly. You didn't need a car. You didn't have to like cars. You didn't have to like driving. You could go to the movies in the middle of the afternoon. Or to a hotel lobby just because. Because it was nice to sit someplace cool and clean and well-decorated. Nice to have someone attend to your needs.

And that's what she often did. On weekday afternoons when she didn't have classes, she'd leave a note for her roommate, Natalie, a polite girl from a wealthy Cleveland suburb who never could understand Carolyn's efforts to describe Wells.

"It's like this, Nat. The most popular boys own rusty used cars with their backsides jacked up with oversized tires. You get it now?"

She'd leave nice Natalie who nodded dutifully yet never could quite see the line-up in the high school parking lot, a chorus of old cars with raised rear-ends. Carolyn would hop the bus from Coral Gables to Miami's South Beach. She especially liked South Beach, the art deco district brimming with people— tourists, musicians, models, businessmen, business*women*, photographers, artists. If the day were cloudy or rainy, she might go to the Casa Grande Suite, ensconce herself in its rich mahogany and teak furnishings while she breathed deep the musty smell of the wood. On a brighter day she might step into the Astor, sleek and shiny, or the festive Cavalier, where palm trees brushed the lobby's ceiling.

She'd ranked the hotels according to the weather and her mood. A Temperament Ranking, she called it. She got so familiar with the list she referred to the hotels simply by their ranking. Misty #1, she might sing as she stepped lightly into the Continental Alexandro.

The waiters were Latin there. And male. She liked that, especially on a misty, romantic kind of day.

"Can I get you something? Perhaps a drink, miss?"

He was dark and thin. He wore black pants, a white shirt buttoned all the way to the top, a black bow tie, thick black-rimmed glasses that looked almost studious. White socks peeped over the rims of his black suede bucks. A nice touch, she thought, glancing at the shoes. Casual and independent.

"Let's see," she said. "A vodka tonic, please?"

"Anything else?"

"No. Thank you."

"Thank *you*."

And when it arrived, he bent over, graciously handing her the drink. He stood for a moment, tipping in her direction, attentive and patient, smiling kindly, waiting until she sipped it.

"All right?" he asked.

"Yes. Fine. Of course."

"Anything else I can get you, miss?"

"I think I'll just sit a while. Is that okay?"

"Of course. Sit a while. If there's anything you need, I'm here."

"How nice."

He was there, for her, waiting to hear if there was anything she needed.

That night after dinner, a quick and quiet affair, she lay on her bed, staring at her childhood things. Her old teddy bear, pilly and worn, still adorned the bed. Her mother must have dragged it out of the closet for she hadn't seen that bear since she was eleven or so. Inside the closet she could see some old clothes that she hadn't brought to college, blouses and dresses too good to be discarded but not fitted to the more experimental style of her new life either. There were photographs of her and Hannah on her dresser, propped alongside her wooden jewelry box filled with bead necklaces she'd made at camp, or leather and bead necklaces she'd made for herself during high school. Hannah, to the degree she wore jewelry at all, still wore that kind of thing, she knew.

She lifted her hand and traced the bumpy texture of the hammered silver medallion she wore now. Her head felt relieved of the throbbing. Dinner hadn't been so bad. Quick, quiet, and cordial. Roast chicken, salad, baked potatoes. A pleasant enough combination. Predictable and easy. Hannah hadn't come home, though. She'd been away all summer living with their grandmother at the beach. Since she'd returned, she practically lived in her boyfriend Jackie's bedroom, her mother had explained as they'd set the table before dinner. Jack had even cut back his hours at his job to make more time for Hannah. God only knew what the two of them did together all the time, her mother added.

"Yes, it's a huge mystery," Carolyn answered, thinking, *sex, what else?* And she laughed. But a moment later, envious, frowning, she hastily switched subjects.

Still lying on her bed, her eyes were closed, her head finally at ease, when she heard her father.

"Carolyn!" he called. "Come downstairs! I'd like to talk to you!" She knew what he wanted to talk about. Money. This would be their annual talk to discuss how she would make it through the year.

She would make it through largely with his money. He knew that and she knew that. But still he liked to sit her down and tell her so.

"Carolyn!"

"Yes! Down in a minute!"

"Meet you at the dining table at eight-thirty?"

"Fine!"

So it was set. The invariable, excruciating appointment. It will only last five minutes, she told herself. I just have to sit still, smile, look grateful, say the right things and it will be over in five minutes. Then I'm free. Free! Better to have it out of the way. Better tonight than any other night. Yes. This is good. This is fine.

Her head began to pound again.

She hauled herself down the stairs, her head throbbing, her right arm slapping the banister, her medallion swinging. When she arrived, her father, already seated at one end of the dining table, motioned to a chair catty-corner to his. She slumped into it. He was still in his exercise clothes, but he'd covered the blue shorts with a pair of gray flannel sweat pants, and he'd taken off his running sneakers, leaving his toes visibly wiggling inside his thick cotton socks. His rusty hair, the same color as hers, was now streaked with gray and looked lighter in tone than she remembered. The most curious thing about him was the new pair of reading glasses with thin brown rims.

"What do you think?" He pointed at the glasses.

"Nice," she said, barely glancing his way. She resumed staring straight ahead at the floral wallpaper before her.

He cleared his throat while she sat still and waited. She

noticed the faint smell of chicken lingering in the air. She noticed a tiny tear in the wallpaper at its lower edge.

"So, how are you?" he began. The sternness of the question felt more like the beginning of a cross-examination than a friendly conversation.

She crossed her arms over her chest. "Fine."

"Anything new?"

"No. Not since dinner."

"Well, of course. I didn't mean that." His tone relaxed some. "I meant at school. How are your courses? Your grades are fine."

"Courses are fine too."

"How do you like school?"

"I like it."

"Anything special?"

"No. I just like it. That's all."

"Picked a major?"

"Business."

"Hey!"

"Hmm." She knew he'd be interested in that and she didn't want him involved. "It's okay," she mumbled. She wouldn't tell him how much she actually liked it, how good she was at crunching numbers and coming up with organizational schemes. This withholding was a kind of power, the only kind she had vis-à-vis her father. She wasn't about to give it up.

"Meeting interesting people?"

"Sure. It's full of people."

Her voice was tight, her arms just about wrapped around her entire body, her crisp answers clearly meant to end this. Stop the chit chat. Get to the point. Refusing to look his way, she stared resolutely at the wallpaper. Her left foot tapped at an impatient clip, and, in her mind, she began to count the wallpaper's flowers.

"So," he said after another pause. He sat still too, and seemed to be staring past her, out the window. "How's your bank account?"

"Fine."

"Enough money?"

"Yes." She paused. Taking a deep breath, she smelled the chicken again. She added, "Thank you."

"Oh, well. What's a father for?" He leaned forward then and she saw that he tried to catch her gaze. The eagerness was back.

No. She wouldn't be engaged. She wouldn't grant him one moment of satisfaction. He was his history, and his history was despicable. Didn't he know that? His history was about hurting her mother, controlling her mother, always making himself appear smarter than her mother. And he wasn't. And he wasn't smarter than her either. He was better than no one. Flustered by her rising rage, she lost count of the flowers on the wallpaper and began over again.

"Well," he continued, "just wanted to let you know how I've managed to afford your education. You know, it's a question of planning and earning. Hey, the green stuff doesn't grow on trees!"

"Of course I know that. And I don't spend unnecessarily. I work part-time too, you know."

"I only meant to say that I'm happy to do this for you. I always said I'd pay for your education." He paused. "And it takes some doing."

"I'm grateful," she snapped. This time she faced him with a ferocious stare.

"You ought to be!" he howled back. She could see he was fighting the urge to burst into his old habit of intimidating by raising his voice. His neck was tense and the veins in it bulged. He'd pursed his mouth into a tight ball, a kind of dam holding back a flood of hostile words. She wasn't afraid of that anymore. A part of her wished he'd fall into the old way of yelling. It would legitimize her relentless anger, prove he was getting what he deserved.

She paused, then mumbled, "What are you going to do? Hit me?"

"What's that?" he asked. "Say what?"

She stared at his hands resting on the tabletop. "Nothing," she sighed.

They both stared at the table top now. She saw him off to her right, upright, solemn, his hands stiff and barely touching the table's surface. By now her arms were clenched even tighter around her body and she was pinching the skin on her waist. It stung in a way that was helpful, giving her a focus of pain different from the pain of being hurtful, of being the mean, bad, ungrateful daughter she couldn't help being. Of realizing the kind of feelings her mother never could. Was she feeling them for her?

"Glad you're set up then," he finally said. His tone was flat, emotionless.

She released a deep breath of air. She hadn't known she'd been keeping it in. "Anything else?" she asked.

"No."

"See you later."

"Hmm," he answered.

Collapsing on her bed, she grabbed her teddy bear. "I'm free," she whispered in its ear. She clutched the toy to her chest, squeezing it almost as much as she'd just squeezed herself. She repeated, through her tears, "Free."

Like everybody else that summer, her sister was reading *Sophie's Choice*. But nobody but Hannah did so in the dressing room at Loehmann's.

"Is it good?" Carolyn asked as she tried on blouses. Sitting cross-legged on the bench in front of Carolyn, Hannah murmured something that sounded more positive than not. The blouses Carolyn had brought in were white cotton, from India, some with interesting, large buttons, others with flowery embroidered collars, and she kept imagining herself wearing them in the lobby of Misty #1 or Cheer-Me-Up #3. Hannah didn't look up.

"At the choice yet?" Carolyn asked.

"Not yet."

Every so often she'd ask Hannah about Sophie's choice.

What was it, anyway? But the choice, apparently, wasn't obvious. Hannah would read and read, and still she had no clue what Sophie's choice entailed although Sophie's flashbacks to imprisonment in Auschwitz were as foreboding as possible. Someone had to die, they figured. Sophie was Polish and the majority of the prisoners were Jewish. Carolyn's and Hannah's intuition was the same: Sophie had to choose who would die and the Jews had to compete for her favor. That's why she was so guilt-ridden. Right?

"Carolyn," Hannah asked, closing the book. "What's with the frills?"

With irritation, Carolyn gazed at Hannah, who wore rubber flip-flops, cut-off blue jeans, and a plain green t-shirt. Hannah scowled back at Carolyn. Her sister didn't like her new style, the hand-made medallion, the double French braid, the strappy sandals. That morning, Day Five of The Week That Meant Nothing, Hannah had gawked, then grimaced when she caught Carolyn in the bathroom with a pair of especially dangly earrings.

"Is that necessary?"

"It's what I do."

"I'll never."

"So what."

Somewhere along the line they'd grown vastly different and Carolyn couldn't figure when that was. Her first year in college Hannah had written almost every week, but slowly the frequency of the letters let up and by now Hannah was almost a stranger. She barely came home all week and when she did she lived inside one book or another. Their agreement about the nature of Sophie's choice was their first agreement in a long time.

"What do you think of this, girls?" Their mother stepped between them wearing a moss-green pair of baggy cotton pants and an even baggier matching cotton top. She glanced from the mirror to them, then back to the mirror. When she rolled the pant legs up, the look improved. Comfortable and Californian, thought Carolyn.

"I like it," she said firmly.

"It's gross," Hannah rejoined.

Her mother pivoted between the girls. "Hmm. . . . So confusing. . . . I just don't know."

This was the side of her mother that frustrated Carolyn. The person who couldn't make a decision. Who didn't know what she wanted to be. Who didn't know if even an outfit, a piddly outfit, was right for her or not. Who depended on her daughters to answer her questions, large and small, and who got confused when the daughters didn't agree.

"Naomi's Choice," quipped Carolyn, surprised to find herself suddenly angry at this parent too. "You can agree with Hannah or you can agree with me. Come on. Choose, Mom. Hannah or me?"

"Naomi's Choice!" Hannah jumped up, excited for the first time that day. They now stood in a row, their mother in between them, staring into the mirror. "What'll it be, Mom?"

Her mother looked unnerved, flustered. "Oh, stop," she began, "I don't need this anyway. What was I thinking? You're my girls. Both of you." Dressing in her old clothes, she continued to chatter. "No, I couldn't get this anyway. So it's no big deal. Now we're even. Okay girls? Okay, girls." She sighed, clearly relieved to have neutralized the scene.

Carolyn snapped up two of the white cotton blouses. Facing her mother, she snarled, "Well, I know exactly what I'm going to do. I'm getting *these*."

The lobby of Cheer-Me-Up #2 abounded with glittering chandeliers, formal floral arrangements, a grand piano, and a veritable army of young, male waiters.

During the ride home from Loehmann's, she envisioned herself in one of her new blouses, seated away from the piano, near a window, the low light of the afternoon casting an enigmatic glow around her.

"Miss?"

"Yes."

"Is there anything I can get you?"

"Tea?"

"With lemon?"

"No. Milk and sugar, please."

"Of course. Anything else?"

"No. Thank you."

And when he brought the tea he would linger near her. It would be a Wednesday. Hardly anyone would be around. There'd be no time pressure. No pressure at all.

"Are you from here?" he'd say.

"No. But I feel as if I'm from here."

"Just passing through, then?"

"No," she'd confess. And she'd tell him about her life at the university, about her business major, how she was sure she could manage a place like this.

And he'd sit by her, smiling, assuring her it was all right, there were no other customers, he had all the time in the world. He'd sit back and ask her about herself in a calm, interested tone, a tone that worked magic, coaxing answer after answer until she finally blurted out her dream of owning and operating, oh, she wasn't too sure really, but something, you know?

"Yes."

"Yes?"

"Of course. I see it. Don't you?"

"Yes," she'd say, smiling as she leaned over, casually sipped her tea.

When they arrived home, her father was in the living room in his blue nylon shorts and white t-shirt doing sit-ups on the rug. He was grunting and panting as he counted out loud. The three of them filed past him toward the stairs.

"I won't be eating supper," he called. "Town meeting." A deep breath. "Starts soon." Another breath. "I'll eat later." A grunt as he exhaled.

"Fine," her mother said without pausing. "I'll keep it warm."

181

After he left, they ate a cold meal of salad and rolls. Then Carolyn went to her room, curious to try on her new blouses. She especially liked the one with the lacy embroidered collar. Inspired, she re-braided her hair and put on her longest silver earrings. In the bathroom, she shaved her legs, then dressed in shorts and sandals.

"Where you going?" Hannah asked. She was reading again, this time on the back steps under what remained of the day's light.

"For a walk. No place really. At the choice yet?"

"Not yet." Hannah flipped a few pages ahead and Carolyn smiled down at her. "Hey, Han, want to come?"

She didn't, so Carolyn walked by herself out of the yard, onto the sidewalk on Route 27, turning mindlessly toward the center of town. The evening was pleasantly cool, and she could sense fall creeping forward, trekking toward town. Seasons were like this, she mused, their arrival both new and old, exciting and familiar, something to experience and recollect all at the same time. The trees along Main were tall and sprawling, an old lot of oaks, and ambling past these well-known friends satisfied a certain longing in her heart. Soon she strolled dreamily, the paradox of seasonal shifts giving way to the reverie of the waiter in Cheer-Me-Up #2. Wasn't he perfect? Of course, he wasn't real and she'd never had a conversation even remotely like the one she'd imagined. But it was possible, she told herself. You never knew.

"Is that Carolyn!" someone shouted.

Looking up, she realized she was almost at the elementary school. Ahead of her, Mrs. Oberry, mother of her classmate Ted, rushed toward her with outstretched arms.

"Hi Mrs. Oberry. Yes. Hi. How are you?" Carolyn sighed.

"Coming to the meeting?" Mrs. Oberry looked the same as ever, tall, flushed, bursting with energy to spare. "We're voting on where to put the new elementary school. You know, grades five and six only. This old school's a wreck. Too crowded, not enough books, never enough money. At least we voted to build the school. You have no idea how hard that was. Your father helped. Spoke powerfully for it."

"I can imagine."

By now Mrs. Oberry had her arm around Carolyn's shoulder and the force of her pace pulled Carolyn along. They filed past the parking lot, filled already with station wagons, a few sedans, and several pick-up trucks. "It's just a matter of putting it somewhere, you know? A place to build the thing." Mrs. Oberry beamed as she talked and she clutched Carolyn's shoulder. "You look good, honey. Nice to see you. I'm glad you're here. We need all the support we can get. It's just plain *good* of you to come."

Others walked past them, and a few turned to Carolyn and waved. A driver she couldn't quite catch the sight of honked at her in recognition. How did this happen? she asked herself as she dropped onto the hard seat of a metal folding chair. The elementary school's auditorium was crammed and noisy. She could smell lingering dinner scents, hamburgers and macaroni casseroles.

Seated beside Mrs. Oberry in a back row, Carolyn scanned the crowd. Even from this distance her father was easy to spot, sitting on the stage with what had to be the other committee members. He was dressed professionally in his business suit and chatted with none other than Mr. Flint, that nosy pharmacist, who sat with one leg crossed over the other, his head tipped toward her father as they conversed. On reflex, Carolyn ducked, then relaxed when she realized Mr. Flint couldn't possibly distinguish her from this distance. On the other side of Mr. Flint sat Mrs. Tucker, the retired teacher. Carolyn had heard she'd taken to local politics, but she was still surprised to see her there, dressed in a bright yellow suit, reading intently from a pad that she held before her. The stage itself looked drab and bare, garnished with only a line of folding chairs for the committee members and the stick of a microphone. Off to one side stood a squat, wooden easel, obviously borrowed from a classroom, with a map clipped to it.

183

From what she could gather, the evening's first problem stemmed from the fact that the new school would serve several smaller neighboring towns, in addition to Wells, just as the middle school and high school did already. Most of the early questions dealt with how much money these other communities would chip in.

"So what you're saying," someone near the front hollered from the floor, "is that we're hog tied on the whole deal until there's agreement, right?" A murmur of assent snaked its way to their back row. The person added, "So what's the point of talking about location when we're hog tied on the money side?"

Her father was standing now, fielding questions, and he leaned into the microphone. "There's disagreement on this matter, yes, but I wouldn't say hog tied exactly. Negotiations are moving along."

Carolyn stifled a laugh. *Hog tied!* She couldn't wait to test it out on Natalie. "Wells is a place where you can use the verb *hog tied*. People *do. Comprende?*"

When she tuned in again, the conversation had drifted into a discussion of the school's location.

"Precisely," her father was saying. "The committee has a preference. It's this land, town owned, out there by the river." He pointed at the map clipped to the easel. Then he added, "It's the boonies. Plenty of space not used for anything much."

The room was quiet for a moment while people seemed to consider the proposal. On stage, Mr. Flint and Mrs. Tucker nodded their heads as if to encourage consent. Even Carolyn agreed that it appeared reasonable enough. Mrs. Oberry whispered, "Practical."

The next thing she heard was someone shrieking, "*Boonies!*"

Carolyn jumped at the sound of the sharp, critical cry. Three rows ahead of her she noticed that a woman now stood. A chorus of squeaking chairs mounted as others began to shift, struggling, too, to see.

"*Did you say* boonies?"

Carolyn didn't recognize her: a small, thin figure wearing worn slacks and a solid peach-colored t-shirt. From the way she yelled, vigorously and at the top of her voice, and from the way she stabbed at the air with her right arm, occasionally stopping to point toward the stage, Carolyn might have thought she was young. But her gray hair, knotted in an old lady's tight bun, indicated otherwise.

"*Who do you think you are, anyway? Who the hell gave you the right to say* boonies? *I happen to live in those boonies. Of course, you'd never think of that! No, Daniel Kahn. Not you!*"

The woman was no more than a few feet from Carolyn. As she raged on, Carolyn studied the color of her neck as its tone deepened into a blood red. She could practically touch her, she realized. Instead she lifted her hand to cover her mouth. It had been her father's comment, yet she felt oddly connected and exposed, as if she'd made it too.

"*You don't belong here!*" the woman now cried. Her yells became a series of short verbal jabs. "*I-said-you-Jews-don't-be-long-here!*"

In a flash, she dropped down to her seat. Carolyn stretched her neck but could no longer see her.

The woman's presence lingered, though. Her fury had worked like a vacuum, draining the room of even the smallest scraps of other kinds of energy, imposing in those first moments a silence that echoed with an odd, hollow purity. Even Mrs. Oberry's faint, sad, "Ah," seemed like overkill in that hushed cave. Dizzy with confusion, Carolyn hung her head. *You don't belong here*, the woman had told her father, and though Carolyn knew it was a spiteful, hateful thing being said, the phrase nevertheless resonated with what she knew to be true for herself. She didn't belong there. Not at that meeting, which she hadn't meant to attend anyway, and not in this town. She hardly felt part of her own family. She lived independently now. Away from here. In as different a place as different could be. Tomorrow, The Week That Meant Nothing would end. She'd fly back to Miami at precisely 4:35 p.m. She repeated the phrase, *4:35 p.m.*, as if it were a healing mantra.

The sound of her father clearing his throat interrupted her thoughts. She did as everyone else did: sat still and faced forward.

"You're right," he began in a measured tone. "I shouldn't have used the word *boonie*. I'm very sorry for that. That's my mistake."

He pulled the microphone close to him, holding it on an angle. As he paused to consider what he'd say next, nobody stirred. The microphone wobbled when he let it go. He then tipped forward to speak into it.

"But you're wrong about one thing. I do belong here." He looked out, directly toward the woman. "This is my home."

Maybe *he* lives here, but not *me*, she thought. As soon as she returned, she began hurling her clothes into her suitcase. She lifted the teddy bear, hugged it to her chest, and decided to bring it with her.

A while later she heard his car enter their driveway. Then she heard him in the kitchen, fixing himself a late dinner. Her mother, she knew, was in the bedroom, already asleep or pretending to be asleep, and Hannah was in her room reading. Carolyn had dashed down the hall toward the bathroom to gather her toiletries when her father began to climb the stairs.

She turned. He didn't know she'd been at the meeting.

She didn't have to get involved in the whole thing. She could feign ignorance. Tomorrow she'd slip away, leave all the hate of this place behind her.

"How you doing?" His voice was low, tired.

"Fine." She took a step toward the bathroom but something—a fleeting sense of identity, or sympathy, something she couldn't quite define—caused her to hesitate.

She stopped and slowly pivoted around. She spoke quietly. "Anything exciting happen?" "Oh, you know. Same old thing." He shook his head. "What can I say? Same old thing."

She inched a half-step toward him, hearing in her mind

186

what she could say, *You handled it well, Dad. I saw. I was there.*

But when she opened her mouth to speak nothing came out. Her vocals chords were knotted, her voice, hog tied.

When she got back to Miami, she immediately settled into a rigorous study schedule focusing on her business courses. She was more determined than ever to become some kind of master of her own design. To stay away from home. To not need anything from anyone. She stopped frequenting hotel lobbies. She stopped—or tried to stop—the incessant fantasies of dark, handsome waiters. Occasionally she still ventured into the city, but these were business trips, less fanciful than practical, she told herself, walking mile after mile. She steered away from South Beach and explored other regions, Surfside or Little Havana, say, on field trips aimed to alert her to the kinds of business opportunities that awaited her.

Once, early that fall, while ostensibly studying the restaurants and shops along Collins Avenue in Miami Beach, but while actually, simply, walking–walking and despite herself dreaming romantically—she felt a calm settle over her. She liked the feel of it, thick like the clouds she stopped, briefly, to gaze at, carrying with her as she did the image of the tan, smiling, busy people in Miami Beach, the people she'd just brushed past as she drifted down the street, the people on the bus and the people at the crossroads, the people in the cars and the people in the shops. They were like a thick skin surrounding her, this dense and protective mass of people—people she didn't know, people she'd never know.

Doubles

(Hannah Kahn—Summer 1983)

On Hannah's first day home from Europe, in early July of 1983, her mother didn't wake her and she slept until noon. So, too, on her second day home. Even though she rose earlier on her third day she still spent her waking hours wandering throughout her house, restlessly flicking on and off lights, the stereo,and the TV, occasionally telling her mother about some incident in Paris or Lucerne, then moving to another room where she'd slump onto a chair, or couch, or bed, and fall back asleep. Her mother assumed she needed rest. Then she'd find a job.

But Hannah's lethargy continued and by mid-July it was clear: she wouldn't work this summer. Her timing was off. Seasonal offerings had come and gone.

"I'll just hang," she concluded. She was in her parents' bedroom, lounging on their bed, watching a soap opera on their new color TV. It was one o'clock on a Monday afternoon and her mother had suggested she go to the lake for a swim. It was a perfect July day, her mother pointed out. Wasn't she sick of being inside? Her mother would be leaving soon to run errands. Or so she said.

"Why don't you call a friend?" Her mother filled a leather pocketbook as she talked. Lipstick. Hair brush. Change purse. Hanky. Hannah watched each item disappear.

"I will." She yawned, then turned back to the TV. "Soon," she added.

"It's been two weeks. Your friends know you're back. I ran into Jan Littleton the other day and she said Marty's eager to hear from you." Her mother paused. "I didn't tell you yet." She paused again. Hannah still stared at the screen but her ears were perked. "Hannah, he's sick."

"Sick?" She lifted her head from a pile of pillows.

"Lymphoma. Began in his arm pits."

She shot upright. She'd known Marty Littleton intimately—since kindergarten–and the thought of him seriously ill seemed as preposterous as the thought of herself in the same condition.

"He's been operated on already. Now he's in chemo. The Littletons are optimistic. They say he's strong."

Though a buzz had started in Hannah's ears and she felt dizzy, she didn't move or speak. She merely transferred her gaze from the TV to her mother, watching as her mother faced her dresser, reached for her comb, smoothed her hair. With these few gestures, so familiar, Hannah felt the return of the easy indolence she'd become used to. She breathed calmly again. Hers was a beautiful mother, with everything—clothes, make-up, hair cut—simple and classy. That day she wore a tailored skirt and a crisp, white blouse closed by a pin at the collar. Her put-together appearance was convincing: their world was still okay.

"I should be home around five." The snap of her mother's pocketbook caused Hannah's leg to twitch slightly, and she turned from her mother back to the TV.

"You'll be okay?" her mother asked.

"Of course."

As if to avoid witnessing her mother leaving–did she really think Hannah believed she were merely running errands?–Hannah held her gaze on the soap opera. In the distance she heard a car door slam, then a car engine grind into life. She sighed, yawned, and "stayed tuned," though she didn't know one character from the next on the blinking TV.

She spent the evening alone. She phoned Carolyn in Miami but there was no answer. She called her ex-boyfriend, Jackie—since college they'd been on-again-off-again—but, as his mother explained, he was spending the summer doing a camp counselor gig in Maine. Her father wasn't home either. As usual, she figured, he worked late. And her mother hadn't returned as planned.

She thought about calling Marty, but instead she phoned her high school friend, Francine. Yes, Francine heard about the arm pits and surgery, but she hadn't seen Marty yet either. The ordeal gave her the Willie Nillies, Francine said. Big time. Like Hannah, Francine had just finished her junior year in college. And, unlike most of their old classmates from Wells, Hannah and Francine were immersed in the likes of art history, psychology, literature, and anthropology. Though a quarter of their class had gone to college—a record for Wells—only she and Francine pursued liberal educations, and because the curriculum didn't lead to specific jobs, the open road didn't make sense to their friends, even Marty, the most brilliant of their old crowd. Two summers ago, after Hannah's freshman year, she'd organized a reunion. There, Marty had said: "So, what's it for?"

"For?" Hannah had asked. She'd been talking about "Religion 1.1" and the concept of "the numinous." When she'd learned of it her heart had flipped. She'd been having numinal experiences, she realized, all her life—whenever she'd look at the stars. She'd been avoiding planetariums for years. Within minutes of star gazing she'd get that sense of infinity, forever, the awesome feel of timelessness, the incredible breadth and scope of her own death. The Willie Nillies, big time. She'd panic, her heart thumping, her body tensing and sweating, and she'd have to shake her hands and stamp her feet, pulling herself away from the feel of perpetual floating, back to solid ground. The numinous was vastness itself and totally frightening. Yet she sensed it as important too. It was *her* death, *her* unique experience of it. She wondered, if this is part of me, how can it feel so far from me? It was confusing, how she was associated with it and disassociated from it at the same time. When Marty asked, "What's it for?"—she'd looked to Francine, who, stubbing out a cigarette, had shrugged.

"It's for me, I think," Hannah answered. She sipped a beer.

This time Marty shrugged, then downed his scotch which he'd ordered straight up. "Hey, Hannah, what's it going to get you?" Though they considered him their class genius his sensibility didn't translate into top grades. For one thing he wouldn't do his homework. In high school he'd read anthologies of short stories throughout math class, then study math, teaching himself trigonometry, through English. He'd forget to hand in papers. He'd smoked so much dope and drunk so much beer that even before they'd graduated he'd grown a little dull in Hannah's eyes. Despite himself, he'd stayed on the pre-college track—where else could they have put him? But he hadn't the GPA nor the desire for college. After high school he graduated from pumping gas to lawn care.

And his mother, Jan Littleton, hated that. She had ambitions for Marty, her only child, just as she did for herself. Her own life represented, if not success, then at least "a move in the right direction," as she sometimes put it. She still talked about her single years when she worked as an ad writer in Hartford, climbing from secretary to administrative assistant to assistant editor to ad writer. "I stuck my neck out, made it happen." This could be said while crossing her arms and glaring at Marty.

Unlike his mother, Hannah and Francine never faulted Marty for the stubborn way he had of undermining himself. They understood him, completely. He was brilliant. A star too bright for dim-witted Wells. And, worse for a boy, he was artistic. For example, when he reluctantly starred as Don Quixote in their ninth grade production of *Man of La Mancha*, he'd sung "To Dream the Impossible Dream" in his beautiful, natural vibrato, accompanying himself on classical Spanish guitar. Afterward he was laughed at for weeks. The guitar was okay, Hannah heard, but the vibrato was faggy. So Marty changed. He lost the vibrato. He replaced his nylon guitar strings with steel. He bought a used amplifier just to have around. Frank Zappa became his sole acknowledged musical influence.

Now that she'd been to Europe—four months of Eurail and youth hostels; of bread, cheese, cheap wine, and chocolate; of

constant companionship with two girlfriends from college—
Hannah's vision of Marty's plight was more keen. It was
Wells's fault, she told Francine. The town— "the *townyness*,"
she called it, spitting the word into the phone—was killing him.
It had given him, ultimately, cancer. Francine agreed. They'd
visit him together—next week.

Later that night, as Hannah was re-reading the "People"
section from *Time* magazine, the most companionable reading
she could find, Jan Littleton phoned.

"Your mother told me you were back," she began. Hannah
recognized the high pitch of the voice and its brisk, energetic
delivery.

"I'm sorry," Hannah said. Lying on her side, leaning on an
elbow, she hadn't yet budged from her parents' bed, not even to
make herself dinner, despite her stomach's growls.

"To be back! I know how you feel!"

"No. About Marty." She shifted, pushing herself upright.

"Yes, of course. He wants to see you. But that's not why I
called. I'll be straight with you, Hannah. We're desperate for a
fourth. It's only me, Glenda Oberry, and Clare Gorden. We lost
Carol Wheeler to a sprained ankle. We play doubles at the lake-
side courts at seven-thirty. What do you say?"

She wasn't surprised at the offer. Jan Littleton had been at
her for tennis games for years. She loved to compete, and
Hannah's court-side hustle and reliable backhand made her a
choice target in Jan Littleton's eyes.

Hannah flipped some pages of *Time*, then answered, "Seven
thirty? A.M.?"

"Do we have a problem?" By her laugh, Hannah knew she
couldn't argue.

"I haven't played in a while. Not since way before Europe,
Mrs. Littleton."

"Think of it as a comeback! An opportunity! A chance to
run a bunch of old mothers ragged!"

"Tomorrow? Seven-thirty?" Hannah closed the magazine.

"See you then. And, Hannah, no need to call me Mrs.

Littleton. On the court I'm Jan."

Jan Littleton had a strong serve, a persistent cross-court fore-
hand, and a budding Chris Evert two-handed backhand. That
next morning, despite the haze in Hannah's head, she learned
her tricks fast. Jan Littleton would serve, then hang deep, waiting for a possible cross-court smash. She was always looking
for a smash and if it was successfully executed she'd be the first
to yell, "Hey! Did you see that?" If she didn't get the chance to
swing cross-court soon she'd lose patience, rush the net.
Hannah watched Jan Littleton's green eyes rake the court eagerly, the clipped strands of her pixie haircut lifting in the wind.
She could run fast—faster, anyway, than Glenda Oberry, who,
though tall and lean, was neither quick nor coordinated, and
faster than Clare Gorden, who lacked Jan Littleton's cut-throat
athleticism. Jan talked a lot too.

"Good serve, Glen!"

"Hit it Clare. Whack it hard, girl!"

"Hannah, what's the matter? Still asleep? This is tennis,
hon. Not the *Louvre*."

Hannah barely responded to the joke, feeling awkward in
this gang of mothers—mothers of children her age. Glenda
Oberry had two children, just older than Hannah. Kim, her oldest, was a nurse. Ted, the youngest, had been in Hannah's sister's class. Before moving to Oregon to join a Buddhist commune two years ago he'd been a long-distance runner, then a
Jesus freak. Before all of that he'd been just Ted, a thoughtful,
polite, good-looking boy. He liked to take long camping trips,
Hannah recalled, her eyes set for a moment on Ted's lean mother, crouching now as she tightened a shoelace. Ted liked being
with nature—something he called "simplicity." Perhaps the
urge toward simplicity had motivated those solitary, long runs.
And they, in turn, were linked to his severe religiosity. Once,
after she'd studied Greek drama in college, Hannah described
Ted's departure for the commune as a kind of tragic inevitabil-
ity, the seeds of the disaster—or so people thought of it—there

all along. The take was oddly satisfying.

Clare Gorden had three kids, all doing fine. Two in techno-logical college, one in business. Clare Gorden's children had never been showy in high school, yet here on the court they had a certain clout. Clare had only to say "Jenine" or "Frank" and the other mothers would raise their eyebrows, nod. They might say, "Knock on wood, Clare," or, "Lucky you." These com-ments weren't meant to undermine Clare Gorden, Hannah soon realized, but when it came to talking about their children—which, to Hannah's surprise, they rarely did—the mothers showed a remarkable and strange detachment, as if they were mere observers of their children's lives, not the ones to shape them by their meals, their lists of chores, their lectures; to infuse them with their aesthetic tastes, their senses of humor, their ver-bal inflections; or to console them by the daily rituals of their lives—spaghetti on Thursdays, the way they cupped a comb in their hands as they smoothed their hair.

That morning Hannah and Clare Gorden lost the first set, six games to two. They lost the second as well, but Hannah's serve improved and the score was six-four.

"Next time we tie," Jan Littleton said, patting Hannah's back as they parted. Jan was half-way to her car when she turned. "Marty-boy says hi. He said to tell you to beat me with all you've got." She laughed and rolled onto her toes. "He's always had it in for me. You know what I mean."

She ducked inside her car, a blue Chevy with a small stick-er on the back windshield of a pair of overlapping blue and pink hearts. The words *Marriage Encounter* ran across the hearts in black italicized print.

Hannah straddled her bike. She knew it would be downhill all the way home. She pushed off, exhausted, ready now only to cruise.

But the joy of an easy ride eluded her. In an instant Jan Littleton's words, "You know what I mean," plagued her mind. She did know. She'd heard about the ongoing clash between

Marty and his mother endlessly from Marty. And she'd witnessed the worst of it once, several years ago. It was a Wednesday, late afternoon, mid-January. The sky had already darkened. Hannah was dropping by to see Marty. But when she'd arrived he was outside the house by their weeping willow and Jan Littleton was hanging out a window. Marty was drunk.

"You louse!" she was yelling. "You're wasting your life!" Her face was red, knotted. She glanced at Hannah, but in her fury barely registered recognition. Hannah looked away.

"Bitch!" Marty yelled back. "You don't know what you're fucking talking about." He was standing still, yet tipping every so often to one side. On his nose, his glasses sat askew. He took a few steps, regained his balance, then inhaled from a cigarette that dangled from his hand.

"Call me what you like. You're grounded—for life!"

Stupid, Hannah thought. *You're always grounding him. You're always setting him up for another go-round with you. Don't you see how hard it is for him?*

Marty yelled, "Bitch, bitch, go away!"

He hadn't seen Hannah. He stumbled off into the woods behind his house. Jan Littleton slammed the window shut.

Hannah left. That evening, the cool distance between her own parents seemed like a mere crack in a sidewalk as compared to Marty's and Jan Littleton's battle across opposite sides of a main street.

They played Mondays, Wednesdays, and Fridays. By August, Hannah was waking up promptly at six-thirty a.m. She'd eat breakfast after tennis, then ride her bike to the lake for a swim, then come home and read. She'd chosen Dostoyevsky's *The Idiot*. "A title I can relate to," she explained to her mother, rolling her eyes and grinning. Her mother laughed.

Yet by her verbal reticence court-side she still gave the appearance of being sleepy. "What's the deal, Hannah, cat got your tongue?" Jan Littleton once teased. But Hannah was stuck, as unsure as ever about how to talk to these middle-aged women, these mothers, these friends of her mother. When forced to talk she still called them *Mrs.* Once, taken aback at Clare Gorden's winning overhand, she'd shouted, "Nice shot, Clare!"—despite herself. But after the game, her self-possession intact, she returned to the old formality. She'd said, "See you Mrs. Littleton. Bye Mrs. Gorden. Bye Mrs. Oberry. Yes, I'll tell my mom you said hi."

She and Francine hadn't visited Marty as planned. Francine couldn't get out that evening and Hannah felt vaguely fatigued at the thought of visiting by herself. She rationalized her resistance by telling herself that she and Marty had grown apart. There was her college major, a religion-literature double, the point of which he couldn't grasp. And there was his lawn care work, which struck her as odd, though it had forced his wiry frame to bulge with muscle. He'd never looked better, Hannah noticed, since he'd begun to fully deny his genius. College had given her this: irony. And now there was Europe, a season abroad, the other world she'd witnessed. When she'd landed in Paris she half-expected the continent not to be there. Europe was still only a word on map. And a map, Hannah thought, looked more like a beautiful design, an abstract expression, a work of art, than it did a tool of reference. But she'd stepped out of the plane, onto solid ground, inside a modern airport, where electronic monitors listed arrivals and departures, where people smoked cigarettes and spoke French. Europe was real, after all. When she thought of her travels, of how easy it became for her and her college friends to spot other, less sophisticated, possibly *mid-western*, American tourists— the Nike sneakers, the sporty wind-breaker jackets, the bright knapsacks, the relentless enthusiasm, those starry-eyed, ever-friendly, American smiles—she shook her head. She told herself this: she'd gone too far to talk anymore with Marty simply about drugs, "doing it," or Frank Zappa.

But he came by to see her. It was a cloudy afternoon late in July. She was downstairs, alone in the house, mid-way through *The Idiot*, the names of the Russian characters swirling in her mind. Glancing out the window, she thought she saw an apparition. Before his work in lawn care Marty had always been thin—which she knew only increased the despair already caused by his multi-talented, intellectual, artistic nature—but now he was just one strand of spaghetti. He wore jeans and a button-down shirt, tucked in, but in his frailness it flapped like a loose flag about his bony frame. On his head he wore a strange, black hat, like an older man's business hat. If she hadn't known why he wore the hat she would have been tempted to tell him how awful he looked. Silly. Ridiculous, she might have said. Marty, take it off.

Instead, she jumped from the living room couch and dashed out the back door.

She rushed at him, forgetting he might be weak, or shy— they hadn't seen each other in more than a year. She forgot her own resistance too.

"What's up?" he asked.

"Nothing. Absolutely nothing. I'm reading *The Idiot!*" As usual, naming the book's title made her laugh. She showed him the book, still in her hand. But the portrait on the cover wasn't so funny. It pictured a man who looked as gaunt and haunted as Marty. She quickly tucked it under her arm.

"How are you?" She tried to focus on his eyes. Except for the new wire rim frames surrounding them, and the thick bags underneath them, their unique gray-green glow hadn't changed. A few limp wisps of what used to be a mass of wavy ginger hair, always collected into a stumpy ponytail, dangled from underneath the hat.

"Shit. What can I say?" He tapped his torso. "My nodes nearly exploded. It's under control, though. Totally."

He explained his control in terms of statistics. It would all work out. Mathematically, he had his cancer just about licked. It was only a matter of working through the chemo, he said.

They went inside for coffee and he stayed about an hour. She gave him a lift home. During the drive he said, "You wouldn't believe how bad I need sleep. Shit!"

He didn't want her help, though, moving from the car to his house. Arriving home had awakened him some. At the door he turned to her, grinned, and gave her the thumbs up sign. She recognized that grin in an instant: an American tourist grin. Unswervingly optimistic. Not a hint of irony. Innocent. Hopeful. Almost nerdy, almost sweet.

He's going to die, she thought.

All summer Jan Littleton's energy wouldn't let up. It could be the most languid of days and she'd be batting tennis balls with verve, the pompon at the back of her sneakers bobbing madly. Likewise, Glenda Oberry and Clare Gorden gave it all they had. For Glenda Oberry's part, she continued to ride her bike four miles to the court, serve her games, and pat her partner's back with an agreeability that to Hannah was almost inhuman in its constancy. After the games she'd go off for a longer bike ride around the lake. By ten o'clock she'd be at her job as a dental hygienist.

"It's amazing," Hannah told her mother. She was sitting on the back steps watching her mother plant marigolds. They'd just finished unloading groceries. She didn't ask her mother where she'd been all day. She simply basked in the ease of having her there, at home, with her. "The energy. The organization. The determination."

"You're telling me!" Her mother looked up, nodding her head, smiling.

"And Mrs. Gorden. She's becoming tough. She'll throw herself on the court before she'll let a shot pass. You should come by." Hannah patted her mother's shoulders.

"Maybe sometime. I'm busy too, you know."

"I know," Hannah said. She snapped a petal from a stray marigold. "I know."

The next morning it was Jan Littleton who wouldn't let a shot get past. She was especially jumpy, shifting from foot to foot in between serves. She yelled "Fucking-A" once, at Glenda

Oberry who'd just missed an easy backhand. She continued to criticize her throughout the first set. The two were winning, but to Jan Littleton that didn't matter. Whenever she could, she'd yell, "Jeez, Glen. What's with you this morning? Hustle!"

When they rested after the first set, Glenda Oberry decided to go inside to the nearby rest room, to drink what she called "fresher" water.

"Oh, my God," Jan said. "My big mouth."

"What's with you?" Clare asked.

"Marty-boy's worse. He was up all night vomiting. Then again this morning. Had to drink beer, the fool. *Had* to." Beads of sweat dotted her forehead but otherwise Hannah thought she looked cool, composed. She'd been running and hopping, not to mention belting insults at Glenda Oberry, but her t-shirt was tucked into her navy shorts that fit snugly around her trim hips, and she looked more like she was at the start of a match rather than midway through it.

When Glenda returned, Jan reached up, wrapping an arm around her. She looked first at Glenda Oberry's pale face, then at Hannah's. Her voice was firm, adamant. "He's killing himself," she said.

The muscles in Hannah's back tensed. She began to tap the face of her tennis racket, which she held in her left hand, against the heel of her right hand's palm. No way, she thought. This wasn't right. This wasn't fair.

"It's the town," she said quietly. "It's too small. He's too brilliant. See what I mean? He doesn't fit in." She mustered the will to stare directly at Jan Littleton's all-too-complacent face. "*Wells* is killing him. It's always been killing him."

Jan Littleton's expression stayed dead-pan as if Hannah hadn't revealed anything like real news. But she began to rapidly bounce then catch a ball. "Wells," she quipped. "No, that's not it." This time she caught the ball and didn't bounce it further. "Hannah, that's not it at all."

Hannah tapped her racket harder and faster. *Stupid*, she thought. Then, *You'll never change.*

The next day was Saturday and Hannah dropped by the Littleton's to visit Marty. He'd called that morning.

"It's a good day," he'd said, and she'd agreed, quickly, to go.

Marty was lying in the living room on a navy blue corduroy couch. Jan Littleton didn't have her own mother's eye for festive interior design. The Littleton's house was crammed with solid, functional furniture, no frills. It always smelled the same, as though it had just been sprayed with a perfumed cleaner. That day Venetian blinds blocked most light.

"I've been sleeping," Marty explained. Then he laughed, weakly. "And fucking throwing up. You wouldn't believe."

He didn't wear a hat now and Hannah could hardly bear the unsettled feeling she got looking at his bald head, the long sprigs of hair jutting forth from it like rare growth in a desert. She adjusted herself in the Littleton's upright recliner and handed him a gift, a "Super" Harlequin romance.

"Just what the doctor ordered," Marty said, grinning. His determination to be hopeful was unflagging as ever. This time, though, the relentless optimism struck a new chord. Sitting across from him, watching him do what he did best—deny the reality of who he was, of what was happening—she thought he never seemed more at home. And by that she didn't mean anything critical. This graciousness, she saw, was a kind of courage.

They sat in the dim room talking in increasingly hushed tones. Marty's voice was fading. As he reclined further into the couch, Hannah sat more upright.

At one point she went to the kitchen to get him juice. Then she began reading him the Harlequin. He chuckled some at first, but by page five—despite the steamy love scene—he fell asleep. She'd been there twenty minutes.

She carried his glass to the kitchen sink. She ran some water in it, then turned to leave.

Before she did, Jan Littleton entered the room. She'd been

sleeping herself, she explained, on the back deck. She wore her navy tennis shorts and the top of a two-piece bathing suit. She'd covered her short hair with a floral print kerchief and she still had on her sunglasses, big plastic circles that gave her eyes the appearance of vast black holes.

Her compact body, lithe and muscular, seemed small here in her kitchen, a mere shadow of the presence it cast those early mornings on the court. She barely filled the shallow cups of her bikini top. Her bony shoulders were slouched and her face, despite the sun, was pale. She looked gaunt. When she took off her sunglasses, briefly, disoriented by the indoor light, Hannah stepped back, stunned at the likeness between the dark folds around Jan Littleton's now-blinking green eyes and Marty's. As if confused, Jan Littleton put the glasses back on and resumed her feeble posture in the dark.

"I'm hungry," she said, yet she didn't reach for food or even move.

"I've got to go," Hannah said. "I'll see you Monday, right?"

"Right. I wouldn't miss it for the world." Jan Littleton's voice, faint and flat, betrayed the conviction of her words.

Hannah turned to leave. Her head ached and her palms were sweaty, tingling. She'd become tense in this dull house with her dying friend and this woman in tennis shorts and a flowery kerchief and a bikini top who wasn't Jan Littleton. Not the Jan Littleton she'd always known. This woman was someone with qualities beyond Jan Littleton's range. She was tired and sad, pale and helpless. Just yesterday she'd said about the cruelest thing Hannah could have imagined: Marty was killing *himself*. On the court her composure had been as formidable as her claim. Yet here in the kitchen she stumbled to a nearby chair and dropped into it with a thud. Her head fell to the table. She was so reduced she couldn't even get herself a bite to eat.

Hannah opened the refrigerator, pulled out bread, mayonnaise, bologna. She cut the sandwich in half. She poured Jan Littleton a glass of milk.

She sat with her while she ate. Jan took slow bites and they

201

didn't talk. After she was through, Hannah clutched the woman's light upper torso to keep her afoot, carrying her through the dim living room, past Marty sleeping on the couch, down the hall, and into her bedroom.

Hannah drew the shades and pulled the bed sheets down. She returned to the doorway where Jan stood, leaning against the frame, silent, waiting.

She lowered her onto the mattress.

She looked down and a pair of black holes stared back. She began to feel it then, the numinal liftoff from the ground, the sense of floating in a sea of perpetual nowhere, perpetual nothing.

Infinite nothing. Forever.

As Jan raised her arm, offering Hannah a weak wave of thanks, she said, "He's a good boy, you know?" She sighed, removed her glasses, and closed her eyes.

Hannah began shifting lightly from foot to foot, a familiar, nervous, court-side hop. Though she answered out loud, "I know," and "Take it easy," what she told herself was, *I'm here. On firm ground. Right here. Now.*

Neither her mother nor father were home that evening. When her mother did get home, past nine, Hannah was on her parents' bed, watching a sitcom on TV.

Her mother tried to make small talk but Hannah got off the bed, switched the channel, and said, "Shoosh. It's a special I don't want to miss. Either watch TV or come back later."

She was surprised at how quickly her mother complied. She didn't even question Hannah, much less put up a fuss. Like a child following her own daughter's orders, her mother sat on the bed and watched TV.

Early on Tuesday afternoon, the next week, her mother walked into the living room where Hannah was lying on the couch, working through the last third of *The Idiot*. The doorbell had just rung. "It's Marty," her mother said.

Hannah jumped up. "Impossible!"

But he was there, grinning, as always. "The worst is over," he announced. "Let's cruise."

He was driving his mother's Chevy. As Hannah passed behind it, she glanced at the familiar *Marriage Encounter* sticker.

"Why is it only Catholics are doing this Marriage Encounter thing? I see the sticker all over."

"It's our way of saying 'get it together.' *Marriage Encounter*—like a bridge over troubled water." He began to hum. "It works, though. You should have seen my parents go at it two years ago. Fucking drove me bananas." He shook his head.

Since high school they'd been talking about how bad the family lives in Wells were. They'd look around and see virtually no good families, no happy, peaceful ones. Was this turmoil unique to Wells? Was it the times? Or, they wondered, was this what growing up was about—this seeing?

He drove half-way around Lake Topaqua, then parked at a clearing. They settled on two rocks by the lake's edge. A breeze blew Marty's wispy hair, highlighting his frailness.

"Your Mom still doing it, well, extra-curricularly?" he asked.

She shrugged, and then he shrugged. She gave him a weak smile, and he tousled her hair. She smelled the lake's familiar algae smell.

"Beats me. What do I care? I'm only here for two more weeks." She kicked off her sandals. The cool water felt good on her feet.

"I've got to get back to work soon," Marty began.

Though she questioned his judgment, she didn't say anything. From the corner of her eye she saw him reach into his pocket and pull out a pack of Camel cigarettes.

By then she was in the water, up to her calves. "I wouldn't do that if I were you." She spoke cautiously, quietly.

If he heard her he didn't show it. He flicked on his lighter as he raised it toward his mouth.

"Are you nuts?" Her voice was still calm. Whatever she felt she took out on the water, which she reached down to touch with her hands, dropping them in and out in quick exchanges, flicking light splashes in front of her.

"What do you mean?" He gave her that smile. That maddening American tourist smile.

"What do you think I mean?" She startled herself by shouting. Her voice hadn't reached this pitch all summer.

"You think this cigarette is going to make or break it? You really think that?" He shouted back. "Hannah, look at me!"

He unbuttoned his shirt, revealing his pale, skeletal chest. A scar, still raw and fleshy, stopped at his rib cage. When he glanced up from his wound, his face looked bewildered, as if it surprised him as much as her, as if he were only a tourist following the strange map of wherever this scar would take him.

She looked at him, her friend since kindergarten, the reticent bookworm she'd sat next to in third, fourth, and fifth grades, the person she'd teased by placing her hands over whatever he was reading and asking, "Am I bothering you? You know the last thing I'd want to do is to bother you." Marty, laughing, would always take a break for her.

Now he was saying, "And I'll tell you something else. Even before this," he pointed again at his scar, "I had the body of an old man. I trashed myself a long time ago, Hannah. And you know it too!"

She did know this. All the dope, the drink, the constant cigarettes. But without the dope, the drink, the invariable cigarette, the constant way he had of undermining himself, he wouldn't be Marty, she thought. Not the Marty she'd always known.

She reached for her sandals and began walking around the lake, toward her home. She was crying, and stumbling because she couldn't see clearly, and when she'd gone a certain distance she yelled behind her, impulsively, "Go ahead and kill yourself. See if I care!"

In the two weeks before she left again for college, Marty's

health continued to improve. By February of the next year, when she was safely back at school, away from her parents and from the summer's mistakes— "the whole summer was a mistake," she wrote Jack, "my timing was off"—Hannah would have heard that Marty's prediction was correct: he'd have beaten his disease. Time would tell if the healing was for good. Even Glenda Oberry's son, Ted, would change. That year he'd come home from the commune for Christmas, then again in the spring, this time "just because."

Hannah played tennis with the mothers until the last possible August day. She and Jan Littleton stopped pairing up. Together they could cream Glenda Oberry and Clare Gorden.

"What's the fun in that?" Jan said. "Divide and conquer. *We* divide—*I* conquer!"

Her mother never showed up to watch them play. But Hannah didn't mind. Her mother's presence wouldn't have been right. Over the summer weeks the tennis foursome had become a quartet, used to each other's ebbs and flows, playing, always, in tune. Their song went like this: "Good get! Holy Mother of Jesus! I need one. Take two. Thirty-forty. Deuce! Here we go . . . love, love. Come on now, girls, we've only got ten more minutes. Your serve, Glenda, babe. Love-love. Love-fifteen. Fifteen-thirty. Hit. Smash. Hey! Did you see that?! I know it's my game! I know it's my game!"

Every game began with *love, love,* and because of the nature of the game, Hannah grew to realize, of all the words they shouted, *love* came out most often.

After Marty had lit that cigarette, Hannah had hurried home, the hot asphalt burning her bare soles. It took her ten minutes to realize she could stop the burning by putting her sandals on her feet rather than carrying them, swinging them in violent strides.

When she walked into her yard, sweating, frowning, hating herself for what she'd just yelled to Marty, she saw her mother unloading groceries from the back of her car. It was late afternoon. Her mother had been away since early morning. Hannah suspected what she was doing, but she wasn't sure.

"Hi, sweets. Can you help with the groceries?" Her mother smiled at her. Hannah scowled back.

"Don't help then. See if I care." Her mother walked into the house.

That was as close as they got to a direct clash.

Hannah spent the afternoon reading *The Idiot*. The words meant nothing to her, though; she couldn't concentrate. "Idiot! Idiot!" she kept repeating, screaming in her mind at her mother, her father, and, most severely, herself. But by dinnertime, exhausted, she'd calmed down, and when she heard her mother playing the radio in the kitchen, Hannah wandered in, like a stray cat, drawn by her need for this parent, the one she knew the best, the one who was home most often, the one who'd always been her good friend. Her mother, singing, was preparing salad, a supper Hannah knew was meant just for the two of them—a kind of peace offering—light, easy, fun.

Later, when her father came home, she and her mother were fully reconciled. He walked in on them lounging on the double bed, watching TV. Their bowl of salad was on the floor, along with some plates and two empty cans of Fresca.

"What'd you do all day?" he asked.

As her father fidgeted awkwardly with his necktie, Hannah turned to her mother for a cue. She knew that her mother might mouth a few words while staring at the TV. Or she might get up, discover some new chore she just remembered. When she didn't do either of these things Hannah was prepared, as she'd been for years, to handle the situation.

"We were busy. It's all we can do to help Mrs. Littleton take care of Marty. You wouldn't believe. Mom's a life-saver, Dad." She pointed at her mother, then at the TV and said, "Shoosh, Dad. This is good! Kind of girly. Not your kind." Then, to clinch it—to get him to believe her and leave—she gave him an American tourist grin: false, painful, and so automatic she wondered, how'd this happen? where'd this come from? and what would it take to get it off—this smile that marked the unknown terrain of her face?

Here's To You, Mrs. Robinson
(Carolyn Kahn—1994)

We were watching a movie on TV called *Mrs. Cage*, starring Anne Bancroft, whom I'd seen when I was a child as the unhappily married "Mrs. Robinson" in *The Graduate*. Unlike her former self, the desperate and manipulative Mrs. Robinson, Mrs. Cage was what one of my feminist professors back in graduate school would have called a "good patriarchal wife"—you know, stays at home, cooks her adored husband a nice meal, irons his shirts, *believing in the value of what she's doing all the time.* The story was about how invalidated Mrs. Cage felt in the new world of the emancipated, "uncaged" woman. Mrs. versus Ms. The early 1980s woman. We were only about a third of the way into the show when my step-father, Louis, suddenly shot up and edged a pillow under Mom's and my feet.

"Carolyn? Naomi? You all right?" he asked.

Yes, we were fine. The pillows made it even better.

There he was, listening to poor Mrs. Cage—she'd just committed murder by the way, and it's no coincidence that the woman she eclipsed was one of those young, confident, career-oriented types—and now, despite sixty-two years of being relatively thoughtful toward women, Louis, sorry for Mrs. Cage, felt like the lone bearer of male oppression, male guilt.

Mom and I burst out laughing. This was fun!

It was a brilliant show and there was the silence for about a minute afterward when it's hard to say a smart thing about a smart thing.

"Tea?" Mom finally asked, rising from the couch we shared. Then, "No, no. Don't get up. Honey, I'll make it."

"Okay," Louis said. Which was exactly what I was about to say. Wasn't I *honey*? How weird, I thought, for my mother to show affection toward her husband. It wasn't what I was used to; she'd never shown anything like this toward Dad. The Mom I knew shared certain attributes with Mrs. Robinson: she was unhappily married, and in so being, manipulative, desperate.

Louis sat still in a redwood rocker and smiled pleasantly my way. He was bald, and the shine of his scalp matched the one emanating from the rims of his silver glasses. Behind the glasses, his eyes were bright, engaged. "That was some show, Carolyn. Don't you think? Here's to you, Mrs. Robinson." When he started laughing, his pudgy body rocked as much as his chair.

Mom fixed us tea, and we drank it while nibbling cookies she'd baked earlier. Oatmeal raisin.

When had Mom resumed the role of Betty Crocker? I wondered as I lay on the pull-out sofa bed a few minutes later, the insides of my stomach humming with sugar and spice and everything nice. It was a calm June evening and the breeze straying in from the living room's open window surprised me; it was cooler in Connecticut than I'd remembered. These days I did little traveling from Miami. In fact on just two other occasions had I seen Mom's and Louis's quaint cape, their compact turn-of-the-century abode set on a woodsy plot on the outskirts of Litchfield. It wasn't the expense or time that kept me away. It was the feelings such visits stirred. It was the confusion, the sorting out—like when did Mom start serving tea again, anyway? Didn't she want to put all that behind her? Wasn't that what her long-awaited divorce was about? No more cookies! No more rigid sex-defined roles! No more serving! Period! No more!

"Care, all I can say is, love has a weird way of changing things."

She said this the next morning after explaining how she'd cut back on her already part-time work hours. In the last years she'd worked at an upholstery shop, marketing with great success her intuition for home improvement. Her home, I noted, functioned as a kind of laboratory. Thus, the slightly heavy, but interestingly textured, woven drapes in the living room; the distinctive wrought iron bed frame cloaked in a flowing Italian-print cover; the snappy mini-blinds in each bathroom. Mom could make a mint, I figured, except she had no motivation. She was in love. In the years of my absence she'd gone, oddly, from being Mrs. Robinson to Mrs. Cage, except unlike Mrs. Cage, Mom wasn't threatened by all the young women around her, self-actualizing and making money, to boot.

"What do you mean? You don't really want to work?"

"Yes, sure. But I really want to be around Louis. We got a late start, you know. I feel good around him. I do. And I want to take advantage of the time we have." We were in her bedroom sprawled across that distinctive wrought-iron-framed bed. We were talking and—I don't know why—looking at the ceiling. A crack in the paint here, a spider inching along there; otherwise a perfectly typical ceiling. Mom had just dumped a load of fresh laundry across the mattress and she sat up to begin folding. The skin on her hands was dry and just beginning to show the random age spot. Her clipped nails shined with a clear-colored polish. Her face bore wrinkles now, around her gray eyes, at the folds of her neck. Still, she looked pretty with her warm olive glow, her ever-exotic angled features.

She lifted a towel and in one efficient gesture shook and straightened it. She couldn't help it, I figured. That's why she hummed.

A few minutes later we were into it:

"Why don't you meet someone?"

"Who? How?"

"Why don't you go to Club Med? You've slimmed down. Care, you look good!"

"Ugh." I folded my arms over my chest.

"There's the ads. The ads! Totally respectable. Why don't you put one in? I'll pay. My treat!"

"I've tried it. It doesn't work. Unmarried men my age are either self-absorbed or socially inept. It's expensive, tiring, depressing."

209

She snorted and crossed her arms, then folded the last t-shirt in the laundry pile. Louis's shirt, size extra-large, Hanes. She squared the shirt on the pile of other shirts and turned to me. I held my breath, pretending to have never veered from staring at the ceiling. I didn't want to be having this conversation that I'd had so many times before, so many that it was my prime reason for not visiting, not daring to call much. *She'll start in*, I've told Hannah. *It's hopeless, she'll start in. The pressure's unbearable. And I feel like such a failure.*

She started in: "Carolyn, honey, I love you. But how can I help? I try and I can't. Let's face it. You're just going to have to get a life." She got up and went to the kitchen.

"I have a life!" I shouted. Then added, rolling onto my stomach, more subdued, "of sorts."

I sighed, and found myself trotting down the hall, my feet heavy on the pliant original pine, each creaky step propelling me forward, toward the kitchen, toward *her*. It was less a masochistic impulse than that I knew what she was talking about, had a need to talk about it myself. My life, my career as a business consultant, included an obvious negative consisting of years passing, a biological clock ticking, intimate male companionship lacking. There was something missing at its core.

But did she have to keep pointing that out? Did my mother have to *define* me in this way? Wasn't there a way to talk about it and be affirming? If I were a man, wouldn't she be proud of my professional accomplishments, at least mention all I was in the same breath that she mentioned all I wasn't?

"Feminists would hate you," I said, standing cross-armed in the doorway, watching her wipe down a counter near the sink.

"Even feminists need love, and you know it." She filled a copper tea kettle with water. She raised her thin eyebrows, obviously proud of her comeback. She nodded. "Yes. They do."

I grunted. I always did this, carried feminism's shield when the going got rough. Me and my other single women friends. Power to us, we'd cry, toasting ourselves with expensive red wine at a fancy restaurant, fancying ourselves the apples of our mothers' eyes, our mothers, whose early lives lacked the opportunities we've had. We could ignore for a moment the stigma that attached to us by virtue of being thirty-plus and single, a stigma that even our mothers—the very same women pushing us out the doors—conveyed. *What's wrong with you?* Weren't we asked that in a myriad of different ways all the time? It took an inner core of steel not to buy into the notion and I didn't know one friend who could put the idea entirely out of her mind. Mom looks at my life and thinks it's the loneliness that's hard, and at times it is, sure, but that's nothing compared to the stigma. *What's wrong with you?*

"You're passive, Care," Mom said. "I've heard about a lot of women like you. On Oprah. *Mirabella* and all the magazines. The *New Yorker's* cartoons. Thank God we live in an age when we can find out about each other, you know? You're smart, sure. It's easy for you to ride the professional elevator, Carolyn. Up, up, up. But to make a decision, stop at a certain floor and say, `Enough! There's some other things I have to do!' That's hard."

I watched Mom loading the sink with dishes, her rendition of "New York, New York" reaching a not-too off-key pitch. The day was cloudy and she'd flicked the lights on despite the double window in front of her. *Hey*, I thought, my back stiff as steel, my mood metallic, defensive. Hadn't Mom retreated behind feminism too?

Back in the seventies she'd cruised in feminism's wake, pining for a career, career—but from what I was seeing now I knew it was all talk. She just wanted to leave Dad without a direct confrontation and the choices opening up for women, thanks to the brave work of feminists, provided her with a nice cover for doing that. For Mom, finding herself and finding a career was a way out of something but never a way into something. Not with any real conviction. And the confident way she plunged her hands into the hot water, pulling up a plate, swiping it clean, rinsing it, and dropping it nicely into the dish rack—not to mention her decade-old obsession with my marital status—didn't that say it all?

"Let's put it this way," I said. I stepped toward her and began peeling an orange. Some spray shot in her direction, I noticed, happily. "You don't tell Hannah to get a life. And what does she do all day? Before the baby, virtually nothing! She's got a God-given gift for music and did she ever develop it? You don't tell her to get a life because she's married. It's that simple and it's not fair."

"I'm worried for you, that's all. And I never thought of Hannah that way. Doing nothing. Is everything all right with Hannah?" She held her wet hands in front of her face, causing water to drip down her forearms onto her rolled shirt sleeves.

"You know what?" I said, splitting the orange in two. "I need a breather. Before Hannah comes I think I'll go for a drive."

"If that's what you want. But tell me, please. Is something wrong with Hannah?" She was wiping her hands.

"Be back soon." Before I left, I placed the peeled orange by the sink's edge. I said, smirking, "For you."

Loehmann's. Like a magnet, it drew me toward it. I zigged across Route 84 East, then zagged for a short spin on I-91 North. In rain, in snow, in sleet, in hail—without fail, isn't that how we shopped at Loehmann's? This was my childhood, when Mom was married to Dad and didn't really want to be. This is where she came to escape, to try on clothes, to find out who else she could be.

It took a long time, this figuring. And I was already in graduate school when they finally divorced.

And by then divorce was common. And by then I had my own life. A life, of sorts. And by then Hannah and I were so used to their unhappiness. It was the air we breathed. It was our childhood.

"Really?" I said to Dad on the phone the day he called with the news of their divorce.

"No one's to blame," he said.

"I know."

"This was a long time coming."

"I *know*."

"This isn't easy, is it?"

I didn't say anything. It didn't seem so hard. It seemed like a huge relief. It seemed like the moment after a sneeze.

"The thing of it is, Care," he said. "You never know what will happen. What I mean is, make sure you can always support yourself. Angel, at a minimum, you have to have that."

"Carolyn?" It was my mother this time. She'd phoned separately, from her now separate home. "Don't do what I did," she said. She whispered this, as if Dad were in the next room and might hear it. "Don't marry too young. Carolyn, I've had what, a piddly job or two. Honey, at your age you can have a *career!*"

I have a career. I'm my own provider now, and I attribute my success in this role to taking both Mom's and Dad's advice. Through my career, I can support myself; I've taken care of the minimum. And in Miami, whenever I go to Loehmann's, which is a lot—whenever I don't know what else to do, whenever I need a reward for working hard, or whenever I need to be soothed—and my antenna for married-women-who-are-spending-money-not-earned-on-their-own starts buzzing, I feel superior and head to the accessories to pick up a little something extra because my work and my income have given me this much freedom: I can buy whatever I want.

Walking through the parking lot toward Loehmann's entrance, I breathed in the June air, heavy with moisture, perfumed with spring. On the way, I'd pruned my mind of the self-criticism I always felt after a morning talk with Mom, filling it with lyrics of the radio's "easy listening."

Inside I breathed deep the stale smell of Loehmann's. It was something like my closet's musty odor, only less concentrated, and it made me smile. Now I'd really come home.

But the place had expanded some and was more rigidly organized than I remembered. To my dismay I realized this was not the Loehmann's of my youth but the Loehmann's of Miami.

An exact replica. Coats to the far left. Toward the back, a new department for shoes, another for lingerie. A "Just In!" sign greeted me, a modern, commercial touch. Breezing past it, recoiling some, I found myself longing for the plain, no-comment, racks-upon-racks warehouse look of the Loehmann's of yesteryear.

As usual I stopped at the sweater aisle first, then the skirts. There I noticed a woman, about my age, her wedding and engagement rings glinting, her face drawn in a grim expression as she determinedly made her way through size six. Immediately I began to flip through size ten with more ease, relishing the view, having found what I really came for: the sight of a married woman on a hasty, mad hunt. In a near frenzy, this woman whisked garments past her, quickly sizing them up and dismissing them. Occasionally she'd pull one out, hold it to her waist, sigh, raise it to eye level, then shake her head. This was it: my childhood revisited. This frenetic, cantankerous, unsatisfied shopper: wasn't she a vision of Mom?

Despite my lingering, in no time I'd accumulated six garments of my own for trying on. This was another new Loehmann's rule: only six garments per person in the dressing room. Long gone were the huge, unmanageable piles, full of extraneous maybes and hopeful possibilities, that Mom dragged in during the 1970s. I carried my light, neat load into Dressing Room Three.

The room was divided between its old public area—hooks and mirrors and open space—and newly installed private booths. On principal I hung my items on a hook in the still-public section, the *historically-correct* public section, right beside a pair of chatty, college-aged, Generation X'ers. The Gens, as I called them, were trying on jeans, jeans jackets, and a series of tight black dresses and tight black shirts. Immediately I wished I'd chosen another spot. Their unabashed sexiness, not to mention their youthfulness, was terrifying.

I slipped out of my clothes, my back to the Gens. I'd just found my way into my first garment when something different happened. I was spoken to. I looked up, confused. Women did-n't usually do this with me. At the Loehmann's in Miami I was all business. I'd try on, take off, get out.

Yet a lady, about Mom's current age, had approached. I was zipping myself into a pleated skirt. It was a bit staid, I thought, but possibly useful for work.

"Looks great!" She spun me around. "Adorable. Darling, what legs!"

The Gens stopped to notice. They looked absolutely dead in all that black. Dead and sexy and young. I was timid beside them, and critical of myself for being so.

I thought about moving to a private booth, but the older woman wouldn't leave me alone. She suggested a cinch belt would do the trick with the dress I wriggled into next. After she arranged for a saleslady to bring me one, she asked me if I worked.

"I consult," I said. "Offer help to start-up businesses."

"Marvelous!" She studied my waist. In her heels she stood as tall as me, and her silvery hair highlighted my own few grays. "I'm a court reporter. I love it out there! Out of the house, I mean. Working. Don't you?"

I work twelve, thirteen, even fourteen hour days, and often weekends. "Half the time," I sighed. One of the Gens was real-ly staring now. "It's true," I added, suddenly emboldened with the verity of experience. "Work's no picnic," I told her. "You'll see."

The older woman stepped in front of me then, laughed shrilly, and said to the girls, "Don't believe everything you hear!" Cheerfully chatting on about her work, she wrapped me in a cinch belt.

"Looks even better. Sexy," she said, winking. The comment enlivened the dead; the Gens winked back. Before she left, she tapped my shoulder. "Sweetie, lighten up." She pointed at the mirror, at me. "Look how you watch yourself. There's no joy! It's cross-examination!" She laughed. "Oh, what I'd do for your legs," she finally said.

Another customer then approached. I was obviously being mistaken for somebody else, somebody popular. Watching as she sauntered toward me, I smiled.

She was of medium height, about thirty-five, no wedding ring. She wore a conservative red suit. She was not particularly pretty. She had a round face, accentuated by her hair, straight, and cut short. She was noticeably chubby and had especially large hips. The tailored suit she sampled wedged angles into her round figure, but the skirt was cut short and her legs couldn't withstand the exposure. Eyeing her in the mirror, I was reminded of one of Mom's few maxims: fashion tells.

The woman said, "What do you think? It's a good price, useful, a good color." She hesitated, weighing her appearance in the mirror. "Too . . . stylish?"

I thought I'd tell her no, it was short, but she could probably get away with it, assuming she bought a suitable shoe.

"This skirt would look fabulous on you." She nodded at my mirrored reflection. Still gathering my thoughts on her, I stood in my white cotton panties, cut high on the sides in the French style, giving my slim hips new shape. My body had changed over the years. I'd lost all my softness. With the aid of aerobics, even my old pot belly now had a hard core.

Though I didn't like the comparison, I couldn't help but notice several similarities between us. Our age, of course, and our marital status. From her suit, I guessed she was a working professional too. But there was something else, closer to home. The way our arms hung limply by our sides, how we each turned slightly sideways as we gazed in the mirror, how we were so serious as we glared at ourselves, studying, scrutinizing, worrying.

I took a hasty step back, and, folding my arms over my chest, I stopped eyeing her in the mirror.

"The skirt," I began, facing her from this new, safe distance. "It's too short. Your legs are unshapely, and you need to work on that. My recommendation? Regular exercise. Discipline! There's no way out for you there."

216

She straightened her back and followed my mirrored image.

"And the jacket," I continued. "You need the tailoring, but the cut is too short. Your hips are wide, and you need to know this."

Her wrists flicked as she began to unbutton the jacket.

"Your hair," I said. "Think about growing it. Think about your femininity. You're obviously someone not comfortable with that side of yourself." I paused, then added in my sweetest voice, "You're still a bud. You need to bloom."

I unfolded my arms and placed my hands on my firm, slender hips. "Another thing . . ."

Other women targeted me as they stared into the mirrors. The Gens eyed me warily, then walked out of the room, glancing over their shoulders as they did as if I might burst forward suddenly and chase them.

My acquaintance was out of the suit and scrambling into her own clothes.

She faced me. "I'm sorry I asked!" Her clothes were on and she reached for her purse. "I don't see what's so obvious about me. You don't even know me. Why, you hateful person!"

"Not hateful," I said. "I say these things to help you."

"You hateful person!" She ran from me and out of Dressing Room Three.

The room was silent except for the brush of fabric against skin and the rattle of a few metal hangers. The remaining women looked to the tawny, carpeted floor or at themselves in the mirror, rather than at me. But for my underwear I was naked and felt a chill. I reached for my clothes—snug, black leggings and a long, cotton sweater—and watched myself in the mirror as I put them on.

What had I done? Helped or hurt? Or simply hated?

Once dressed, I looked different, like a stranger. No one there could answer this question, but I wanted to ask it anyway: "Is it me?"

It felt like a necessity, the way I drove home, my eyes encased in dark sunglasses despite how thoroughly cloudy the day was. I flipped the car's radio on, then tuned out the offer of easy listening. For a while I drove too fast, then, as I approached Mom's, too slow.

Once there, I slid inside and snaked my way quietly past Mom and Louis, cheerily sipping tea together in the kitchen. Locked safely inside the bathroom, I scrambled out of my clothes, my jerky moves as rushed and desperate as those of the woman whom I'd just uncontrollably slandered at Loehmann's.

Was it me?

Looking at my face in the bathroom mirror I couldn't deny it. Between the angles and the freckles and the coloring and the worry lines, my face had become a perfect blend of both Mom's and Dad's. My parents were like two opposite points on a coat hanger and I was the twisted pinnacle in the middle, the hook, arched in a curve that ached. My personality was all-business like Dad's, and desperate like Mom's. Like Dad, I worked long hours to avoid my problems. Like Mom, I shopped whenever I could to avoid my problems.

I was a bud. I needed to bloom.

And I hated that.

I entered the steam of the shower, stood under the hot rivulets, and said to myself, "No, no, no."

"Change of plans," Mom said. I'd dressed and joined them in the kitchen. "It's easier for Hannah if we go see her." She threw me a set of car keys. I threw them right back. "Too tired," I said. She then threw them at Louis who pretended to throw them at me. Then he said, "Just kidding. I'll drive." And so he did.

Like a kid, I sat by myself in the back seat, silently staring out the window. It was late in the afternoon when we arrived in Wells. Hannah had documented the changes, but now I saw it firsthand.

Our old house. According to the sign on the front porch it

was a day-care center on the first floor and the second floor was rented out as office space. Newly painted a cream color, its mushroom and maroon trim impressed Mom. "How come I never thought of colors like that?" she said.

I stared, and stared, and even when Louis pulled us around the corner, off Route 27 and onto Main, I turned back to stare some more. A wave of something terrible and heavy overcame me. It was as if all our old anxiety, all the tension, all the years of unresolve, had been lurking there, waiting to get sniffed out. I caught the overwhelming drift. "Whoa," I moaned from the back seat.

"Driving too fast?" said Louis.

"Too slow. Keep going." Despite my words, I couldn't peel my eyes away.

Our house faded in the distance and soon, as we reached the downtown, my anxiety transformed into wonder. Where there used to be a pizza house, a drugstore, two tiny groceries, and a gift shop, there was now a boutique, an art gallery, two tiny antique stores, and a patisserie. Where there used to be our sole bank, there was a "professional services" building filled with doctors and accountants, lawyers and a masseuse. Where there used to be a stop sign, there was a blinking light. Where our town sign used to read, "Wells, Connecticut, Population 3,000 (I was five then), later changed to "Population 6,000" (I was twelve), it now read in larger, fancier print, "Population 12,506". And where there used to be a package store, Delaney's, there was a second-hand bookstore with a poster on the door, "Poetry Readings, Monday nights, 7:30."

"Darling! Isn't it?" Mom said, pointing.

But I was too confused to answer. When did people in Wells start reading, much less writing, poetry?

"Carolyn, you won't believe this," Mom said, "but sometimes I swing into town to shop!" I noticed how she eyed the two tiny antique stores. "Maybe we could—"

"No!" Louis and I snapped in harmony.

"Just kidding," Mom quipped.

It was picture-perfect, this new, quaint downtown. And this made me uneasy. Sure, the seeds of change were there, even before I'd left for college. But the changes back then—a tiny shopping mall, a second car dealership, a cheap Italian restaurant—were modest in nature. These new businesses, charming and oriented toward leisure, were for whom? Tourists? Summer people? People passing through? The used bookstore was painted blue with yellow trim, and its pretty sign—also blue and yellow with purple triangles forming a jovial border—looked like a clown's happy makeup imposed on an otherwise sad, worn, but more interesting and authentic face.

"Are we late?" Louis asked, steering us out of the downtown.

"No. Not late," Mom said. "Hannah's invitation was casual. She didn't mean for us to arrive at any particular time. But time's passing."

Mom was right. Time *was* passing. All these changes drove that message home. Time passing. . . That would mean that this, this present time, the time I spent living in Miami, working and working, shopping as consolation, not daring to call home. . . *Was this really my life?*

Hannah's place was set deep in the woods on the outskirts of town, and before we arrived it had begun to rain, a placid steady stream. I didn't understand why Hannah and Jack chose to live so far away from things but Hannah insisted she liked the privacy of this plain little cabin that she and Jack had built—their joint design. "Plain and private," she said. "I can't get enough of it. I drink it up."

Now she said, "I'm so glad you're here." She waited for me to step out of my damp coat before squeezing me hello. Mom was out of her coat in a flash and grabbed Jenny, Hannah's five-month old. "Where's Jack?" I asked.

"Having a boy's night out tonight. A much deserved one, I think. If it isn't me, it's Jenny. If not Jenny, me. We need him a lot, and he knows it!" She laughed, a sad sort of laugh. Her hair was frizzy, and I noticed she had a few grays, like me. Her usually rosy cheeks, covered in freckles, were pale. She hung our coats on the rack in the hallway, and I followed her to the living room, dimly lit with Sabbath candles. Recently Hannah had begun practicing a modest Jewishness, as she put it. It felt good, "more complete," even this little bit, and Jack, who was not religious, was taking to the candles too.

Mom and Louis stayed in the kitchen, playing with the baby. They cooed and laughed.

Hannah dropped down on her natural weave couch like she was exhausted.

"Feeling good?" I asked. She was forever fighting with something inside her. She was moody, solitary.

"Most of the time. It's weird, though. With the baby, I've felt I had to pull myself together. Quick! In exactly nine months. Had to have everything about myself neat and tidied up so I'd be ready for her. Completely for her. Only it hasn't been that simple. Jack didn't know what to make of me. I'd grown so weird."

Louis walked past us then to go to the bedroom, he said, for a quick snooze. He held his glasses in one hand and rubbed his eyes with the other. Mom stayed in the kitchen with Jenny, still ogling over her. We both listened for a while to the sound of Mom squealing, and Jenny squealing, then Mom and Jenny squealing in sync. Hannah and I laughed.

"I'm weird too," I said.

"You? You're the straightest arrow I know. You always know what to do. You're always in control."

"Oh my God, Hannah," I said. "What you don't know."

Mom came in then, carrying Jenny. She placed her in my lap, a warm bundle covered in yellow terry cloth. She wiggled a bit before settling down, and I wiggled too at the strangeness. There had been nothing in that lap in so long.

"Looks pretty good." Mom winked at me.

"Don't start," I said.

"I'm not starting." She backed off, seating herself away from

221

me, beside Hannah. "I have the two touchiest girls in the world."

Hannah spun around and glared at her. "Don't you dare criticize!"

"I'm only trying to help! Really!" Mom looked so earnest, I felt for her. And I felt for Hannah. Where was this line between helping and hurting, anyway? Did the two always have to be this inextricably mixed?

Jenny pulled on my pearl stud earring, then rubbed her head against my shoulder. I held her there, began rocking gently. I couldn't tell if it actually looked good, but it felt good, this little life I held.

I sighed.

"That's the saddest sound in the world," Hannah said. "It makes me sad." She sighed, a deep, melancholy exhalation.

Mom, staring bleakly at the two of us, also sighed.

When Louis came in a minute later he exclaimed, "You three! It must be horrible! What's *wrong*?"

Later, when Hannah and I were alone again, she said, "Carolyn, I married so young, like Mom. Jack's the steadiest guy in the world and still I'm afraid all the time, it seems. I fought hard with Jack about *not* having the baby."

I was surprised. I never knew that. And it helped. There was something missing at her core too. Some block to the present. We weren't so different, Hannah and I. Mom had left to start making dinner, a treat for Hannah, and I sat closer to Hannah on the couch. Jenny was still in my lap, sleeping in my arms. The candles cast a warm glow, and a lush smell of garlic and onions began to stream in from the kitchen.

Pretty soon I felt drowsy too. Hannah leaned her head back on the couch, and I did the same, moving gingerly so Jenny wouldn't wake. It was wonderfully quiet here, I noticed, in Hannah's snug house in the woods. I could see why she liked the rich sound of her privacy, her solitude.

"Know what?" she said. She was speaking quietly.

"What?"

"Mostly I feel like I've never lived a life. I've just been holding my breath for so long. I watch Jenny breathe and I feel like she's teaching *me* to breathe." Hannah smiled, but it was more sadness that came through.

I watched Jenny breathing in my lap, her face snug against my chest, her eyes closed, her tiny lips just parted. She breathed in, expanding some inside her yellow terry suit. Then, breathing out, she fell against me even more securely. It was the calmest, simplest gesture. In. Out. I turned to Hannah and reached for her hand. I felt calm too. And serene, like I didn't want to be anywhere else but exactly where I was.

I closed my eyes. Perhaps it was the sound of silence— "The Sound of Silence"—that led my thoughts to drift to ones of Mrs. Robinson. Hers was the role I identified with, not Mrs. Cage. What did she do once she'd smashed her marriage to pieces and damaged her relationships within her family beyond repair? Hadn't I done that too with my father? Was she wretched? Forever lost and grieving? Maybe, I thought, she slowly, *slowly* began to forgive herself. Maybe she took a job, one she really liked. Maybe she took long, consoling walks, talking to herself, getting to know herself better. Maybe one day she woke up in her own place, her own bed, and smiled.

I opened my eyes and turned to Hannah. "I know what you mean," I said. In. Out. This breathing was perfectly uncomplicated, frank, and direct. "I've always wanted to tell someone. And maybe I'll tell you. About my life. The real one." I snuggled deeper into the couch's folds as if readying myself for the longest talk ever. "Hannah," I began, "it's the one I never lived."